Dedication

Many people have contributed information for this novel, either by direct advice or personal contact in times long past. I thank them all for being part of my pleasant memories.

My thanks to Gressenhall Farm and Museum, Dereham Norfolk, who gave me free access and allowed me to use photographs of their exhibits in this novel. Thanks also to an acquaintance who allowed me to use some of his photographs concerning Norfolk history.

Invaluable help was given by a family proud to bear the name 'Foster', including my parents Oscar and May, and my siblings Brian, Dick and his wife Hilary, Graham, Mary, and nephew Ashley. Six of whom have since gone to a new life.

Finally, my heartfelt thanks to both whatever and whoever gave me the gift of a life full of interest, activity, happiness and the pure joy of living.

Lung David

BORN AND BRED ON A FENLAND FARM

AUSTIN MACAULEY PUBLISHERS™
LONDON • CAMBRIDGE • NEW YORK • SHARJAH

Copyright © Lung David (2017)

The right of Lung David to be identified as author of this work has been asserted by him in accordance with section 77 and 78 of the Copyright, Designs and Patents Act 1988.

All rights reserved. No part of this publication may be reproduced, stored in a retrieval system, or transmitted in any form or by any means, electronic, mechanical, photocopying, recording, or otherwise, without the prior permission of the publishers.

Any person who commits any unauthorised act in relation to this publication may be liable to criminal prosecution and civil claims for damages.

A CIP catalogue record for this title is available from the British Library.

ISBN 978-1-78554-477-4 (Paperback)
ISBN 978-1-78554-478-1 (Hardback)
ISBN 978-1-78554-479-8 (E-Book)

www.austinmacauley.com

First Published (2017)
Austin Macauley Publishers Ltd.
25 Canada Square
Canary Wharf
London
E14 5LQ

Contents

PREFACE 9
THE FENLAND RUNNER 16
THE SMITHY 25
THE HERD 46
PLOUGHING 75
SUGAR BEET HARVEST 94
THE HOLE 107
POTATO HARVEST 115
WHEAT HARVEST 142
THRESHING 162
THE DANCE 180
GERALD'S STORY 187
LILLY 223
REMINISCING 257
THE DINGHY 272

PREFACE

The main character in this book is Simon, as a boy; his accounts are in the present tense. The narrator is Simon as an old man, he relates in the past tense. Additional versions from Gerald and Lilly, a sister born when Simon was eight years old are also in the past tense. Few people had cameras. Old photographs are difficult to reproduce, even with the incredible technical devices of today. The writer asks the reader to accept the poor quality, and illustrations that are not directly relevant to the text; for example, the family in this introduction were perhaps five years younger than the time of the story. The photo of the brothers in The Herd chapter was taken on a trip to the seaside, and is included for its charm, and the absence of a contemporary photo.

***

In the far-off days of the nineteen thirties, English Fenland hamlets were isolated from the world beyond the village and local town; the inhabitants struggled for survival in the period between the Depression and the Second World War. Contact with the outside world was by means accumulator powered radios, newspapers delivered from the village, and a twice-weekly bus service to the nearest town. Our village was a mile down the road; going to the village involved either walking, or cycling, or horse-drawn farm cart, or pony and trap. There was a local bus service that left for town at nine in the morning and returned at six in the evening, two days a week, for those who could afford the few pence fare. Those who hadn't the fare either cycled or walked the seven miles, braving the strong winds.

The roads were long with few bends and the uncut grass verges bowed and rippled, leaning away from the wind, unlike the people who struggled bent-backed and head down into the buffeting. Some children were more attuned to nature and walked backwards bowing away from the wind. Those who were unable to face the fare and the wind stayed in the hamlet, engulfed in the flatness of the earth and the enclosing skies.

The elusive close horizon was defined by the low cottages, farm buildings, and trees; out in the fields divided by drainage ditches, only scattered trees and bushes broke the shallow curve between sky and earth. On stormy days, the trees and church propped up the heavy cloud-billowed sky. On fine days, the blue sky seemed as a flat transparent skin stretched over the flat Fens; on clear bright nights the stars gave depth to the vertical hole of the Universe. The far-off stars and the roads tapering off into the distance were the only indication of anything beyond the hamlet.

Our hamlet was dominated by the Norman church with its square tower supporting five bells, and a Victorian vicarage. There was a pub, aptly named the Five Bells, and a scattering of family farm houses and farm worker's tied cottages, all separated by beyond shouting range. The population was about the size shown on this photo, taken outside the church in Victorian times. Cars or motorcycles were rare, and the sound of an approaching vehicle would send children scurrying to the main road to watch it out of sight down the long straight Fenland road.

The hamlet had none of the now essential amenities such as electricity, sewage system, mains water supply, telephone and street lighting. We were blissfully unaware of such luxuries, and were quite happy with the earth closet in a shed 100 yards from the house; an underground cistern to store rain water from the roof; candles and paraffin lamps for lighting, and huddling in front of the coal and log fires during the bitterly cold winters. The lack of a shop, school, and communal hall did not justify the designation of village, hamlet was more appropriate for our small cluster of humanity marooned in the vast Fens of East Anglia.

Dad, grey and bowed from farm labour, yet with a twinkle in his blue eyes and a ready nicotine-stained smile, often cuddled Mum. She was taller tending to stoutness yet strong in body, her authority over the family evident in the slight jut of her jaw and steely grey eyes, features that could become tender when looking at her brood of four sons. Gerald, the oldest, taciturn and stocky, lost in his own little world of thoughts, shared the chores of the farm and rearing a family with the parents. Martin, small, sharp featured and cocky as a sparrow was responsible for the cows. Cyril, rotund and happy, cared for the horses. The first three sons had inherited the dark hair and strong body of Mum. I was the youngest, Simon, slightly built, blue-eyed and blond. I was pampered by the family, and still at school so did only light work in the house and on the farm. We brothers wore handed down working clothes, belted and braced serge trousers, white cotton thin-striped shirts and narrow woollen ties, a Fair Isle woollen sweater and a serge jacket that did not match the trousers. Mum's clothes were hidden under a large flowered pinafore. All the family put on their Sunday best to attend church and when they went to town. We lived in the farmhouse next to the graveyard that protected the church. We were used to the clanging of the weekly bell practice and twice on a Sunday call to church, but visitors often complained, "How on earth can you tolerate that din?" The dairy herd and three horses grazing in the back pasture occasionally twitched an ear, but that was probably due to persistent flies and not the tolling. Apart from the bells all was peaceful, until sleep was disturbed by the throbbing roar of German bombers on the way to blitz cities, and later when they returned, chased by fighter planes spitting bullets and death. After the Battle of Britain, allied bombers reciprocated the damage wreaked by the blitz, by the cruel and wanton destruction of enemy cities. The steady hum of English and American four-engine bombers instilled relief instead of fear. One night, Martin, being unable to sleep, looked out of the window to see a ball of flames plummeting from the sky towards him. The blazing bomber passed just over the roof and crashed with a loud bang on the house of the poorest family in the hamlet, leaving a great crater rimmed with fractured pieces of house, aircraft and flesh. The actual fighting during the war was a distant horror, reported on the accumulator radio, remote from the peace of the Fens. Later it transpired that the bomber was in fact a Flying Fortress, limping back to base. The captain gave the order to abandon the aircraft too late, and parachutes barely had time to open. Some crew survived, but one smashed into a neighbouring barn; he managed to crawl to the neighbours' house, but they were afraid that the Germans had invaded, and did not answer the tapping at the door. Next morning the dead airman was found, arms stretching to the door. Three days later Gerald went looking for mushrooms in the back pasture, and found another airman with a half-opened parachute. Neither Gerald nor Martin fully recovered from that trauma.

The nearest village was over a mile up the main road from the hamlet, and had grown by the side of a deep wide canal to drain excess rainwater from the Fens. The village huddled around a village green that straddled the main road, the smaller section just grass with a rough track to a pub and the blacksmith's workshop, house and yard. In the middle of the grass, a brick turreted tower with a chiming clock to commemorate Queen Victoria's glorious sixty years asserted its alien urban dominance in such rural surroundings. It was about ten feet square and contained a room used as a headquarters by the Air Raid Wardens during the war. It was quite large enough for the six local members to sit and smoke and play nap during the non-active hours of duty, whilst one unlucky member patrolled the village shouting, "Put that light out!" at every crack in the blackout blinds that covered the windows. Small houses, the village hall and shops, including a harness maker, butcher, haberdashery and barber lined one side of the main green. Mature horse chestnut and elm trees spaced on and around the green provided shade for the Salvation Army gatherings, and the village brass band that performed at fetes and other village events.

Down the road from the green, towards the hamlet, the petrol station swung cantilevered hoses to reach cars parked by the kerb; next was the school and then a grocery and bakery and after a couple of big houses, the Victorian edifice of the church, its size and sentinel tombs and gravestones setting it apart from the everyday affairs of the village. The church was used only for Sunday services and weekday weddings and funerals.

Alongside the graveyard wall sat the small squat brick and slate Methodist chapel. It was near the road, and more intimate than the church. Not many villagers converted from Church to Chapel. The majority preferred the awe and mystery of the Church rituals rather than the homely cosiness of the Chapel. Farther down the road, big houses in large gardens gave way to much smaller worker's cottages with small vegetable gardens, sited near the road in the corners of the fields edged with ditches and hedges that divided and drained the flat expanse of the Fens, the deep alluvial soil being the most fertile in England.

THE FENLAND RUNNER

It is a cold January Saturday afternoon. I am squatting in front of the coal fired cooking range in the kitchen of our farmhouse, on the rag rug that my mum made from a pea sack and strips of clothing. The rest of the family has gone to town. Mum is shopping, Dad is in his card club, and my brothers Gerald, Martin and Cyril, have gone to the pictures to see Snow White and the Seven Dwarfs. I am only just nine, and not allowed to see Snow White because the wicked witch would give me nightmares. Anyway, I have more important things to do, I don't care that I am not allowed to see Snow White. It's only a stupid film. I could be doing my fretwork, but I want to go skating, so have to get ready for that. It has been freezing hard all week long. The ponds and ditches and canal are covered with a thick layer of ice, strong enough to stand the weight of a man. So, I am going skating, and I don't care about the film.

I have everything ready; my hobnailed boots, a meat skewer, a pair of pliers and of course the skates. They have been handed down through all my brothers. I don't care that they are old; all my clothes and things are handed down, and old. When I am old, and rich, I will buy myself new clothes and things. I will buy my mum a nice new dress. I open the door to the range and push the skewer between the vertical grate into the glowing coals. I hold a boot, sole up, between my knees. I use the pliers to pull out the red-hot skewer. The heat is fierce on my face and hand. I push the red-hot tip into the middle of the heel, and it goes in a little way. The stink of burning leather makes my eyes water. My eyes watered from the smoke of the bonfire on Guy Fawkes' night. My brother said I was crying because he would not let me hold a sparkler, but it was the smoke from the bonfire. Sometimes dust gets in my eyes and makes them water. It's very strange that sometimes my eyes water when I think about things in bed; there must be invisible dust floating round the room.

I blow away the smoke, and re-heat the skewer and push it into the heel several times until the hole is about an inch deep. I am very careful not to let the skewer slip and burn a hole in my knee. It could slip from the pliers and burn a hole in Mum's nice rug, and then I would be in trouble; Dad would give me a clip round the ear. Later Mum would give me a cuddle to take the dust out of my eyes. Girls are allowed to cry. Big boys don't cry; I want to be a big boy, so I cannot cry unless I get something in my eyes.

I burn a hole in the other boot, and then close the door to the range to stop me from sweating. Mum will be cross if she smells this stink of burned leather, so I open the window and door to the conservatory. The east wind will blow away the smell; it will also make the kitchen cold, so I open the hob on top of the stove and shovel in coal from the brass coal scuttle. The kitchen will soon be warm again. I have to polish the scuttle sometimes, but I can only really help my brother. It's too big for me to manage; it would take all day. I have to polish the brass candlesticks and door handles. My big brother told me that gold does not need to be polished. Why don't they make coal scuttles and doorknobs out of gold?

I stop daydreaming and carry on fitting the skates to the boots. There is a screw on the heel of the skate and I turn and push it into the hole that I burned in the boot. It is a good fit and holds the skate tight to the heel. The soles of the skates have steel spikes that should dig into the sole of the boots, but they cannot reach beyond the hobnails. I wedge the spikes among the hobnails and hope that the skates will not slip sideways. I then buckle on the straps over the toes and round the back of the boots and pull them tight. Some people fix their skates onto Wellingtons and shoes. When they try to skate, their ankles bend inwards and the wooden part of the skate scrapes on the ice. Boots support the ankle, so I won't have aching ankles. I am almost ready to try out the skates. I close the window and go to the conservatory closing the door after me to keep the heat in the kitchen. I put on my thick green overcoat, woollen scarf and gloves and cloth cap and Wellingtons. I tie the bootlaces together and sling them over my shoulder and go to the pond in the pasture behind the stackyard.

The air is cold and my breath makes a fog. I pretend that I am smoking. My dad smokes all the time. It's grown-up to smoke and I want to be grown-up the same as my dad. I can't wait to skate, and run to the pond. I usually run when I go anywhere, walking is too slow. I pull off my Wellingtons and sit on the frosty grass to put on my boots. I carefully step down to the ice. It has been too cold for snow, and the ice is clear as glass. I can see mud and weeds on the bottom of the pond, but everything is still. In the spring, after the thaw, the ponds and ditches are full of clear still water. Everything moves, the weeds sway and newts crawl on the mud and stir up little clouds, and beetles and minnows dart around, and water boatman skate across the surface. I look at the fish; there is no dust in the water, so how do they cry? They can't blink so perhaps they can't cry. Anyway, you couldn't tell if they were crying because you can't see tears under water. If I ripple the water the things change shape, just the same as my reflection in the 'Hall of Mirrors' at the March Fair. When the water is smooth, it reflects the sky so I can see two worlds at the same time, one under the water and one in the sky. It is a magical world in the ditches when spring arrives. Now it is winter, and everything in the water is dead; I feel sad.

The cold makes me shiver and I stop daydreaming. I stand on the ice. Last year I could stand and slide the skate on the ice to go forward. Now I am a year older I am going to try to lift up each foot and skate properly. I push forward with one foot and lift the other, and both feet fly up and I fall flat on my back. My thick coat softens the fall and I am not hurt. I remember to lean forward with the next step and I glide forward on one foot. I change my weight to the other and glide forward on that one. I am skating. I am so pleased with myself. I get my feet in a tangle and go sprawling down again, but this time I laugh. I remember a picture in a book with a woman in fancy clothes falling down and the heading, 'Pride comes before a fall', and I laugh again. The sparrows in the hedgerow are not interested; they just carry on twittering and hopping among the twigs. I try again and again, and finally manage to skate slowly forward and even to turn slightly. I am very pleased but don't want pride to make me fall again.

I am cold and my ankles ache a bit. I take off the boots and put on my Wellingtons and go back to the stackyard. Two years ago, when I was young, my brothers cut a slide across a frozen puddle in the stackyard. With a good run and a jump, I could slide on my hobnailed boots several yards, but my brothers could slide much further. They poured water on the frozen ground between puddles and when it froze they had a very long slide almost the width of the stackyard.

Friends from other farms came to slide on that. We all had a good time.

It is almost teatime. I stop in the hen house and feel under the hens for an egg. They just cluck, but don't move. My hand is warm under one hen and I take an egg and go back to the kitchen. I put a small saucepan of water on the hob, wait for it to boil and use a tablespoon to lower the egg into the boiling water. I open the fire door, and use a long fork of twisted wire to toast a round of bread while the egg is cooking. After four minutes by the alarm clock, I spoon out the egg, put it in an eggcup and slice off the top. I spread margarine on the toast and cut it into fingers. Hot toast fingers dipped into a boiled egg warm from the nest is delicious, a real treat. We have many treats; trifle for tea on Sundays; going to church; playing games in the evenings; riding our bikes, and sometimes listening to Children's Hour on the radio. I have seen people collecting money on tins marked 'Waifs and Strays'; they are children who do not have homes and mums and dads, and do not get enough to eat. I am very lucky to have a family and a happy life.

***

It is now Monday. There was heavy snow on Saturday, and a slight thaw on Sunday. The snow drifted up the banks of the canal, and later thawed a little and then froze into a curve from the ice about one yard up the bank. Work on the farm stops in freezing weather, except for looking after the animals, so my brothers have time to take me to the canal near the village this afternoon. We go on our bikes with our skate boots hanging from the handlebars. A small crowd is on the banks of the canal and on the ice. They are having a good time, talking, and laughing as skaters fall over. Two girls with special skates are very good at figure skating. Our skates are for going forward very fast and are no good for twisting and spinning. If you want to turn quickly you have to jump up off the ice and turn in mid-air, but you have to be clever to do that. We ride further along the embankment and find a clear stretch of ice. We slide down the frosty grass, put on our boots, and step on the ice. My brothers are much better than I am and glide along. I remember falling on the pond, so I skate slowly across the canal.

I swallow down my pride when Gerald calls out, "Well done! You couldn't even stand up last year. Who taught you?" He skates near me. "Why don't you try this?" He points to where the ice has crept up the banks to form a curve about two feet high. He gets up speed and glides up the curve of ice. Martin and Cyril join in and they have a fine time laughing as they swoop up and down the curves.

I think that it would be the same feeling as riding on the vertical 'Wall of Death' at the fair. I imagine myself on a crackling motorbike and skate as fast as I can at the curve. My brothers shout "No!" and gasp as I turn a somersault and land flat on my back. They laugh with relief when I get up grinning. We stay at the side to let a line of speeding skaters swoosh past. They are very graceful as they take long swishing strides, leaning far forward, with their arms crossed behind their backs. Their skates are new and shining as they flash past, without a glance at us. I want to skate like that when I grow up.

There is a commotion back at the village. We skate back to see what it is going on. The crowd is not laughing now. They cluster round a drainpipe outlet from the main road. I overhear some men talking. "That outlet is below the frost level in the ground. Warm water must have run under the ice and weakened it."

They looked at the jagged hole in the ice. "Arthur must have skated over it and it gave way."

"Yes! He is a bit overweight."

I squeeze through the crowd, and see the hole. About three yards from the hole, a man under the ice looks at me. His face is purple. He must be very cold. He is not moving, just floating with outstretched arms with his face pressed against the ice. The blacksmith comes running with a big sledgehammer. He is very strong but he has to crash the hammer on the ice several times to make a hole near Arthur. A man lies on the ice and reaches under and manages to grab Arthur's hand, and pull him to the hole. More men help to pull him out of the water. Both holes already have a thin layer of cat ice. The doctor comes. Everyone is very quiet while he examines Arthur. The doctor shakes his head. "I'm afraid that he's gone. There is nothing that I can do."

I feel someone pulling my sleeve; it is Martin, "Come on. It's time to go."

We wait while men carry Arthur to the doctor's car. They lay him on the back seat. The doctor says, "I will take him to the undertaker in town." He looks very sad, "Somebody must ask the vicar to tell his family." We change our boots and cycle slowly home on the slippery road in the fading light. The cold gets under my gloves to my hands. I think of how lucky I am to be going home to a warm kitchen. Arthur will never be warm again.

In the kitchen, my brothers tell Mum and Dad about Arthur. Dad is very serious and says "Poor old Arthur. He played a good hand of solo. We shall certainly miss him in the club."

Mum shakes her head, "Oh! My forefathers! What will become of Elsie and the little ones?" Mum always says strange things when she is upset; one is 'Ye Gods and little fishes.' I don't understand what she is saying. Gerald once told me that people spoke that way in the First World War. We have a photo of Mum in uniform standing by a very large car with wooden spoked wheels. She told us that she used to drive a general around; perhaps he used to say those strange things and Mum copied him. I know Arthur's children; Sheila and Phillip are my school friends. They have no dad to look after them now. He will lie cold and stiff in the churchyard. I feel sad. The invisible dust gets in my eyes again.

THE SMITHY

I am Simon and I am eleven years old. Cyril is the horseman on our farm. Our three horses are Shires, but we think of them as carthorses because they pull carts and farm implements. Martin looks after the herd of thirty Friesian cows. When I said to him that Violet is pretty, he retorted scornfully, "How can a cart horse be pretty? My black and white cows are much more beautiful, just look at their gentle eyes."

This morning, we sit as usual round the big table eating breakfast of thick sweet milky porridge, and slices of fried fat pork. The butcher comes to slaughter one of our pigs every year and we salt the joints of meat and hang them from hooks in the kitchen ceiling. The meat has to last until the next pig is slaughtered. Dad talks to my brothers about the day's work. He turns to me, "Simon, you take Captain and Violet to be shod, tell the blacksmith to put it on my bill. Don't waste any time. We have to make a start ploughing the ten-acre this afternoon."

After breakfast, I help Mum with the washing up, and then go to the stable. Cyril has already fed and brushed the horses and put on their leather bridles with heavy blinkers over their eyes so that sudden movement will not startle them. He has not removed the halters, and tied the free ends together; he always does that when he has to work two horses side by side. He leads the horses to the road, and tells me, "Don't try to rush them, they know the way there and back so you shouldn't have any trouble. I've put a short jerk line on Violet, so you can ride her. You know the signals, a short tug and say 'Reest Reest' for turning right; four quick tugs and 'Cup Cup' for turning left and a long steady pull and 'Whoa' for stop. Just let them walk at their own pace and do not let them trot or gallop. Now up you go." He cups his hands and gives me a leg up onto Violet's back. He pats Captain's neck and grins at me. "None of your daydreaming now. Off you go."

I have handled one horse pulling a cart, a hay rake and harrows on the fields. When I go with my brothers in our pony and trap on the road, they sometimes let me take the reins, and I have ridden our pony to drive the cows down the road to the pasture in the green lane, but I have never been in charge of a cart horse on the road. Cart horses are much too broad to straddle, even adults have to sit sideways. I settle myself on Violet's back and click my tongue and slap the jerk line on her neck as the 'Go' signal. Both horses move obediently forward and we are on our way. I feel the stolid roll of the broad back and the sound of each mighty hoof taking turns to slump down with a hollow thud and swish as it slides forward a few inches on the tarmac. Captain has a loose shoe and that makes a loud click as it touches the road. It is quite different from working horses in the fields; then every muscle bulges as each hoof thumps on the yielding ground, forcing it in to gain a purchase to pull a plough. Gentle beast becomes straining rippling muscular power. Once Dad was telling stories in front of the kitchen range after supper; he said that a one-horse-power rated internal combustion engine is only a fraction of the power of one healthy cart horse.

I am bored sitting on the horse with just the road and fields to look at. I know the road very well; I have to go to school in the village. I don't like being bored; I prefer to think about all sorts of things. My brothers don't know what I think about and tease me for being a daydreamer. Now I am thinking about school. When I started school, Martin gave me a lift on the crossbar of his bicycle; now that bike has been handed down to me so, I ride it to school. It often has a puncture and if my brothers haven't time to mend it, I have to walk; then I get scolded for dawdling on the way home instead of rushing back to help with the chores. I like school and learning about everything, but I don't like the milk; we have to drink a third of a pint bottle of it during morning break. I don't understand why I have to drink it; there is plenty of milk on the farm and it tastes much better from the cow instead of out of a bottle. The teachers make us drink it because it is good for our bones. How can milk get into bones?

Mum makes a jam sandwich for my lunch. She wraps it in newspaper and tucks it into the cardboard box for my gas mask. We always have to carry a gas mask in its cardboard box slung on a cord over one shoulder. The headmaster says that it is in case the Germans drop a gas bomb, but I think that is stupid. Why would anyone drop a gas bomb on the Fens? There are no soldiers, just a few people working the farms. I also have to remember to wear a slab of camphor under my vest on a piece of string round my neck to keep away scarlet fever; that killed some children. I'm only eleven. I don't want to die. Some children have goose dripping plastered on their chest and they have to keep the vest on all winter to stop being killed by pneumonia. Mum says that is an old wives' tale. Why do wives have to be old before they tell a tale? My mum was a nurse in the Great War; she says that having goose dripping on your chest all winter is smelly and unhygienic, whatever that is. She makes us have a bath every week, in a galvanized tub in front of the kitchen range, and then we put on a clean vest and shirt. We wear a very itchy thick wool vest in the winter, but we don't wear a vest in summer.

A bark makes me pay attention. We are about halfway to the village. It is the big Alsatian dog. I am so afraid of that dog when I walk to school. It's chained to a tree, but I know that one day it will break loose and bite me. I keep to the far side of the road, and run as quiet as a mouse, but it still barks loudly. I am not afraid now; Captain will kick it to death if it breaks loose. Once Captain stepped on my foot, but he immediately lifted it and he didn't hurt me. Captain would never hurt me and he won't let that dog bite me.

We pass the doctor's house, and the grocer's shop. The grocer is a kind man; he is also the baker. Once he let me see the oven behind his shop, and all the dough; he showed me how to knead the dough and press a little into a tin. When it's cooked it swells up over the tin to make a loaf with a crispy top. He makes buns too. My dad gives me one penny pocket money every Saturday, and I sometimes buy a bun, for one farthing, on the way back from school, but I prefer to buy a big gobstopper or ten aniseed balls or some Val's sherbet with a liquorish tube to suck it out of the yellow triangular packet.

I don't see many people on the road; it's the school holiday and most children are working on the farms, leading horses with cart loads of sheaves from the fields to the farmyard for stacking, picking fruit, and breaking their backs bending over to pick potatoes. It is easy to climb fruit trees but the branches of the tall elm and wide conker trees are too far apart and beyond my reach. I am not really interested in watching the fields go by. I think about odd things so I won't be bored. I like to polish my brothers' leather shoes. Work boots and Wellingtons are left in the veranda at the back of the house. Best shoes, worn at school and church, are stored in the bottom cupboard of the kitchen dresser. I take them out and lay them in a row on the quarry tile floor. I polish my brothers' shoes because one day they will be mine, and I polish my mother's shoes because she works very hard and I like to help her a little. I carefully put them back in the cupboard in neat rows on the shelves; if I don't keep that shoe cupboard tidy I know that something bad will happen, perhaps a bomb will drop on the house.

Not many people visit our house. The grocer makes weekly deliveries with his horse and van. The butcher sold his horse and bought a new small Ford van to deliver his meat. Men come on motorbikes and sidecars to take orders for seeds, fertilizer and meal for the chickens. They all stay and chat with Mum and Dad. Mum's sister comes to visit from London every year. She always says something like, "Look at that fair hair and those wistful blue eyes, what an angel, a picture of innocence."

Mum would always explain. "Yes, he's lovely, but after three boys, we really wanted a girl." I just feel uncomfortable and rush away to hide in the barn. I am a boy; I don't want to be a girl.

Another auntie brought an Indian family for a visit. I recognised them from pictures in the encyclopedia. The women had coloured sheets wrapped round them, and the men had tight white trousers and strange jackets, but their dark faces and black beards and hair curling from under their turbans made me sure that they were Indian; not Red Indians from America, but proper Indians from India. I was frightened by their dark skin and black staring eyes, and I ran away to hide in the barn. I climbed up the ladder to the loft; they would never find me there.

When I get hungry, I have to go back and brave the Indians. After dinner, the auntie was very haughty. She looked down her nose when she said, "These flies are filthy. They get everywhere. It's disgusting to see them crawling on the food. They have probably come straight from the earth closet and the dung heap." She wrinkled her nose. "God only knows what sort of germs they are spreading."

Dad laughed, "They never bother us, and they never bothered our ancestors."

Mum points to three fly-papers hanging from the ceiling near the open window. "They catch most of them."

I overcome my shyness and say, "Wasps are much more dangerous. I catch them with a jam jar of water with some jam stuck round the edges. The wasps fall in the water and drown. After a few days, there are hundreds in the water."

An Indian man spoke in a strange way, but I could understand most of the words. He said, "You should come to our country. We have enormous insects, including wasps and hornets. You would have a fine time hunting them." He had a nice smile as he spoke, and I was not afraid of him after that, and even admired his curly whiskers.

The clang of the blacksmith's hammer on his anvil rouses me. We have reached the village. I give the jerk line four quick tugs and call, "Cup! Cup!" and we turn on to the small green and cross the grass to the smithy. I give a long steady tug on the jerk line, "Whoa, Violet! Whoa, Captain!"

The blacksmith comes out of his workshop, wiping his face with a dirty cloth. He is a large powerful man in a sweaty shirt with rolled up sleeves, his muscles ripple the same as Captain's, and he must be very strong. He looks at me and his kind eyes show that he is a good man; he would never hurt me. He reaches up and lifts me down, my knees scraping against his torn leather apron burned by hot sparks. "What's your dad doing, letting a young lad handle horses on the main road?" he asks.

He ties Captain's halter to an iron ring in the doorframe, and then leads Violet inside and ties her halter to a steel ring in the back wall.

Two old men sit on a bench outside the workshop; one looks at me in a strange way and says, "It's criminal to send a young boy on the road with horses." He looks at the other man. "What if a car or motor bike came, they would surely frighten the horses into bolting away, and how could a small boy control them. He would probably fall off and be kicked to death."

The other replies, "His father should be reported to the policeman, and he could tell the boy's father that it is a criminal offence and a danger to other people as well as to his son."

I don't like people to say nasty things about my dad, he works very hard and I am happy to help him. I look at the ground and say nothing. It is rude for children to talk to grownups, unless they are asked a question. I feel angry, and follow the blacksmith into his shop. My anger soon goes. There are so many interesting things to see.

The blacksmith smiles at me. "Stand

over there and don't get in the way. I don't want to shoe you by mistake." He laughs and I giggle and stand by a stack of horseshoes. "I make those when there are no horses waiting and when I am not making harrows or repairing implements." I nod. I once watched him when Dad brought me with him when he wanted a new toe to put on a ploughshare, and he stayed to chat with the blacksmith while he worked.

The blacksmith makes his own tools, but he buys nails from the town. He makes the shoes from a strip of iron; he pumps up the forge with big leather bellows with a handle longer than me, until the coals glow orange. He pushes the strip in with his long iron tongs until it is red hot, and then quickly lifts it onto the anvil, spiked to a chunk of tree trunk, and beats the strip to a horseshoe shape, and then plunges it into a trough of dirty water beside the forge. He then reheats the horseshoe and pierces holes for square nails and also forms the lip at the front of the shoe; he plunges it into the water again and throws it on the stack of shoes. He makes the shoes in several sizes and puts them in separate piles at the back of the workshop.

It is murky in the workshop. The forge makes it very hot, and great clouds of steam hiss from the water trough when the red-hot iron is plunged in. The rough brick walls, rafters and underside of the roof tiles are festooned in cobwebs; the earth floor is littered with bits of metal, and a thick coat of dust has settled in every nook and cranny. When the blacksmith shapes iron on the anvil, he hammers the red-hot metal, and then bounces the hammer four times on the anvil. He told me that if he hammers hot iron without the bouncing, the hammer would get very hot and lose its hardness. The rhythmic thump and tapping echo around the village green, but no one complains. Blacksmithing is noisy work, and people just put up with it. I like to make things out of scrap materials; mostly model planes and boats, and I have tried casting molten lead into shapes, but I have never tried to play with red-hot iron.

The blacksmith strokes Violet, and then with his back to her head, he lifts her front leg and holds the hoof between his knees. He uses a claw hammer to un-cleat the old nails and prize off the worn-out shoe, and then cleans the underside of the hoof with a short, curved knife. He eases the hoof back on the ground. He selects a shoe from the pile and lifts the hoof again to check the size. He takes the few steps to the forge, pumps the bellows and pushes the shoe into the glowing coals with his tongs. When the shoe glows red hot, he grips it in the tongs puts it on the anvil and taps a special spike into a nail hole to act as a handle. He carries it quickly to Violet, lifts her hoof and presses the still glowing shoe to the underside of the hoof. A cloud of acrid smoke billows up to engulf the heads of the blacksmith and Violet; neither seemed to mind, but I gag and cough. The blacksmith plunges the still hot shoe into the water trough and when it is cold puts it, with the claw hammer, on his wooden tray of nails. He lifts the hoof again, fits the shoe and carefully hammers nails at an angle through the hoof, to protrude about an inch though the top. He then places the hoof on a three-legged iron stand and bends over the ends of the nails to cleat the shoe firmly to the hoof. He then takes a rasp from the tray and trims the outside of the hoof to the curve of the shoe. All the while he talks softly to Violet and often reaches up to stroke her ears. He is very gentle and kind with horses, and children.

The blacksmith finishes shoeing Violet and leads her out of the workshop and tethers her, and then brings in Captain and re-shoes him. He leads him outside and ties his halter to Violet's bridle. He grins at me. "Come here, young man." He lifts me on to Violet's back as though I am thistledown. He unties the jerk line, gives it to me, and leads Violet to the road, "Off you go. If a car comes, just stop the horses and talk quietly to them until it has gone." I shake the jerk line and click my tongue and we start down the long road. We go through the village, and I start thinking again.

Martin sleeps on the landing. It's a big room and has a large bookcase, and a fat leather trunk full of Mum's and Dad's old clothes. It is my pretend magic horse. I like to sit astride it and ride it to all those places over the sea. The bookcase has many books and papers, and bound copies of the London Illustrated News at the time of the Great War. I spent a lot of time absorbed in those books, looking at the drawings and reading about the trenches where my uncle was gassed, and many soldiers killed. Mum bought a set of encyclopedias from a man who came to the door. She talked to me when we were alone in the kitchen. She had her stern look and said, "Now that Gerald has been called up in the army he will change his ideas about his future, and may not want to work on the farm when he comes home. Martin and Cyril did not pass the scholarship, and have no choice but to stay on the farm; anyway, they like farming and don't want to do anything else. You seem to be interested in everything, so Dad and I have bought these encyclopedias. We really cannot afford them, Dad will have to pay the salesman every month, but if you learn and understand everything in the books you will not have to slave on a farm when you grow up; you could either work in an office or be a doctor, sheltered from the weather with a regular income and no worry." My brothers are not interested in the encyclopedias, but I am fascinated by using cow's blood in humans to stop smallpox, pictures of the inside of bodies, and stories and pictures of strange people in foreign lands. I read of people with strange names, Freud and Descartes who know about the mind and how it works, I cannot really understand but I read and read all those books because I don't want to work on a farm and not go anywhere all my life.

Martin once bought two white guinea pigs from the market in town. I had not seen such animals before. Gerald told me, "If they are held up by the tail their eyes drop out." I am very puzzled because I can't see a tail. My brother laughs and says it is a joke. I do not think that a guinea pig not having a tail is funny. Perhaps when I grow up I will understand his joke.

The guinea pigs were put in one of the rabbit hutches. After a few months, they were crowding out the rabbits. Their numbers grew and white guinea pigs and rabbits soon shared all the hutches. They ate the rabbits' food. Rabbits make a tasty stew, but guinea pigs are no good for eating. My brothers could not kill them so they collected them into potato sacks and carted them to the orchard. There was a stack of twigs and dead branches, and the guinea pigs scuttled for shelter under it and burrowed holes to live in. There was a glut of fallen apples and plenty of grass and weeds and the guinea pigs continued to breed, until there were hundreds forming a white carpet as they foraged for food. Winter snow came and it was difficult to see the white animals. After the snow and frost thawed there was no trace of the guinea pigs, they had disappeared. Dad commented, "It must have been the hard winter. They're foreign animals and cannot stand the cold. No doubt the frost killed them." We nodded and Dad added, "It's just as well, they would have eaten all the winter wheat. With no crop to sell, what would we have done?" I didn't want to think about that and went to the hen house to collect the eggs, warm from the nest. I like to cook them for our five o'clock tea. Mum showed me how to wait for the water to come to the boil, and to lift out the eggs with a tablespoon after four minutes. More than four minutes and we can't dip bread and butter fingers and have to spoon the hard yolks out.

I see and hear a motor cycle approaching and pull the horses to a halt. The driver halts and stops the engine and then beckons me on. As I ride by he gives a smile, "They're fine horses you have. I don't want to frighten them so I will wait for you to pass." I am shy and do not speak to strangers, but I am pleased that he stopped, and I smile back. I look carefully at the bike with its wide curving handlebars with levers and wires and a horn, and round green petrol tank. I have seen pictures in the encyclopedias of cars and motorbikes cut away to show the inside and read how they work, and I imagine the piston and gears inside the motorbike. After we pass, I turn to watch the rider kick start the engine and drive off with a clatter and cloud of smoke. I love Captain, but carthorses are slow; I will drive a fast motorbike when I grow up and have a lot of money. When I am a man I will look after Mum and Dad and Captain when they are old and cannot work anymore.

We arrive home; the horses naturally go to the stable. I slide off Violet. I tie the halters to the stall and climb in the manger to take off their bridles. I stroke their manes and then climb down and take Violet and Captain to the back pasture. I open the five-barred gate, let them loose, close the gate and look through the rails. There is a water tank there but they are not thirsty and prefer a good gallop. Dad joins me and leans on the gate. He looks cross. "Why did you let them loose? I've been waiting for you. I want to use the carts." He has a funny look and put his hand on my shoulder, "I'm proud of you, Simon. You didn't see me, but I followed you on my bike. I saw that you reached the smithy safely, so I came home. I knew that you would come home safely by yourself, but I kept an eye on you from the bedroom window when you came back just in case anything happened." I am pleased that he looked out for me. I will tell the blacksmith next time I see him, and then he will tell those men that my dad is not a criminal.

We are all sitting round the table after supper. I get up and start to clear the dishes, but Mum tells me to sit down. She looks at Dad and then me, "We had an important letter today. You have passed the Scholarship and can go to grammar school in September." When I took the exam six weeks ago I did my best, now I am so pleased that I can go to grammar school. Mum turns to Dad. "He's very bright and should be given the chance to have a good education."

Dad sighs. "He reads a lot, but he's also good with his hands. I had hopes that he could drive the tractor when we can afford one, but I suppose you're right as usual. It's going to be a struggle to find the money. It's been a bad year for potatoes, and although we had a good crop of wheat the price is down."

Mum smiles. "Well! We always manage to pull through somehow, I'm sure we will cope with this, even if we have to put off buying a tractor for a year."

Martin and Cyril had been looking at their plates. Martin looks up. "When you get a tractor, I want to drive it. I saw an orange Ford Standard in the village. I think that a tractor would be better than horses."

Cyril looks angrily at Martin. "Don't you say anything against my horses; they're more useful than your cows; all they do is poo everywhere."

Mum raises her voice. "That's enough. There will be no quarrelling in this family."

Dad adds, "Do as your mother says. When we do get a tractor, I will drive it." He smiles at Martin, "When I am expert I will teach you." He looks at Cyril. "When we get a tractor, I will keep the horses, so you don't need to worry. There will always be work for them that a tractor cannot do." He looks at me. "You, Simon, will go to grammar school and when you have finished, you can help me with the books; that is when you can spare time from polishing the seat of your trousers on an office chair."

We all laughed. Mum said, "That's settled then. Simon, just clear the table and help me with the washing up, then we can have a nice game of cards."

After we have finished playing cards, Dad talks to me. "I hope that you make the most of your chances at the grammar school, but in life you also need a bit of luck. The blacksmith's son Rupert, when he was just a bit older than you, made pictures by gluing feathers onto a pane of glass. I saw a few and I was very impressed, but the blacksmith ridiculed them and said that his son had to follow him into the blacksmiths' trade and eventually take over the business. His mum was upset; she liked the pictures and showed them to the headmaster. He said that he had never seen anything like them and wanted to show some to his friend who had an art shop in town. The friend was very impressed and bought one for half a crown. Rupert's mum encouraged him to do more and he developed his technique. The art shop sold the painting for five shillings. The headmaster opened a joint bank account with Rupert, and persuaded the smithy to let Rupert make more pictures. The headmaster became Rupert's agent; he bought the material and the boy mixed oil paint and feathers to make pictures of farm life. The pictures sold well at auction and to private buyers and bank account grew."

Mum adds, "The smithy changed his mind when he saw how much Rupert was earning. He had his eye on the money."

Dad continues with his story. "The blacksmith needed more income. When Rupert left school, he persuaded Rupert to spend some of his money on welding equipment. He made wrought iron gates for farmers. Rupert became very interested in welding and made fancy ironwork garden ornaments. His artistic gift enabled him to make very intricate patterns, and his reputation spread to the town. Eventually the welding brought in more money than the blacksmith. Rupert was loyal to his father; all his earnings went into the family income. Rupert's Mum and Dad were very proud of him; because of his earnings they were able to buy a car and have a good life."

Mum completes the story. "Rupert still did his paintings, but paid another artistic boy to help with the simple bits. The headmaster continued to be his agent, he took twenty percent commission and when Rupert needed money they both signed the withdrawal cheque. Everyone was happy. The headmaster sadly died from pneumonia just before he was due to retire. Rupert was very upset, and made a special pair of gates for the school with the headmaster's name included in the design." Mum looks intently at us. "Big oak trees from small acorns grow. Just remember that if you work hard at something that you like, success will follow. Never work just for the money; if you are good at what you do the money will come in, and you will also enjoy working for it."

Dad laughs. "Yes, but you also need a bit of luck."

One day I go to watch the blacksmith after school. He is busy with some men putting an iron rim on a wooden wheel. I am told to get out of the way, and can't really see what they are doing. When I arrive home after fetching the cows from the pasture I ask Dad to tell me about it.

He says, "My dad was a wheelwright; he made wooden carts and lorries, including the wheels. He took the wheels to the local blacksmith to have the rims put on. My dad wanted me to stay at home and help him with his business, but two of my older brothers were already learning the trade and there was not enough work to support all of us." He smiles at Mum. "After I came home from the trenches, I met Mother. I was very lucky. After we married, her dad set us up in this place. I had always wanted to be a farmer, and my dream came true." He looks fondly at Mum. "No' only that, I also found a wonderful wife."

Mum blushes and mutters, "Not in front of the children."

Dad grins, "Anyway, I know about putting rims on wheels. I had to take them to the blacksmith several times. The blacksmith has to make the rim. It is a very skillful job. It has to be perfectly round and just the right size. It has to be too small for the wheel, and will only slip over the wood rim if it is made red hot. The wheel is laid on a concrete pad with a hole in the middle to take the hub. Next to the concrete is another slab. The iron rim is supported on bricks on the slab, and a coal fire is lit all round the rim. When the rim is red hot, four men lift it with big pincers and quickly fit it on the wood rim and hammer it in place. The wood burns, and the flames are put out with water that also shrinks the iron and it squeezes the rim and tightens all the joints in the wheel, and the rim cannot come off."

I interrupt. "I read in the encyclopedia that metal expands when it gets hot and contracts when it gets cold." I look at Cyril, "That's why the rim fits tight on the wheel."

Martin smirks, "Clever clogs." Cyril just looks at his plate.

Mum says sharply, "That's enough. Simon, stop showing off."

Martin says, "Dad! Tell us again about painting carts."

Dad smiles. "Again! Never mind there's not much on the radio until 'In Town Tonight'. I didn't really like working with wood, I preferred painting. Mind you it was interesting to see Dad do it. The wheels were special; the hubs were ash, the spokes elm, and the rims oak; that oak was very hard to shape. It took several years' experience to make a wheel, every joint had to be perfect and a tight fit, otherwise the wheel would collapse under load. The rest of the work on the cart was comparatively easy, and I must say that I liked carving the angles of the shafts and main timbers with a spokeshave. I varied the depth of the cut to give a series of curves to the angles. They were picked out in paint. The carts were usually painted in either orange or dark blue and the decorative bits picked out in black and yellow. The flat bits were decorated with scrolls and straight and curved lines. It took me a long time to get the hang of using horsehair brushes in a goose quill handle. The hairs were up to six inches long and some quite thin. It was an art to fill the brush with paint and then flick it on the cart and pull it along in a straight line. The curves and scrolls were done with a shorter brush, but all the work required a very steady hand." Dad holds out his hand. "I've still got that. You've seen me touch up the paint on my carts, so I haven't lost the knack. The bit that I really didn't like was grinding the paint. It took hours to grind the slabs of lead paint, and then add the linseed oil, chalk filler, and colour. It was a bit like the sausage mincer, but much harder to turn the handle." Dad pauses. "The most satisfying thing was painting the name and address of the owner on the front panel of the cart. The curlicues and scrolls were always the same, but the address was always different, and I could use different types of lettering to suit the owner."

Mum glances at the kitchen clock. That was good timing, it's just in time for 'In Town Tonight'. I always smile at the beginning of the programme when the man says, 'We stop the mighty roar of London traffic, to bring you what's happening tonight.' We also enjoy listening to Cyril Fletcher and his 'Odd Odes'. Another funny man is Arthur Askey, and another man does impersonations of many things; I like his impression of a steam train, and the clatter and click as the train runs over points in the rails. We like Ronny Ronald, the whistler, and Larry Adler who plays the harmonica, but it sounds the same as a mouth organ.

THE HERD

The Recession, we knew it as the Slump, was still biting during the thirties. The dairy herd of thirty Friesians was subsidizing the arable farm, but more income was needed to feed four hungry sons. Dad heard of a milk round for sale in the town. He talked it over with Mum, and they decided to take out a bank overdraft to buy it. More money could be made by selling milk direct to customers, rather than to bulk wholesale buyers. Dad paid the village jobbing builder to help him to lay a concrete base, and erect a timber and corrugated sheet shed in the yard opposite the house for use as a dairy.

The farmhouse, outbuildings and yards occupied a rectangle of about three acres, behind the yards was lush pasture, where cows and horses grazed and chewed the cud under the shade of chestnut and elm trees. Arable fields were beyond the pasture; more fields including an orchard and worker's cottages fronted the road that passed through the hamlet. The pasture was separated from the farm buildings by a timber rail fence and five bar gate that opened to a yard used for stacking hay and straw, and large enough for the massive steam driven threshing tackle to come in after harvest. At the sides of the yard were a henhouse, stores, and another fence and gate to a crew yard bounded by cowshed, calf house and barn. The barn had doors to the cowshed and yards, and then another gate beside the calf house leading to another yard with a door to the barn and calf house, bounded on one side by a shed for the car, a lean-to shed for paraffin, grease for the carts and other bits and pieces included a coal fired boiler next to the dairy. On the other side of the yard was the back garden of the farmhouse and door to the conservatory, then a gravel driveway to the main road, flanked by the front garden of the house and a large vegetable garden. The road boundary was hawthorn hedging with an opening for a five-bar gate that was never closed.

During fine weather, the cows were brought into the cowshed for morning and evening milking and spent the rest of the time in the pasture. In bad winter weather, the pasture was frozen and covered with snow, and the cows had to be fed. They spent most of the time in the cowshed and crew yard with only occasional visits to the pasture during spells of fine weather. The cowshed had a concrete floor had three levels; a two-yard wide walkway, with a door to the barn, ran the length of the floor down the side near the crew yard, and had double timber doors for the cows to get in and out. Alongside the walkway opposite the doors, was a double depth trench, to form a nine-inch deep by one-foot wide trench for liquid drain off and a shallow thirty-inch wide channel for cows to deposit dung. The concrete alongside the channel was divided into cow size bays by galvanized tubes set in the concrete to form stalls for the cows, with a concrete manger and a slated wood hay rack above. The wall above the racks was glazed with no openings. Chains round the neck with quick release catches restrained the cows. The dung channel and stalls were bedded with straw from the stack yard. The cow's urine spurted as far as the deep trench and flowed out through a hole in the wall into an open ditch at the side of the stack yard; and the solids were deposited on the straw spread on the channel.

During the summer, grazing on grass gave cows diarrhea, so that when they came in for milking a wary eye and quick side step was needed to avoid a splattering. In winter with more solid food, the end result was more solid and easily disposed of. The soiled straw was forked into a wheelbarrow and carted to a muckheap in the stack yard. At the end of the winter, the heap was very large. It rotted all summer, and by the autumn had changed into manure. After the harvest, it was carted to the fields and put in small heaps that were later scattered and ploughed in as fertilizer.

The walkway and both channels were hosed down; the waste drained to a ditch bordering the pasture and contaminated a pond where the cows used to drink. The cows later drank from new galvanized tanks with a ball valve fed by mains water, placed near the gate to the field, and in the crew yard.

***

Across the road from our house is a bigger farmhouse next to the churchyard. Dad often has a faraway look when he gazes at it during Sunday dinner eaten at midday Cooking a main meal at midday and having a high tea around four-thirty, and a light snack at eight in the evening fits the workings of the farm and is handy for Mum. A school friend gave me a sketchpad with a pen and Indian ink. I drew a sketch of the Old Henry's farmhouse from our dining room window. I had never tried drawing things as I see them, I was very pleased that I could do it at ten years old, but no one said anything. Pride and praise have no place in our lives.

Dad says dreamily, "When Old Henry goes we will live in that house." Old Henry doesn't work now; he just sits by his dining room window as though he's waiting for a visitor. Dad continues, "When you boys have a sister we will need an extra bedroom."

I ask, "Why do we need a sister Dad?"

Mum replies, "After Gerald we wanted a girl, but had only boys." She looks at me. "We were certain that after three sons, you would be our little girl." She pats the bulge on her stomach, and smiles at Dad. "I'm sure that we will be lucky this time."

I feel angry. "I'm glad I'm not a stupid girl. I would hate to play with dolls. My Meccano is much better." The same as our clothes, the Meccano set had been handed down from my brothers Gerald to Martin, to Cyril and to me. I was very lucky, an aunt gave me her son's clockwork Meccano motor, so I can make things that move.

I am happy living on our farm. The house is small, cool in summer and cold in winter when the east wind finds all the cracks in windows and doors. Old Sam works on the farm. When the east wind blows he shivers and says, "This comes from Siberia. It doesn't blow round a body; it blows right through. It chills the marrow in your bones." I don't understand why he says it so often. Dad says that we need the draught to make the fires glow in the closed kitchen range and open grates in the dining room and parlour when the doors and windows are closed against the cold. He says the draught works in the same way as the bellows in the smithy's forge. In the winter, we sit in front of the fire and our faces and legs go red with the heat, but our backs freeze in the draught. Upstairs is very cold so we quickly get undressed and snuggle in the feather bed. When it's really cold Mum fills a stone vinegar bottle with boiling water to warm the bed before we get in. The elms in the neighbouring vicarage poke into the sky higher than the church tower. I like to listen to the wind make a loud sigh through the trees while I am snug in bed. Rooks and crows live in the elms. When they build their nests high in the top branches, we know that it will be a fine spring.

The gardens at the back and front of the house are grass with a few laurel bushes and roses. The laurels have big thick leaves on the outside, and I like to sit on the branches inside them and play pretend games. When

Mum goes on at Dad to make pretty gardens, he just laughs and says, "Good farmers make poor gardeners. Get the children to help you." Mum has no time for gardening; anyway, we brothers prefer growing vegetables rather than flowers, although I do like the roses. We have to cut the grass with an old cast-iron hand mower. It is very hard work and impossible to cut long grass, then someone has to mow it with a scythe.

Gerald is seventeen; he has left school and is learning the seed business with an uncle's firm in the town. He lives in digs. I thought that he lived in a hole until I visited him with Mum and saw his room in a boarding house. Gerald cycles home at weekends, and helps with odd jobs. This Saturday he is making it easier to push the mower by slicing the long grass with a scythe. He is taller than Dad and very strong. He thinks a lot and has a serious face, but it lights up when he smiles. Old Sam taught him how to use a scythe. He is very skillful. I like to watch his slow smooth swinging stokes. He keeps the blade level and just above the ground, it cuts and also gathers the grass and leaves it in a neat row.

He has to sharpen the blade often; he puts the long, curved handle behind him with the blade sticking forward over his right shoulder, then he grips the end of the blade, and strokes each side with a rub-stone. One day I will be tall enough to do that, but I will be afraid of cutting off my hand. One of our neighbours was scything in his orchard. His foot slipped in a rabbit hole and he fell on the blade. He walked half a mile to our house with a gaping wound on the front of his leg. I was afraid, but also curious. I had never seen gore before. The man was very brave and did not cry. Mum said the wound needed stitching together, and although she was a nurse in the First World War, she said it was too deep for her to sew it up. She took him in the family car to hospital in the town. She wrapped the leg in newspaper to stop the blood dripping in the car.

Martin is nearing fifteen. He is smaller and more wiry than Gerald, and wears cord trousers and a flannel shirt and a knitted sweater under a Harris Tweed jacket; he generally wears heavy hobnailed boots with leather leggings, but in very wet weather wears wellingtons. Of course, all his clothes will be handed down to Cyril and then to me. Martin is the cowman. Most of his work is done during early morning and in the late afternoon, and at other times he helps on the farm. Part of growing up on a farm is learning how to work on one. My brothers, and sometimes Dad tell me how to do things. Today Martin shows me how to cut into a stack of straw. He uses a large broad blade with a wooden handle eighteen inches long at right angles to the blade to cut out chunks of straw and haystacks for bedding and fodder. I help him to carry a long wooden ladder to the stack. Martin lays it on the ground at right-angles to the stack, and tells me to stand on the end near the stack, He then lifts the far end above his head, and then walks to the stack lifting the ladder hand over hand above his head as he goes, until the ladder falls forward onto the stack about four feet from a corner. He jumps on the bottom rung to make sure that the ladder is bedded in the soil, and climbs up, taking a pitchfork with him, sticks it in the top of the stack, and then comes down. He goes up again carrying the broad bladed stack knife on his shoulder with the blade down his back. "If I slip and fall this could cut off your head, so stand clear until I am on the stack then come up after me." I climb up very high.

Martin is waiting sitting on the sloping top of the stack. The pitchfork and knife are stuck in the straw beside him. He gives me a stern look, "No playing around. This can be dangerous. Straw is not so bad, but hay is very slippery. You just stay on the ladder and watch carefully." He sits on the slope, digging his heels into the straw to stop him from sliding down, and forks off the straw below him to the yard, so that he has a level space about three and a half feet square. "That's the tricky bit, especially if it's wet," he says as he stands on the level part.

Martin reaches up and takes the stack knife from where he pushed it in the slope of the stack. "Be very careful with this, it's very sharp. It looks difficult to use, but you soon get the hang of it. Start at the outside like this." He stands on the platform and holds the knife in both hands and works the blade up and down, until it has cut about six inches into the stack and the blade is fully in the straw. Martin looks at me, "Now that I've made a start it's easy to push and pull the knife at a slight angle and force it through the straw." He does that until he reaches the corner of his platform. "You must keep the blade vertical and make a clean straight cut. You have more control if you keep your knees bent, you keep your back straight and go up and down by bending the knees." He lifts out the blade and thrusts it in at right angle to the first cut. "Now do the same on this line." He pushes and pulls the blade until he almost reaches the edge of the stack. "Now be careful, when you are about six inches from the edge just ease the knife to finish the cut. If you are too vigorous you could overbalance as the knife slices through into open air, then you could fall and either break your neck or chop your head off if you fall on the knife."

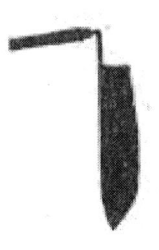

I shudder and look down to the ground about twenty feet below. "Don't be afraid. When you are big enough to do this, you will have more common sense than you have now, and it will be obvious that you have to be careful when working with sharp tools. Just as I told you when I gave you that pocket knife." He smiles. "Now climb up the ladder a bit so that I can get on below you." I climb higher and hold tight to the ladder. "Now pass me the fork, I stuck it in so that you could reach it." I reach out and pull out the fork and lower it to Martin. "Not like that, stupid. Pass it handle first. If you let it slip the tines could pierce my neck or something." I carefully turn the fork and hand it to Martin. He leans over and forks the two-foot deep square of straw down to the ground. He steps back on the now lower level platform and slides the knife horizontally into the cut stack. "That will be safe there, and be handy for tomorrow when I have to cut more straw." He pulls a rub-stone from his pocket and pushed it in beside the knife. "It's best to sharpen the knife before you use it, so keep these together." He pauses and says, "Come on down, and don't fall on me," as he quickly climbs down. Martin tidies the heap of straw and thrusts the pitchfork into the top and levers it on his right shoulder. The long handle of the pitchfork stuck out at an angle in front of him and almost touches the ground. I know it's a pitchfork because it is used to pitch sheaves of straw from the stooks in the cornfield up to the horse drawn carts, and also to throw the sheaves off the cart onto the stack. I follow Martin as he carries the straw about two hundred yards to the cowshed.

"Doesn't that handle hurt your shoulder?" I ask.

Martin waits until he has dumped the load on the walkway. He is panting. "It's heavy. Of course it hurts. Many farm jobs hurt, bending down to pick potatoes and singling sugar beet is back breaking, but you have to get used to the aches and pains." He loosens the straw with the fork and spreads it on the concrete stalls as bedding, and in the trench to absorb the dung. We have to make several trips to the stack to get enough straw. We do the same thing with the haystack, but Martin puts the hay in the racks.

It is time to do my own regular job and go to fetch the cows from the pasture. They wait at the gate and when I open it they find their own way to the cowshed and start to eat the hay in the stalls. I remember to shut the gate. I follow the cows and put the chains round their necks. Martin and I walk to the house, take off and clean our boots on an old besom and a sack, wash our hands and join the others for tea of boiled eggs and fingered toast, bread and jam and sponge cake.

I have been reading about parachutes. It must be a wonderful feeling to float down through the air. Gerald has cut about half way down the stack; the ladder is still there, so I climb about fifteen feet to the square bit and step onto the small space. I have made a parachute of a square of brown paper, with string tied at each corner. I grasp the ends, take a deep breath and jump. Before I know what has happened I am sprawled on the heap of straw that Martin forked off the stack. The paper is ripped and the string has torn out of two corners. I am very disappointed.

Gerald comes running to the stack with his pitchfork. He shouts, "What the hell do you think you are playing at?" He sticks the fork upright in the ground. "You've done some silly things in your time, but this is plain stupid." He calms down. "I had to go and have a pee behind the stack. If I hadn't wanted a pee, I would have already taken the straw in the cowshed and you would have crashed to the ground instead of having a soft landing. You would have at least broken your arm, and probably your neck. Mum would never have got over the shock of seeing me carry your dead body into the kitchen."

I hang my head. "Well! I didn't break anything, but I've bruised my thigh. I didn't think it was dangerous, I thought that I would just float down." Gerald turns his eyes to the sky and says nothing.

When calves are born the milk is very rich and yellow, and is known as beastlings. It cannot be used for the milk round, but Mum uses some to make foamy custard in a pastry flan; it is delicious. After a few days when the milk is white again, the calf is separated from its mother and put in the calf house, and it has to be taught how to drink instead of suck milk. Cyril shows me how to do it. He gets half a pail of milk from the dairy, and we go to the calf shed. It's warm but a bit gloomy in there, and the calf is alone. It is pleased to see us, and pushes its nose against us. Cyril grabs the calf round the neck. "Hold that pail firmly on the floor, otherwise this thing will spill the milk. Calves may be small, but they are very strong for their size." He pulls the calf to the pail and scopes up some milk in his free hand. "Just rub the milk on its nose." He dips his hand in the milk again. "Then put a couple of fingers in its mouth and it will taste the milk and start sucking." With his fingers still in the calf's mouth he lowers its head into the bucket. "Hold its mouth on the milk like this; while it sucks my fingers it will suck up some milk." Cyril lifts the calf's head out of the pail and wipes his fingers on his trousers. "Now you have a go. I will hold its head for you. Keep one hand on the pail."

I wet my hand in the milk and the calf sucks my hand into its mouth. It is a strange feeling; the calf's tongue is as rough as the rasp that I use to shape wood, and a bit painful. Cyril laughs. "It's not going to eat you. Now slowly take your fingers out while I push its mouth in the milk." The calf keeps sucking and slurps up the milk, drinking greedily. "That's good, it's got the idea. It will only need a couple more feeds and it will be come straight to the pail and drink." I didn't like the feel of my hand in the calf's mouth. Now it's over I think about making the Spitfire fighter. I have shaped the body and wings and now have to finish the tail. I enjoy making things. Cyril disturbs my plans. "This has good markings for a Friesian; you see how there is no black below the knees, that's a sure sign of a pedigree. I expect Dad will keep this one. If the markings were not good, or if it was a bull calf, Dad would sell it to the dealer and he would sell it to the butcher for veal."

"What's veal?" I ask.

Cyril grins. "Don't you know anything? It would be slaughtered; calf meat is veal." I know that Mum cooks pork and beef for Sunday dinner; I think that the joints of meat are too big to be veal. I could never eat a calf. Instead of thinking about eating calf, I think about the tail plane. It will be too thin to shape with a rasp, and I decide to ask Dad to get me some sandpaper next time he goes to town.

After tea, I usually help Mum with the washing up, and then go to the cowshed to help Cyril muck out the cows before they are milked. We use four-pronged forks to lift the straw and dung onto a barrow. It is made of wood and very heavy, I can wheel it when it is empty but Cyril has to push the barrow of muck out to the muckheap behind the cowshed. He reminds me, "Don't try to lift too much on the fork." He grins and adds, "This muck is very heavy and I don't want to be blamed if you rupture yourself." I know what a rupture is. Dad has one. It's a lump that pokes out of his stomach. I haven't seen it, but he has to wear a strong spring belt with a pad to keep the lump inside. When the trench is clear, we swill it down with a yard brush and water from the cattle trough in the crew yard. Cyril scrubs and I play with the water. Cyril then spreads more straw in the trench from the pile on the walkway. We have to do that in the morning as well, after the cows are milked.

***

The cows are milked at seven in the morning and at five after afternoon tea. Dad, Martin and Cyril are expert at milking cows. I have watched them many times. They sit on stools about eighteen inches high, knocked up from bits of wood, a single leg of three by three with a three by one seat nailed across the top. They turn their peaked caps back to front, sit on the stool with a pail held between their knees and press their heads against the cow's stomach. The cows are pedigree Friesians, except for one Red Poll, and one all black. The Friesians are docile and only accidentally lash a tail on the milker to brush off flies. Sometimes the milkers tie the cow's tail to a back leg. Cow's back legs are very flexible and they can kick sideways as well as forward and back. The black cow has very tender teats that have to be handled with care. Any roughness from the milker and he would be sent flying in a shower of spilt milk.

Cyril talks as he shows me how to milk a cow. He puts his right hand to the cow. "You put your finger and thumb at the top of the teat." He glances at me. "Like this. Then you press them together and close your fingers down the teat, at the same time pulling gently." A stream of milk appeared. Cyril cups his left hand and catches the milk, and wets his palms and the two nearest teats. "That makes them slippery and is easier on the cow and your hands." He settles his chubby body on his stool, grips the pail between his knees, and takes a teat in each hand. "Start with the two nearest. Squeeze and pull alternate teats and you will have a continuous stream." The spurting milk makes a hollow drumming on the bottom of the pail that changes to a splashy swoosh as the milk froths and foams as the pail fills. It's a nice gentle sound, not as loud as the clanging of the five bells in the church tower; that hurts my ears on Sundays. There are many gentle sounds on the farm; even the church bells can be gentle when I am far away in the fields. When the teats run dry, Cyril changes to the other two. It takes about ten minutes to milk the cow.

Cyril stands up and puts the pail on the walkway. "Cows give about one gallon," he says as he picks up an empty pail and carries it with his stool to another cow. "There we are. Now you have a go." I turn my cap round and sit down. I can't hold the pail properly, and just close my knees round it and let it rest on the straw bedding. I take hold of a teat. It is very big in my small hand. I have to take my head from the cow's stomach to see what I am doing. I pull my finger and thumb down the teat without squeezing and a trickle of milk comes out. The cow hurts my back with its tail. Cyril speaks sharply, "What did I tell you! That just serves your right for not paying attention. Why are you always daydreaming? I told you not to pull too hard. That's stropping and can hurt a cow, so never do it again." I choke back my tears and try again.

After a while I get the hang of it, but my hands seize up with cramp and I have to stop. Cyril is back to his cheery self. He grins. "Don't you mind. My hands hurt when I started, but with practice they get used to squeezing.

"When you get bigger you can make a start milking the heifers after they have their first calf. The teats are small and should fit your hand." When the two pails are full, Cyril uses a wooden yoke with chains to take the weight on his shoulders, to carry the pails to the dairy. He tips the milk into the cooler tank, rinses the buckets with the hose and goes back to milk more cows. Dad and Martin do the same.

During the summer, the cows just eat grass in the meadows and hay from the racks. In the winter when the pasture is frozen there is not enough grass to feed the animals. The cows are fed with a mixture of shredded mangolds and chaff, cow cake and sugar beet pulp. The pulp comes from the factory and is the leftover after the sugar has been crushed out of the roots. The pulp is stored in large sacks in a closed store at the end of the barn near the door to the cowshed. Inside the store is a large galvanized tub of water to soak the pulp overnight before giving it to the cows. If they ate dry pulp it would swell up inside them and kill them. The door to the pulp store is normally closed, but once it was left open and two young heifers got in. I watched as they lay on their sides with bloated stomachs struggling to breathe as the pulp swelled inside them. Their breaths became shorter, then they stopped breathing and their wide-open eyes became cloudy. The village butcher came next day to take away the bodies. He said that the meat was not poisoned and was cutting into joints to sell in his shop.

There is a granary over the sugar beet pulp store. It is used to store lightweight things such as potato baskets and sacks. I climb up there when I want to be alone with my thoughts. It is quiet and comfortable lying on the sacks, and there is nothing for rats to eat, so they don't bother me. Next to the pulp store is a space for linseed oil cake compressed into slabs eighteen inches wide and a yard long and one inch thick. They are fed into a crusher operated by a handle on a large flywheel, Cyril turns turned the wheel and Martin feeds in the slabs of cake, and small bits of cake spill out into a bucket. There is also a chaff cutter that has a similar flywheel but with sharp blades bolted to the curved spokes. As the wheel is turned, long straw is pushed through a slot into the wheel and the blades chopped it into very short lengths.

It's not used anymore and is gathering dust and rust. Now Dad buys in sacks of chaff. I don't know here he gets it; it is just always here.

Every week, Martin takes a horse and two-wheel tipping cart to the clamp in the field and brings back a load of mangolds and tips it into the barn door. Cyril helps him to pitchfork the roots inside the barn. The trick is to pierce a couple of roots, swing them into the barn and jerk the prongs out, so the roots fly the fifteen feet into the barn and make a neat heap. It is rather clever to do that. We have our tea, finish the milking and sit in the barn, wrapped in warm clothes, cleaning mangolds. We sit on fruit boxes, with a folded sack as a cushion, in a semicircle near the heap, and with another sack draped over our knees. We reach for a mangold from the heap, lay it on the sack and scrape off the dirt and mud with a curved sharp scraper with a wooden handle, and then throw it behind us on the floor until we have cleaned enough for the night's feed. The paraffin lantern sits in a pool of light on the floor, and lights up our faces against the darkness beyond the light. Our moving hands cast flickering shadows on the distant walls. The barn is sinister at night. It has a slate roof and brick walls, and is long and narrow. The flame in the lantern cannot light up the barn, and there are dark shadows on the walls and among the rafters. Sometimes I frighten myself by imagining giants in the shadows waiting to catch and eat me. I never go into the barn at night by myself.

Martin looks behind me with a shocked expression. "Watch out behind you. I can see a monster crawling out there." I go rigid with terror and cannot look behind me.

Cyril leaps from his seat, stands behind me, and stares angrily at Martin. "Why do you have to frighten him? It's bad enough for him to wake us with his nightmares. If he has one tonight you will be to blame, and I'll give you a good hiding." Cyril puts his hands on my shoulders. "It's alright. He was trying to be funny. All he has done is to make himself look stupid."

Martin just concentrates on cleaning his mangold, and mutters, "I was only teasing." He knows that he would lose in a fight, even though Cyril is eighteen months younger. It was raining when Martin brought in the last load and the mud is slippery. Martin is careless and a mangold slips on the wet sack and the scraper nicks his finger. He looks at me and shouts, "I bloody hate cleaning bloody mangolds. You're so bloody clever with your hands. Why don't you invent a machine for cleaning these bloody mangolds?" I am very shocked. I have never heard my brothers swear. My Sunday School teacher said it is wicked to swear.

Cyril squeezes my shoulders, it takes away my fear, and he sits down. I look across at Martin and feel sorry for him, and say, "I know that you're not stupid. Please don't swear and don't frighten me again."

Cyril laughs, his cheery smile comes back. "It's alright now. Next time you have a nightmare, just shout out for me, and I will drive your monsters away."

Martin sucks his finger. "That's enough now. Let's get on with the shredding."

The shredder has a flywheel with a handle similar to the cake crusher. The axle goes into the bottom of a steel hopper on a stand. Inside the hopper is a shiny metal disc punched with rows of slots, one side of the slot sticks out and is very sharp. When a mangold is thrown in the hopper it is cut up and the sheds go to the other side of the disc and drop through the bottom of the hopper on to the floor. Cyril turns the wheel, and I use a pitchfork to throw the cleaned mangolds into the hopper. When there is a pile on the floor, Martin mixes the shreds with chaff and fills two potato baskets and takes them to the cows. He empties one basket in front of each cow, so makes several trips; between each trip Cyril and I have shredded enough for the next. A mangold jams at the bottom of the hopper and the disc spins without cutting. I reach in to free the mangold and Martin snatches my arm out. "Now who's stupid? Do you want to have your arm sliced off? Use this bit of hoe shaft, like this." He uses the shaft to press the jammed mangold against the disc and it is quickly shredded; Martin hurt my arm, but it's better than having it cut off. I keep back my tears. I am lucky to have brothers to look after me, even though they tease me sometimes. I feel safe and happy in the barn with my brothers, not talking much; only the sounds of whirring, cutting, and mixing disturb the silence. We finish our work and walk across the yard to the house. I carry the lantern and swing it so that the pool of light jerks around us and we slosh in our wellingtons through the puddles and moving patches of light and dark. I like doing that even more when hoar frost sparkles in the light.

***

Milk, warm from the cow, needed to be cooled to stop it from going sour. The cooler was a galvanized steel stand about five feet high, supporting a holding tank for the milk. An adult could reach up and pour a pail of milk into the tank, but we boys had to stand on a stout wooden box. A tap in the bottom of the tank regulated the flow of milk into a trough with a perforated bottom, so that the milk could trickle through and over a hollow vertical galvanized hollow panel about two feet square with horizontal corrugations on the front and back. The panel was cooled by cold water flowing into the bottom and out from the top, and the outsides of the panel cooled the milk as it flowed over it. The cooled milk collected into another trough under the panel, and discharged through a hole into a churn placed beneath. A long-handled plug acted as a tap to stop the milk whilst a full churn was replaced. The water came from a hose from the tap and another hose from the top lead to the back of the dairy, where it flowed through a hole in the wall to the ground outside.

Some of the full churns were tipped into pails, and the milk was then ladled into pint and half pint bottles, sealed with a press-on cardboard disc, and then put into galvanized milk crates, sluiced with cold water and stacked in a corner of the dairy. The remaining full churns were rolled down the drive to the main road, and lifted onto a wooden trestle platform at the same height as the collecting lorry, so that they could be easily rolled from the platform onto the lorry. Empty churns were left on the platform, later to be filled to await collection every morning. I could roll an empty churn, but it needed someone taller and stronger than me to roll a full churn, and it needed two men to lift it onto the platform. The churns had a tight-fitting lid with a wide flange; that was needed to give a good grip when removing the lid, and also to give a purchase when rolling the churn. Of course, the churns were not rolled on their sides. The trick was to grasp the flange and tip the churn towards your body, and then use a cross arm movement of alternate hands to turn the flange. The tight fit ensured that the whole churn turned, and rolled on its bottom rim. With practice, it could be rolled at a fast walking pace on the driveway, and at a trot on concrete.

Early each morning the crates of bottles were loaded on the back seat and in the boot of the car; a small churn of milk was put on the floor behind the passenger seat and the delivery bucket behind the driver. Dad went off to deliver milk and chat with his customers if they were at home. The bottles had the name of the farm, and 'Full

Cream Milk' printed in red script, to prevent theft by other milkmen. Some milkmen were known to add water to the milk. Dad never did that. He told us to leave the taps on the cooler open and turn the churns and bottles upside down to drain after they were washed to make sure that no water diluted the milk.

Unbottled milk was measured from a two-gallon oval galvanized bucket with a hinged lid, embellished with brass scrolls and tracery. It was a work of art and had to be polished with Brasso metal polish every day. Inside a half pint brass jug hung from a rail, it was used to measure out the milk into customers' jugs. The bucket was topped up from the small churn in the back of the car. Some customers preferred loose milk from the churn; they said it was more natural from the churn rather than the bottle; in fact, it was cheaper; times were hard in the Slump. In those days, before the Welfare State, old people and others with no means of support, gradually sold off their possessions to pay the bills, and when all was gone they were taken into the Workhouse; we talked of it in horror as 'The Grubber'.

Dad took part of his tea and sugar ration in a metal tube divided into two with a screw cap at each end. One old lady would have the kettle boiling for him and make him a cup of tea. He didn't charge for her Sunday half-pint of milk. The delivery of milk and collecting of empty bottles took all morning. Dad would note his deliveries in line with his customers' names in a small ledger during his rounds. After dinner, he would add up the sales for the day. On Fridays, he would enter customer's deliveries for the week and collect payment on Saturdays so he was always late for dinner. Occasionally he had to take family treasures in lieu of payment, and Mum had a good selection of cut glass in the display cabinet in the lounge. There were no ballpoint pens then, and entries were in pencil. Dad showed me how to keep the records, and when he was too busy with farm work, I would add up the figures for him. He was quick with figures and could run his finger down the columns and add up the number of pints quicker than I could read them. I was only ten at that time and money was in Imperial pounds, shillings, pence and halfpence units, and much more complex than the metric system. There were no calculators, except shop tills, and mental arithmetic was an essential part of the school curriculum. Basic book keeping was instilled in me at that early age, and has since helped me to keep firm control of my financial affairs.

***

The dirty bottles have to be washed each day in boiling water with soda crystals and sterilizing powder. It's Saturday, and Gerald is home and we are still sitting at the table, chatting after dinner. Earlier this morning Martin used bits of wood splashed with paraffin to light the fire under the boiler in the lean-to next to the dairy. He stoked the fire with engine coal left over from the threshing machine. It takes about two hours to boil the water. We hear the safety whistle scream. I follow Gerald to the boiler. He looks at the pressure gauge and opens the fire door and rakes out the burning coals. "This thing is ready to blow up. Quick! Fetch a couple of buckets of water from the dairy." As I run off he shouts,

"Half buckets." When I get back he grabs a bucket and douses the glowing coals. The whistle has stopped shrieking, but the gauge is hard against the stop. Gerald shakes his head. "I must tell Martin to go easy on the coal." He fills the buckets with boiling water and caries them to the dairy. "Don't get under my feet. Neither of us needs a scalding." He glances at me, and smiles. "Well! You do when you are naughty." He empties the buckets into a large galvanized trough about two feet deep on legs about two feet high. It takes several trips to half fill the trough.

Gerald puts on a waterproof canvas bib apron that almost reaches the floor and a pair of red rubber gauntlets. I know that they are gauntlets because I saw a man wearing them in an advertisement for a Norton in the Motor Cycle magazine that a friend gave me. Gerald stirs a couple of handfuls of soda crystals and sterilizing powder into the water. He stacks the crates of dirty bottles on his right and carefully floats the bottles from the top crate on the still very hot water. He takes a length of hoe shaft and pokes the bottles under the water. "Get all the air of the bottles so that they sink, otherwise they won't get sterilised. Now move that empty crate and put it down on your left." He pushes the crate a couple of feet with his foot, "Now you stand beside me and as I wash the bottles I will hand them to you and you put them upside down in the crate." He pushes the stiff bottlebrush up and down a bottle and water squirts out, some down his apron. He says, "When we first had the milk round, we had to learn as we went along. Mum washed the bottles then, and the soda made her hands wrinkled and sore, so she bought this apron and these gloves."

He washes the bottles and passes them to me. As he empties one crate he puts it on top of the one that I have filled. Gerald said, "Henry Ford does something like this when he makes his cars. Several workers do the same piece of work all day and it is passed on to the next worker on a moving conveyor belt." He stops to move a crate. "I read about it in a magazine in the guest house. We haven't got the belt, but we are using his idea." I think that it would be a good idea to use conveyer belts to do jobs that I hate. I don't like fetching the cows from the pasture when it's cold and raining and mud everywhere.

I giggle. "Why can't we have a belt to bring in the cows for milking?" Gerald doesn't laugh when I make jokes.

I get bored with handling the bottles; anyway, they are still hot and hurt my hands. When Gerald changes the next crate, I turn on the hose for the cooler and squirt it on his apron. He grabs me and lifts me high up and shakes me. The hose soaks his face. He looks angry, and then grins. He puts me down and gives me a good clip round the ear. "Stop messing about, get on with this, I don't want to be here all day."

When all the bottles are gleaming clean, Gerald washes the delivery can, and buckets in the still warm water into the holding tank of the cooler and then turns on the tap to let the water run over the cooling panel and onto the floor. He gets a besom and uses the waste water to wash the concrete floor. I make a game of standing in front of him, and then jumping out of the way. He swills the water to the back of the dairy and out through a hole in the wall. It flows directly onto the earth, so the land behind the dairy is marshy and covered in large stinging nettles. I keep well away from there, but docks also grow well in the marsh, and when I do get stung I rub dock leaf on the rash and the stinging disappears. Cyril taught me that trick.

***

Running a farm, especially with animals, was a seven-day a week occupation, but only the minimum of work was done on Sundays. Sundays was the only hint of a holiday; in fact, there were no holidays. Industrial worker had their Wakes weeks and similar set holidays, but farmers had no time for that. In the summer Dad delivered double milk on Saturdays and none on Sundays, so Sunday summer afternoons he sometimes took us on a thirty-mile car ride to the seaside. Gerald was the cross bearer in the church choir and could not go on the trips. We younger brothers were also in the choir, and had to get permission from the vicar to miss evensong.

Of course, children had school holidays, but the long summer holiday was spent helping with the harvest. The young children stayed at home helping Mother and playing with neighbouring children. Permanent workers could not cope with the harvests, and work was contracted to gangmasters who organised workers from the local town, and from the farm camps for Londoners. There were also itinerant gypsy-type wanderers living in horse-drawn caravans. When they worked for Dad, they camped near the orchard and we children were not allowed near them. Sometimes genuine Romany gypsies came for work; they were respected and we could talk to them. There were no immigrants in the Fens during the war. The only foreigners were Italians and German prisoners of war who were trusted to work on the fields. They were delivered from the prison camps in the morning and taken back in the evening by lorry. We became very friendly with them, and enjoyed the happy Italians singing arias, but the Germans were much quieter and withdrawn. During winter, the permanent workers did general repair and tidying work, mending potato sacks, hedging, pruning the orchard and ditching.

That was before T.T. milk and all the rules and regulations from the Health and Safety Ministry. The whole process of milk production in the thirties would be illegal today. We were unaware of bacteria, bugs and viruses lurking to spread disease. Rats, flies and fleas were common. Who knows? If a flea bit a person and then a rat, the rat would probably have died? Our immune system, not that we knew about that, must have worked overtime to protect us, and so we became very strong. We did have smallpox inoculations, and Mum made us have a spoonful of treacle like goo from a brown jar labelled 'Radio Malt' because the doctor said that it was good for us.

Our general good health was probably due to a simple diet. During and after the war, food was rationed; cheese, butter, lard, bacon and meat, and sweets were restricted to about four ounces a week per person; that would be insufficient for one meal by present day standards. Of course, being on a farm had several advantages, we had a ready supply of milk, eggs chickens and vegetables, and the ten-bore and twelve-bore shotguns provided rabbit, hare, pigeon and an occasional pheasant. The simple, balanced diet, hard work, fresh air and no fizzy drinks and certainly no drugs, and a strong immune system for the boys anyway, resisted the occasional outbreaks of scarlet fever and meningitis among the children of sedentary parents. The strong immune system of healthy young men called up for military service eventually surrendered to the deprivations of life on the Death Railway in Thailand; of 24 drafted from the village and nearby hamlets, only one returned home.

After the war farming became more stable, Dad sold the milk round. I was burning potato haulm with him in the fields; Mum came running waving a telegram from the bank to say that a cheque for 325 pounds had been cleared. She had a weekly allowance of one pound for housekeeping, so that was a considerable sum. Dad used it to buy a new Ford tractor, which eased the burden of the Shire carthorses, and eventually led to their retirement. Old Henry joined his dead neighbours in the churchyard. A rich uncle acted as guarantor at the bank, so Father could take out an overdraft and fulfill his dream of buying Old Henry's farm.

PLOUGHING

Our three horses are Shires, but we think of them as carthorses because they pull carts and farm implements. They are large muscular animals with hoofs as round as dinner plates. The farm could not operate without them. The horses are kept in a stable in a corner of the pasture behind the farmyard. The stable is open-fronted and has a small barn and tack room at right angles to it. A yard is enclosed on the other two sides by timber rail fencing with a five-barred gate opening on to the pasture.

Cyril cossets the horses with a currycomb and stiff brush to make their coats gleam, and feeds them mixed chaff and ground oats in the manger, and clean hay in the hayrack above it. They drink from a trough in the yard; that is an open space between the backs of two barns on two sides, the stable on another and a wooden fence and five-barred gate to the road. The yard is only used during very wet and cold weather, when it is fine the horses are free to gallop in the grass field. Captain is a castrated stallion, tall and rangy, with a mottled light and dark grey coat and a black mane and tail. He has sorrowful eyes and a large quivery lower lip. He is always happy to lower his head so that I can stroke him behind the ears, and his chin stops quivering when I cup it in my hand, at least part of it as it is too big to enclose in my small hand. Violet is a mare, smaller than Captain, and her hoofs are not so big. She is fatter than Captain so her muscles bulge instead, rippling under her pale brown coat; her mane and tail are white. Tinker is younger and frisky, and I am not allowed to go near him.

I have watched Cyril harness the horses many times, so I have a good idea of how to do it. Today there is no need to get to work quickly; I am only going to rake up the dead potato tops. Cyril lifts Captain's harness off hooks in the brick wall. "Come on then. It's about time that you did this for yourself."

I protest. "I can't. I am too small."

He says, "Don't make feeble excuses. Get in the manger. You can do it from there."

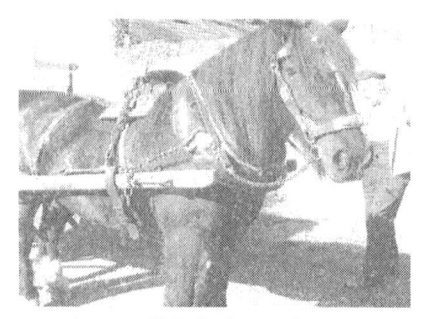

The collar is black leather stuffed with straw, and has iron aimes on both sides, with hooks to hitch chains for pulling carts and things. It is heavy, but I manage to lift it into the manger, and then put in the bridle. I climb into the manger. Captain doesn't mind, he just carries on chomping his oats. I have to untie his halter from the iron ring on the manger, thread it through the collar and then retie it. I have to turn the collar into an upside-down position, and then force it up and over, and behind his head where the neck is thinnest; it is easy to turn the collar upright and push it down his neck to rest against his shoulders. It is easier to put on the bridle but Captain won't open his mouth for the bit, so I have to pull his bottom lip so that he opens his mouth and I can push the bit between his teeth. He champs on the bit until foam comes round his mouth; if it hurts him he doesn't toss his head; that would throw me out of the manger. He is a very gentle patient beast. Cyril has to put on the heavy leather narrow saddle with the top built up into two ridges and a groove to take the chain to support the shafts of a cart. He smiles. "Next time you can bring an apple box to stand on, and then you can reach to put on the saddle. Be sure to tighten the girth; if the saddle slips, the chain might come off and cut his back." Cyril learned all about ploughing from an old man who had been a horseman all his life. Later, when I am thirteen, Cyril passes on his knowledge.

We went to plough in some stubble after the wheat harvest. He gave me a lesson before he started, and told me, "To plough a straight furrow, line up the horses and plough on the headland at one hundred paces from the end of the field and facing the other side. Adjust the wheels of the plough so that it is level. Pace out a hundred paces at the other side of the field, and mark it with a stick. Go back to the horses, and then find a mark in the distance, say a tree, and then use the mid-distance between the horse's collars as a back sight, and the stick and tree as foresights, the same as sighting a twelve bore on a ribbit. Start the horses and concentrate on keeping the sights in line, don't look back or sideways until you reach the other side of the field. When you look back you will see a perfectly straight furrow."

Cyril positions the horses and the stick and draws the first furrow. At the end he says, "The horse needs room to turn round at the end of each furrow." The horse stops at the boundary, he pulls the plough round and back so that he is standing on the brink of the ditch, and the horse is lined up for the next furrow. "Lower the big wheel into the furrow, with the small wheel on the ground so that the plough is level. All that you have to do is to keep the big wheel in the furrow, and you will find that it will be as straight as the first." He adds, "Before that we have to set up a top, just stay with the horses and watch me do it." Cyril paces a hundred steps and puts in sticks at both side of the field. He comes back for the horses, and holds the plough above ground whilst he moves it to a stick. "Now we do just the same as before, and draw another furrow." He does that, and there is another furrow parallel with the first. He grins. "We now have to go to the first furrow, adjust the plough as I told you, and keep ploughing new furrows to the left of the previous one. After each furrow, we have to move the plough along the headland and plough into the second furrow. Eventually all the land between the first two furrows is ploughed, and we will have to set up another top, and another and another, until the whole field is ploughed."

We stop for mid-morning lunch of marmite sandwiches and cold tea. Cyril continues the lesson. "That leaves an unploughed strip about seven feet wide on the sides of the field and is known as the headland. After the field is ploughed the headlands are ploughed along their length; that leaves a square at each corner that has be to dug over with a spade. If the next field is not on the roadside, and you can only get to it by the headland, then it is not ploughed and left as a dirt track."

***

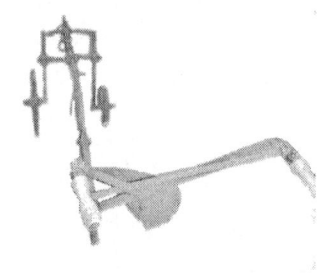

A plough is made of a long iron curved bar. At the front is a ring to hook on the crosstrees from the horse's chains. Behind that is a short crossbar; that holds one big wheel that runs in the furrow, and a smaller one that runs on the unploughed ground. They have bolt fastenings so that they can be raised or lowered. At the back of the curved bar is the plate for bolting on the plough share, and then the long thin iron arms curve back to a small crossbar and beyond them the arms stick out and have wooden handles for the ploughman. The ploughman adjusts the height of wheels to suit his own height and to regulate the depth of the furrow. If everything is set up properly it doesn't take much effort to keep the furrow at a constant depth, but if the chains do not line up right with the share, the ploughman soon gets tired from either bearing down or pulling up on the handles. It is a very skillful job being a ploughman. A well ploughed field with straight and even furrows and constant width tops, so that there is no wedge piece of ground left between the tops, is admired by country dwellers as a work of art, and the ploughman could be justifiably proud of his skills. Sometimes a farmer holds a ploughing match on a field of stubble. The field is divided into strips. Several ploughmen and their horses do their best to win. The winner gets a prize, and sometimes gets an order from a smallholder to plough his plots. It is also a social affair and there is a stall selling tea and sandwiches, and some people bring their own picnics.

After ploughing, the land is broken up with a duck foot cultivator and harrowed to a fine tilth. If the land is intended for spring sowing, the furrows are left to the effect of the frosts, which partially break up the ridges. Autumn sown wheat germinates before the frosts and gets an early growth in spring before spring sown wheat, which germinates and becomes established before the frosts; the ploughed land is cultivated soon after ploughing.

I will have to wait until I am strong enough to handle a plough, so I am just watching Cyril plough our orchard ground. He has already set up two tops and is guiding the plough up one side of the first top and down the far side of the second. When he has ploughed the space between the two tops he will have ploughed the same area on the far side of the second top.

He will then have to set up another top and do the same again, and keep setting up new tops until the whole field has been turned over. I am following Cyril in the furrow and find it difficult not to trip on the sides. I have read in the encyclopedias that Red Indians walk in single file treading in each other's footsteps so no one will know how many braves had walked on the trail. I imagine that I am a brave and then it becomes easy to follow Cyril in the furrow.

I stay with Cyril while he has his midmorning lunch. Mum has packed him a honey sandwich and two of her really hard rock cakes, and a bottle of homemade ginger beer. He gives me one of the cakes. I ask, "Why is most of the ploughed land left until the spring?"

Cyril takes a swig of ginger beer. "So that the frosts can break down the clods, and kill the germs. It doesn't kill worms though. They are very useful. They take air down to roots of plants, and eat Colorado beetle larva." He laughs. "That reminds me of a Max Miller joke. A man had to have an operation to take out one ball. The doctor replaced it with a seed potato, so that he was balanced. Later he went with a whore." Cyril laughs again. "He got pox in one ball and Colorado beetle in the other."

I turn red. "I don't like dirty jokes. I would rather learn about farming." My cheeks stop burning. "So why is some of the ploughed land worked down in autumn?"

Cyril laughs again. "That reminds me of another joke."

I interrupt. "I don't want to hear it."

He shrugs. "Well that's your loss. Anyway, if your head was not so full of learning, you will have seen the duckfoot cultivator in the yard."

I interrupt again. "Don't be so nasty, of course I've seen it. It's that heavy iron frame thing like a gate, with a lot of iron tines on strong curved springs sticking down with flat ends, like a duck's foot."

Cyril says, "If you had looked properly, you would have seen that it's got iron wheels the same as the small ones on the plough; they can be lowered so that it can be towed on the road. They also regulate the depth of the tines in the earth. It is very heavy, so I have to hitch up two horses to pull it. I pull it across the furrows and the feet break up the soil into small bits. Later when the soil has settled, I make the lumps smaller with a set of harrows." He looks down his nose. "You must know what a harrow is."

I am a bit upset. "Cyril! Why are you being so nasty to me, what on earth have I done to make you so unpleasant?"

Cyril looks shamefaced. "Well! I had to leave school at fourteen, and you are getting a good education until you are sixteen. Then you will probably go to university whatever that is. If you are so clever, why do you have to ask me all these questions?"

I say quietly, "Because I want to learn."

He replies, "You are always learning, with your head buried in those encyclopedias, and meeting all those posh people at school."

I look down. "I enjoy it. That's why I do it."

Cyril looks shamefaced. "I'm sorry to be so jealous. I have a hard life to look forward to, yours will be easy just sitting at a desk." He smiles. "I am really very happy for you. I am proud of you." He laughs. "When you earn a lot of money you can buy me a nice new Norton."

We just have a battery radio and don't listen to it much apart from Children's Hour, and a few other programmes such as Sunday Night Serenade and In Town Tonight, and Dad listens to the six o'clock news every night. We make our own entertainment especially during the long winter evenings. There are whist and beetle drives in the village hall, and we sing in the church choir for Sunday morning and evening services. At home we play cards together, whist newmarket, and dominoes and drafts. I like to do things alone, such as fretwork, Meccano, and reading, but have to join in with the others. Mum told us that she was in a concert party in the town years ago, but is too busy bringing us up to do it now. She still has a deep contralto voice; when we have singsongs round the piano, she always sings 'Queen of Angels' and does a monologue 'The Green Eye of the Little Yellow God' that frightens me. I am a bit shy and my cheeks burn when I have to stand up and sing 'Little Drummer Boy'. I hate doing it, but I have to do as I'm told. I am happy to sing in the choir because we all do it together, and nobody looks sat me; I could never sing solo like Gerald did. I miss him now that he is in the army, and worry that he might get killed, and then we would have to listen to the slow church bell. It would be terrible to know that it was for him, and that he would never come home.

The ploughing is finished, the winter wheat is sown and there is not much to do on the frozen earth. The nights are long and cold from frost and icy wilds. Mum lights the paraffin lamp and closes the curtains to keep out the cold, but the wind still gets through the cracks and moves the curtains. Mum and Dad are telling stories; we have heard those tales many times, but still like to listen. We sit round the kitchen table after supper. It is freezing outside with the wind moaning in the elms; Dad says that it comes direct from Siberia, wherever that is, but it must be cold. It is warm and cosy from the heat from the open door of the kitchen range, and our thick woollen socks and pullovers keep out the drafts. Mum and Dad tell stories about the living and dead, about family and about neighbours.

Mum puts on her acting voice. "I went to the grass field to collect some mushrooms for breakfast, and on the way back I noticed that the cows and horses were not at the water trough near the gate. I thought that a rat had drowned and fouled the water." She puts on her shocked look. "The only thing floating was Cyril's hair." Now she puts on a determined look. "I grabbed his arms and yanked him out of the water. His lips were blue. I knelt on one knee and laid him face down on the other and pummelled the water out of his lungs."

Dad interrupts. "Thank God that you were a nurse."

Mum smiles. "Yes! I know what do." Her face softens as she looked at Cyril. "You were only four. It would have been too much to bear to have lost you."

I pipe up. "Then he couldn't have looked after the horses."

We giggle and then laugh when Dad says, "Yes, and I can't afford to pay wages for another man."

It is Dad's turn. "When Martin was small, he would often get in the way. I tripped over him once and grazed my knee. I gave him a good telling off and a box round the ears." He looks at the ceiling. "I thought that would do the trick, but a few days later he got in the way of Tinker. Tinker accidentally kicked him and broke his leg."

I interrupt. "It must have been an accident. Our horses would never hurt anyone."

Dad nods. "Yes, but his leg was still broken. Mum and I had to take him to hospital. He didn't want to go and cried all the way. They plastered his leg and said that he would have to stay the night. We went back next day, and the doctor said that we could take him home and bring him back in a couple of weeks to have the plaster removed."

Martin joins in and speaks quietly. "It was horrible. They put me in a big room with rows of empty beds. I was all alone. I was very frightened and wanted Mum."

He looks at Mum; she has her misty eyed sad look. "My poor little boy. You were so happy to come home."

Martin says, "Those horrible doctors were not nice. They told me to be quiet and stop making so much fuss. Our doctor is always gentle and kind."

The German aeroplanes fly over at night on their way and back to bomb big towns like Coventry and Liverpool. English aeroplanes make a low humming noise, but the German Junkers and Fokkers make a throbbing roar. We like the humming, it makes us feel safe, but the throbbing is frightening, we worry that they might drop a bomb, and we tremble in our beds. Dad had told us that there is nothing worth bombing in the Fens, but we are still afraid. Sometimes a German is shot down by our fighters, and we hear it crash; it explodes and leaves a big crater. Sometimes the Germans unload their bombs and turn back to go home, and they make craters as well. Next morning, we cycle off to see them. It is just a big crater half-full of dirty water with bits floating on top; around the crater we find bits of jagged metal and pieces of flesh and cloths. We take some metal bits home as souvenirs, I swop them a school. My brothers and Tim and me are talking about the latest bomb. Tim exclaims, "Did you hear it? What a bang. My dad said it must have been a land mine; they drop them on a parachute."

Martin says, "Yes it woke us up. It was a bit too close. I think that we should make an air raid shelter."

We all nod in agreement. Cyril says, "We can make an early start before morning service tomorrow."

We stand in the yard. Martin points to the near corner of the grass field. "Over there is a good place, it will be out of the way of everything." We set to work with spades, and soon clear an area six feet by six. About two feet down we have dug out the rich loam, and reach blue clay. Martin mops his brow. "That's enough for today. Tomorrow we will have to use a pickaxe to break it up."

After a few hours spread over several days, the hole is five feet deep with the soil piled up at the sides. We smooth off the top and lay some planks and some old corrugated iron sheets, and then put on a six -inch layer of soil. We leave an opening in one corner and let down a length of old ladder. We climb down into the hole and look around. "This should be safe enough, but it's not very comfortable. We should bring down some planks and make some seats and a table."

Cyril smiles at me. "That's a good idea. We can play cards and have a smoke down here."

I don't like it down here; it's gloomy and damp. I feel frightened and climb out. The fresh air and sunlight drive away the fear, I shout down, "You can do what you like, but I'm not going in there again, not even if there is an air raid."

Three days later at dinnertime we hear a loud neighing and thumping. We all rush out to the yard, and see Tinker's head waving about in the grass field. We all run down to the gate, and see that Tinker has fallen into the shelter. He is lying on his side on a pile of smashed sheeting and planks, kicking the sides of the hole and waving his head. By the time that we have opened the gate and reached the shelter he has scrambled out and trotted off down the field. Dad is very angry. "What on earth have you been doing?"

Cyril shuffles his feet. "Making an air raid shelter for us all to use if there is a raid."

Dad snorts. "Well you made a pretty poor job of it. How could you think that a few pieces of corrugated iron would keep out a bomb?"

Mum looks worried. "Just think of what would have happened if we had been inside, we would have been crushed to death."

Dad says, "Not me. I would prefer to take my chances and stay in the house rather than in that hole." He puts his arm round Mum's shoulders. "Don't worry Mother." He always calls her that, why doesn't her use her name? "It didn't happen and it certainly won't happen in the future." He turns to us and says sternly, "Think of yourselves as lucky that Tinker didn't cut himself; he could have broken a leg. Get those sheets and planks out and fill in the hole. Don't ever do such a stupid thing again. Remember I was in the Great War, and know how to dig trenches and build shelters." It took three days of our spare time to do as he said, by which time Mum's worry and Dad's anger had gone, and we were all happy again.

One Saturday, five years ago when I was about seven, Dad came back from the market; he shouted, "Martin! Give me a hand." They unloaded a pony foal from the back seats; it was wrapped in a sack to keep it still. Dad said, "Promise to look after it, and it's yours." We promised. It took two days' discussion to find a name.

We settled on Nobby. I was a bit too young to care for it, but I was allowed to stroke it and help Martin and Cyril feed and groom it. It grew up with us, and has a lot of attention and is very tame. Martin put a halter on it soon after it arrived and it was quite happy to be led around the yard. We kept the halter on all the time, so when it was let loose in the field it was easier to catch. It was not long before it came when its name was called; it was often rewarded with a sugar lump. I helped Cyril to make a low manger and hayrack, rather I got in his way, but he didn't mind. We fixed the manger and rack in a corner of the barn, and restrained Nobby with a rope tied to his halter. Otherwise he would have eaten the animal foods stored there. If he had eaten un-soaked sugar beet pulp he would have blown up like a balloon and died; that happened to two heifers.

Nobby had to be broken in. Dad told Martin and Cyril how to do it in easy stages, so as not to break its spirit. Anyway, it was already very tame; it was really a case of training it rather than breaking it in. The first stage was to get it familiar with harness. We tried the riding bridle first. We loosened the halter and pushed it round its neck. We took the bit off and just hung the bridle over Nobby's ears for a few minutes. We did that a few times and then attached the bit to one side of the bridle. We then tightened the strap, took hold of the dangling bit and led Nobby round the yard. When it got used to that we gave Nobby a lump of sugar and at the same time eased the bit between its teeth. After three times, we fastened the other side of the bit; it champed another lump of sugar, the bit was in the gap between the back and front teeth, so I don't suppose that it could feel anything; it champed a lump of sugar and nodded its head and seemed unworried by the bit. The next item was the riding saddle. I had often sat on Nobby's back while he was being lead from the barn to the field, so it was used to my light weight. Martin rested the saddle on Nobby's back few a few minutes and took it off. Nobby looked back and tried to displace it with its nose. After a few times, it stopped looking back and Martin tightened the cinch. Nobby ignored the saddle from then on. Mum walked down the yard to collect eggs from the chicken house. She said that we must stop giving Nobby sugar lumps, as they would rot its teeth. Nobby had to get used to more weight on its back. Cyril stood on a milking stool and put his arms over Nobby's back and laid his weight on the saddle. Nobby jiffled a bit, so Cyril stepped down. After a few more times, Nobby ignored the weight, so Cyril stood on the stool and swung his leg over the saddle and sat down while Martin held the bridle. Martin led Nobby round the yard with Cyril in the saddle; Cyril pulled either rein as Martin lead from left to right and pulled both when Martin stopped. Martin then let go of the bridle and Nobby was quite docile as Cyril rode it round the yard. Over the next week, Nobby got used to walking, trotting cantering and galloping with Martin mounted. Later Nobby got used to Cyril's weight. A couple of weeks later I was allowed to ride Nobby with Cyril holding the bridle. Later I rode Nobby walking and trotting. Mum and Dad came to see the first time that I did that; they didn't give any praise, but I knew from their smiles and shining eyes that they were pleased with me, and proud of my brothers for training Nobby and for teaching me to ride. I quickly went from trotting, to riding Nobby at a canter and gallop.

Tim wanted to ride Nobby, so we made a game of bucking bronco. We tied Nobby to the field fence, put Tim in the saddle, and then I let Nobby loose. Nobody had told Nobby about bucking broncos, it just trotted away. Tim had never ridden a pony, and when Nobby made a sharp turn, Tim fell off. His head hit the ground and I thought that he must have broken his neck. Tim just got up with a big grin. We joked about his hard skull and thick neck. He never wanted to ride Nobby again.

The next stage was to get Nobby used to pulling a two-wheeled cart for passengers, we called it a trap. Nobby was used to a saddle, riding bridle with short reins, and a halter, the working bridle was heavier than the riding one, and had blinkers; Nobby accepted it with no fuss, so all that was needed was a collar to complete the harness. I held the halter while Cyril eased the upside- down collar over Nobby's ears, let it feel the weight, and then took it off. Nobby just munched at the hay that I was holding for it, so Cyril did it again then turned the color upright and slid it down Nobby's neck to rest against its shoulders. Cyril attached the long reins, and walked behind Nobby and guided him around the yard. Nobby soon got used to that. We had to get Nobby used to pulling something, so we hitched a log to the chain traces from the collar, and used the long reins to guide Nobby round the yard. It snorted at first but accepted the weight and easily pulled the log. We then tried a heavier log and Nobby strained a bit to start but still pulled it.

We took Nobby to the trap, and stopped it in front of the shafts. I held Nobby's halter and stroked its nose while Cyril lifted the shafts, and pulled the trap closer to Nobby. Cyril then lowered the shafts onto the saddle to let Nobby feel the very light weight of the shaft chain. Nobby didn't seem to notice, so Cyril tied on the underbelly girth; it was always loose to allow the shafts to lift about eight inches. Cyril then attached the chain traces from the collar to the trap. Cyril led Nobby around by the halter, and then sat in the trap and used the reins to guide Nobby. Cyril was careful to use his weight to balance the trap so that the shaft chain just rested on the saddle. I got up with Cyril and we took Nobby to the field, and drove him at a walk and then a trot. Later Martin took Nobby and the trap on the road to get it used to walking and trotting on the tarmac.

We had several rabbits. We bred them and sold them at the cattle market for four pence each; if we were lucky we got five pence. We had up to twenty rabbits and they were always hungry. We took a sack and tramped the fields and verges on the main road, picking dandelions, groundsel and sow thistles. They also liked mangolds and swedes and crushed oats. It was easier now that we had Nobby and the trap. We went out every three days and filled the trap with greenery for the rabbits. My brothers let me take the reins on the road, but always took them back if a car came; that didn't happen very often.

A couple of years after getting Nobby, when I cycled home from school, I left my bike in the yard and harnessed Nobby, and rode to fetch the cows from Green Lane. I imagined that I was a cowboy. I had seen a cowboy film; the cows were spooked and stampeded through a town. When cows run the milk spurts out of their teats. Dad would have been very angry if my cows had stampeded and were dry at milking time. I don't know why cowboys call cows Doggies, they are nothing like a dog. They sing them a song to keep them quiet, so I used to sing 'Get Along Little Doggies' to my cows.

SUGAR BEET HARVEST

Sugar beet was relatively easy to grow. The land was cultivated by the normal method, and then the seed was sown with a drill. When the seedlings were about four inches high they were thinned by chopping with a hoe to leave clusters of seedlings at nine-inch centres, later these were reduced to the strongest in each cluster by hand. The crop was hoed at intervals to control weeds and to aerate the soil. When the roots were fully grown they were loosened with a beet plough and pulled out by hand, the tops were the chopped off and the beet carted to the roadside to be later loaded onto contractors' lorries and taken to the sugar beet factory for processing.

The same drill was used for corn and beet, but the centres of the funnels were widened to make the rows about nine inches apart, instead of the six for wheat. The beet plough was a smaller version of a normal plough but with the share removed; instead two flat bars extended vertically into the soil, the ends were bent at right angles and sharpened so that the blade went under the roots and the verticals loosened the soil around the roots. There were no furrows in a field of beet, so the wheels were of equal size. Apart from hoes, and horse drawn carts, the only other tools needed were a potato forks and beet hooks.

***

Two weeks ago, Old Sam, Jack and Eddy chopped out the beet. It's Saturday morning, and I am helping Martin and Cyril to thin out. Jack and Eddy and their wives have been at it for several days, and have done most of the work, so we will finish the field today. We bend and pull out the seedlings, leaving only the strongest, and press the soil round the stem. It's easy work, but makes my back ache, so I crawl between the rows. The rows go on forever; it takes over an hour to thin out each row.

Martin sniggers. "I keep thinking about that girl I met at the dance last week, I hope that she will be there tonight. I might be lucky and get the last waltz, and may even get a kiss goodnight afterwards." He smirks. "My cock gets hard when I think of her. I wonder how big her thing is?"

Cyril laughs. "My friend Douglas told me that he felt one, and her slit was as long as her forefinger."

Martin ponders and then says, "That seems about right. A cow has a very long slit, and a pig is small, a woman's body is smaller than a cow and bigger than a pig, so the length of a forefinger would be about right."

Cyril giggles. "I might be lucky tonight and find a girl who will let me feel her thing; she might even let me put my finger in."

I feel embarrassed and don't look at them. Sometimes I wake up during the night and my cock is hard, but I wouldn't like to push it in a girl. I have seen a bull mount a cow, and it seems a strange way to make a calf. When the stallion comes to a mare, Dad will not let us look. They have to do it in the orchard, where no one can see them. I don't know why.

Perhaps one day I will ask Old Sam to tell me about it; he knows everything.

Old Sam lives in brick and slate roof building with an earth closet at the back built on the Garden Ground at the edge of the grass verge to the main road. Granddad built it as an office when he started the seed business. It has one small room with an open fireplace. Dad has no use for the office, and he lets Old Sam live there rent-free in return for casual light work on the farm. Old Sam speaks in a posh voice, and knows many things. During our fireside talking, about family tales and gossip, Mum said that Old Sam came from a very good family and had a good education. He did something bad and the family disowned him, but gave him an allowance so that he would not starve. He has lived alone in the office ever since I can remember. It's after Sunday school, so Cyril and I visit Old Sam. He likes to talk to us; perhaps he is lonely, but he always has a smile and is never agitated. I don't understand much but he has a quiet voice, and I copy the way he talks. He has a large leather trunk, and I sit on it. He says, "I used it on my travels when I was young." Apart from the trunk there is not much in the room; a single iron bed, a table and two chairs and a couple of apple boxes to keep his pots and pans and food.

Old Sam often goes for a pint in the local pub during the evening. On his birthday and at Christmas, he decks himself out in a black suit; the jacket is a bit strange it is a funny shape and has tails hanging at the back; he has an almost white shirt and black bow tie, and a top hat. He told us that he wore the dress suit to go to dinner dances when he was young, and that he met many beautiful ladies. The neighbours just smile and nod when he strides to the pub; they are too polite to laugh, especially as he is well-bred. He is a bit smelly but not much more than anyone else. We have a bath every Saturday, but Old Sam only has an enamel washbowl, so never has a bath. He seems to live on sausage and chunks of fried potato, and bread and jam. Mum gives him a treat sometimes and invites him for Sunday dinner. He doesn't wear his evening dress, but he combs his hair and is not so smelly, so must have had a good wash. We have to be on our best behaviour; Mum says that she doesn't want Old Sam to think that we do not know how to eat properly. We have on our best clothes; we have been to morning service, and have to go to Sunday school after dinner. Old Sam must have worked on farms for a long time because he seemed to know all about farming and how to work on a farm. Dad and Old Sam sometimes sit together on the milk stand by the main road, so perhaps they talk about farming, and the best way to do it.

Old Sam, Martin and I go to hoe the sugar beet. We leave our dinner bags on the headland. Martin starts to hoe. Old Sam calls, "Wait a minute. Always use a sharp tool."

Martin looks crestfallen; he doesn't like to be told off. He mutters, "Sorry, I forgot."

Old Sam grins, "Sorry is no excuse. One of these days you will forget your head." Martin grinned back and goes to his dinner bag for the file, and starts to sharpen his hoe. Old Sam says, "Not bad. Here give it to me. Both of you watch this." He takes the file, inverts his hoe and digs the end of the shaft in the ground and holds it firm with one foot. He grasps the steel handle with the blade pointing up in his left hand, and pushes the file firmly along the length of the blade in one stroke. He does it again and says, "Keep an even pressure and angle on the file and make each stroke the full width of the blade." After half a dozen strokes he holds the blade towards us. "See the bright steel is the same width along the edge of the blade. If you use short stokes across the blade you will get an uneven cutting edge that is no use to neither man nor beast." A full-size hoe is too big for me to handle, so I am using an old hoe that has been filed so often it's half the size of a new hoe. Old Sam takes it from me. "Give me that, I will sharpen it for you. Your mum would never forgive me if you slashed your hand."

We all start hoeing and after half an hour Old Sam stretches his back and we stop for a breather. He spoke softly. "I used to go to the ballet at Saddlers Wells and classical concerts at the Royal Albert Hall in London, when I was at Cambridge. I miss them. Watching someone doing farm work reminds me of the ballet." He says to Martin, "Start hoeing and let us see how you do it." Martin gets going. Old Sam's eyes glow. "See how he holds the hoe shaft, steadying it with the right hand and pressing down with the left hand to guide the blade in a smooth sideways action. Watch how his body bends forward from the hips and turns slightly to slice through the roots. It's similar to a movement in the ballet, full of grace and controlled power."

Cyril laughs. "He's only hoeing. Hoeing is just a knack. Ballet is dancing, and I don't think about hoeing when I have my arm round a girl's waist."

Old Sam replies, "I don't see a man hoeing. I see a dancer." I respect Old Sam. He is always kind. I like him. Dad has Martin and Cyril to look after the farm when he is old, so perhaps I will be a ballet dancer.

We work through the rows until it's time for lunch at half past ten. As we eat, Old Sam looks at Martin. "I've noticed that you scratch the backs of your hands a lot, let me look." Martin holds out his hands. "Just as I thought, you've got warts. Do you want to get rid of them?"

Martin nods. "Yes please. This itching is enough to drive me mad."

Old Sam has a solemn face., "Just cut off your hands." Martin looks shocked, and then we burst out laughing. Old Sam chortles, "I'm pleased that you can take a joke." He winks. "Next time you see a fat slug, just rub it hard over the warts, and if you do that half a dozen times, they will disappear." I can't stand those nasty black slimy things.

Martin looks worried. "Are you sure? It sounds nasty."

Old Sam retorts, "Of course I'm sure. There is something in the juices that kills the warts. So, don't put your hands near your mouth until you have washed them. I don't know how the juices affect humans, and I don't want problems with your mum if you kill yourself as well as the warts." He adds, "I don't want to risk not being invited to Sunday dinner again."

Martin says, "Well! If you say it works, I will give it a try." We carry on hoeing. We don't say much, but Old Sam chuckles out loud several times. He must be thinking of all those beautiful ladies at the dinner dance.

Later that evening when Martin and I are working on our vegetable plots, he calls out, "I've found a fat one." I am nearly sick as he crushes it on his hands; when he finishes it is just a nasty grey pulp with bits of black skin, which he throws to the ground. He holds out his hands. "It seems to be working. They have stopped itching already." He grins and starts whistling 'I'll be Seeing You' and doesn't stop until we go for supper. He catches a fat slug every day, and squashes it on his hands. Within a week the warts have fallen off.

Next time we go to see Old Sam, Martin holds out his hands. Old Sam raises one eyebrow and chuckles, "Well I never! I've read about faith healing but never believed it." He adds, "Now I've got second thoughts.

Perhaps that explains miracles." I don't know what he is talking about.

Martin nods. "Yes! It was the juice. I didn't like doing it, but you said that the warts would go, and they did. Thank you very much."

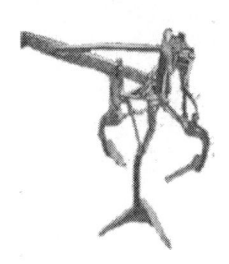

Dad has his leg over the arm of his chair after tea. "The beet leaves have started to yellow." He looks at Cyril, "Tomorrow you can make a start with the beet plough. The others can start pulling out a couple of days later. That will give you plenty of time to keep ahead of them, so they won't be held up."

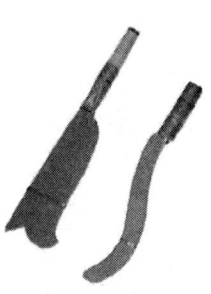

Two days later I call to watch them on the way back from school. I don't have long as I have to fetch the cows from Green Lane. The beet plough loosened the soil, so is easy for Martin and Jack pull up the beet and laying them in rows with the tops all pointing the same way. It is much quicker than singling and takes about twenty minutes to finish a row, and then they take a quick rest before starting on the way back to the headland where they stop again and take a swig from a bottle of cold tea. Eddy and Fred follow more slowly. They pick up a beet by the root, slice off the leaves with a beet hook, and throw the roots into piles. Pulling beet and heaping it is not as graceful as hoeing, but I can see the smooth movement and the knack of making it easy, apart from aching backs. I stand on the headland. Jack hands me his bottle. "Have a drink. My back is giving me gyp; I will have to get the wife to rub on some Wintergreen tonight."

Eddy had joined us. He adds, "I find that rubbing with horse oils, and hot water in a vinegar jar wrapped in a towel on my back does the trick for me."

Jack smiles. "Well every man to his own poison. I will stick to Wintergreen, thank you."

I thank Jack for the drink, and leave. I have stayed too long and don't stop at the house, but go straight to Green Lane to fetch the cows.

When I get back Mum scolds me. "Don't do that again. I was worried when you didn't come home from school. I was just going to ask Dad to look for you."

I reply, "I only went to look at the beet."

She gave me a clout on the head. "That's enough of your cheek, don't do it again. Now go and see if the hens have laid, we are having scrambled egg for tea."

Tim and I are leading the horses. We just hold the halters most of the time; the horses know what to do and where to go. I take Violet to the end of the rows of heaped beet, and we walk slowly between two rows while Martin and Jack use potato forks to load the beet into the cart. When it is full, we walk to the road, cross the bridge over the deep ditch and then Eddy takes the halter and backs Violet to the grave and tips up the load. The grave is the same as a potato clamp, but is on the grass verge, not in the field. The bridge is just old railway sleepers laid across two steel beams. I have to make sure that I lead Violet in the middle of the bridge, so that both wheels stay on the sleepers. While I am at the grave, Tim is getting his cart loaded. It takes about ten minutes to walk from the far side of the field to the grave, so Eddy has time to shape the grave and then have a short rest. Jack and Martin can also rest for a few minutes, but Tim and I have to keep walking. I take a rest sometimes by riding on the shaft.

Work does not stop when it is raining; we fold potato sacks in half lengthw-ays, and tuck the corners into each other; that makes a hood to hang over our head and the sack hangs down our back to keep us dry. In wet weather, the heavy loads churn up the earth near the bridge, and the wheels and horses sink deep into the mud. Then another horse has to be hitched to iron loops on the front of the shafts, and both horses heave and strain to pull the cart onto the road. Cyril does the hitching; sometimes he has to hit the horses with a stick to make them pull harder. I don't like to see him hurt them, especially Violet. He told me that sometimes he cries at night in bed because he is forced to hit the horses.

We don't have to earth up the grave because after a few days, motor lorries come to take the beet to the beet factory. It is an enormous building but I have never been inside so don't know how they take out the sugar, but I do know that all that is left of the beet is a lot of short grey strips. Dad buys some back and feeds it to the cows.

Farmers are usually kind to animals. One evening Dad was telling us some of his stories. "A friend of mine, I won't tell you his name, was worried about getting the beet into the grave. The motor lorries from the beet factory won't wait, they are on a contract and can't waste time waiting around." He gave us a knowing look. "Time is money, and don't you forget that." He grinned. "Anyway, this friend had a stubborn horse, a jibber, it refused to pull, no matter how hard he hit it, so he lit a newspaper and held it under the horse's belly. It moved quickly enough after that, and he only had to wave a newspaper under its belly to make it pull." The others laughed, but I didn't think it was funny to burn a horse. Dad looked at me and then I forced myself to giggle.

Before he came to our hamlet, Eddy lived in Ireland. He said that he had to leave because of The Troubles. He had to stand on a bridge for hours. He could not stand the pain, but they threatened to shoot him if he lowered his hands. He didn't say who they were. He is very serious sometimes. He is serious now. He glares at us. "I believe in freedom."

Old Sam leans back in his chair and looks at the ceiling. "Violence to animals can lead to violence to man. I assume that it was the Black and Tans who tortured Eddy. You heard how that farmer burned his horse. Make sure that you never use violence. The use of violence has destroyed several empires."

I think of Violet and the word violence and how I would do anything to stop anyone hurting her. "How could I stop them without using violence?"

Old Sam looked down at the floor. "You do well to ask that question. Many learned people have tried to solve that conundrum. Perhaps as you learn more you will one day understand that negotiation is better than confrontation." He looked rather sad. "Let me quote you a verse from a poem by Yeats. I read him at university before I was sent down." Old Sam seemed very far away as he quietly recited.

"The days are dragon-ridden, the nightmare

Rides upon sleep: a drunken soldiery

Can leave the mother, murdered at her door,

To crawl in her own blood, and go scot-free;

The night can sweat with terror as before

We pieced our thoughts into philosophy,

And planned to bring the world under a rule,

Who are but weasels fighting in a hole."

Old Sam's eyes are open but he doesn't seem to be looking at anything. He makes me feel nervous; I have never seen him like this before, what is the matter with him? He continues:

"The swan has leaped into the desolate heaven:

That image can bring wildness, bring a rage,

To end all things, to end

What my laborious life imagined even

The half imagined, the written page;

Oh! but we dreamed to mend

Whatever mischief seemed

To afflict mankind, but now

That wind of winter blow

Learn that we were crack-pated when we

Dreamed."

I shuffle my feet and giggle, and quickly get away and run home. I go to my shed, I am happy there. I am making a model Spitfire.

THE HOLE

Our farmhouse kitchen had a large wooden table with turned legs and a scrubbed whitened top. Two Windsor bentwood chairs ranged each side, another at one end and a much larger version with arms at the other end for Dad. I sat to his right opposite Mum. The oldest son Gerald sat at the end opposite Dad, the second son, Martin sat next to Mum, and the third son, Cyril opposite Martin. Mother of course at Dad's left, so that she could have a good view of Dad cleaning his ear with a Vesta safety match after finishing the meal; his farmer's breeches-clad leg would be hanging over the arm of 'Head of the Family' dining chair. I suppose that he was at peace with the world, although he never commented much about that, in retrospect I think that he was preoccupied with anticipated actions upstairs, particularly if it happened to be a Sunday. One Sunday afternoon I was told to play in the adjoining bedroom and look after a baby sister named Lilly, I was eight, and having a rather curious nature I looked through the keyhole to see Mum and Dad doing a very strange thing; I was not really interested, but the memory of the extremely bored look on both faces still remains. However, I digress.

The flickering flame of the paraffin lamp, on its polished brass tall stand, glowed with a soft golden light, reflected on the wind-reddened faces, deepened the hue of the red cheddar cheese, quickening the appetite. The light spread from the soot-streaked glass globe, forming a hole of light in the gloom-filled night, pooling on the scrubbed table, and casting the periphery of the kitchen with sooty shadows that moved in rhythm with the wind-wafted flame, playing hide-and-seek between the exposed blackened floor joists. The coconut fibre matting absorbed the light and stayed a dull brown and cream pattern.

The table and chairs were on a blank wall, and opposite an old plywood sideboard seemed to support the heavily curtained window. The dominant feature of the kitchen was a black-leaded coal-fired cooking range, resplendent with burnished brass levers and knobs, tucked into its high alcove. The table and range took turns in order of importance when in use. Mum gave her full attention to the range when cooking mountains of food brought from the scullery. The table was an altar for the almost sacrificial consumption of sometimes singed, sometimes burnt offerings, depending on the strength and direction of the winds blowing across the Fenlands. The wind rumbled round the farm buildings and soughed through the majestic elms and ancient low hedges. The louder the wind, the more the fire glowed and the ovens and grates overheated. The family could anticipate the quality of cooking by the force of the wind. A mid-strength blow from the northeast gave the best culinary results.

Apart from hard graft on the farm, preparation and consumption of food were the most important activity, and the focus of activity was the main meal at midday. We children were not allowed to talk whilst eating. We each had different eating habits, I was finicky, Cyril smiled in his enjoyment, Martin grimly munched away, but Gerald was a sight to behold. His gaping mouth, rippling jaw muscles and half-closed eyes indicated total concentration on eating. He would demolish a large plate of the day's offerings; he would then nudge either Martin or Cyril, "Pass the stew and vegetables please." He would ladle spoons of second helpings of mashed potatoes and greens on his plate, and flood the heap with thick stew. It oozed over to the rim of the plate, but before it could drip off Gerald attacked with flailing knife and fork, and the pile would be demolished and disappear into his chomping jaws. Pudding would sometimes be jam roly-poly, boiled in a teacloth. Sometimes, if Mum's internal timing had gone awry, it would be a reasonably palatable jam roll but encased in a hard shell that cracked young teeth, resulting in a visit to the torture chamber in the school playground that served as a surgery for the peripatetic dentist and his female masochist; those people of my generation will no doubt recall the noise of the foot operated drill, being held down by the nurse, no freezing injection in those far off days, just sheer terror catching the throat. Mum would serve large slices of jam roll and we would help ourselves to custard. Whatever the state of the wind, the custard was always sweet, thick, and bright yellow. It was coaxed from a large jug to form a glutinous topping to the pastry. On a really good day a spoon would stay upright in it for at least two minutes. Gerald's treble helping was indisputable testimony to Mum's great gift in the art of custard making.

The wind also rumbled around the small shed set some distance from the farmhouse, a wooden feather board structure with single pitch corrugated iron roof. It had a very small fixed window, and a wood ledged and braced door with a six-inch gap at the top and bottom to provide ventilation. A peep through a heart-shaped hole at eye level would reveal whether or not the shed was in use. The internal fixtures and fittings were sparse indeed.

Along the full width of the wall opposite the door, were lidded wooden boxes forming seats, one at adult height, and the other suitable for a small child. The seats were hinged at the back, and when lifted revealed another seat with a heart-shaped chamfered opening giving access to a cavernous hole dug into the subsoil. The hole extended from under the seats to beyond the back of the building, so that the building sat over half the hole; that part of the hole behind the building being covered by wooden planks with a light scattering of soil. This was the second most important building on the farm, aptly named The Hole. It was well cared for; the seats and lids scrubbed white, and the earth floor swept clean. The Hole was for peaceful contemplation and reading, although the latter was confined to scanning the sheets of newspapers torn into squares, pierced at one corner and threaded on a wire hook screwed to the wall.

Gerald was obsessed by his alimentary canal, shovelling food in one end, and emptying the other by spending protracted periods enthroned in The Hole. I could hang on the top of the door and look through the peephole and see him re-reading the news, grunting and straining with in his efforts. His overworked innards often gave up the struggle, and had to be assisted by countless bottles of liquid paraffin, and during one extreme case of rebellious bowels, he was seen to swallow a whole bottle of syrup of figs in one long swig. I think the God Bacchus helped Gerald defecate, he didn't give thanks to Bacchus, and Bacchus was very cross indeed.

By listening for the timing of the splash it was possible for the discerning ear to determine the level of the waste in the hole; of course if the level was too high a splash could reach the exposed portion of the user's anatomy. Slightly before the possibility of that eventuality, Dad ordered the Hole to be emptied. It was usually after a prolonged visit from Gerald. After his dedicated efforts, the level would rise dramatically, and Gerald would have a relieved expression, bordering on rapture, for the rest of the day, but the drifting malodorous mists kept us away from The Hole for at least half an hour.

The Hole could not contain the efforts of the family for long, and the threat of an undesirable splash indicated the urgency to empty it every few months. The method of emptying the Hole, inherited from illustrious forefathers, was foolproof. It entailed digging a pit, some distance away, connected by a shallow trench falling away from the back of The Hole. The boards were removed from the back, revealing the sludge which was ladled into the trench with a small steel bowl affixed to a long ash handle, normally used to ladle water into the cattle trough from a nearby ditch. The ladle was also used to encourage the sludge down the trench, and into the pit. Eventually The Hole would be empty and the pit full. The boards would be replaced, and given a light scattering of soil. After a few days, the liquid would seep into the subsoil, and the pit and trench would be filled in with the previously excavated soil.

A time to empty came imminent, and Gerald was delegated the task, so he, duly fortified with vitals, selected a spot near the rabbit hutches and scratched a rough square in the soil with a spade. I tried to help, but just got in the way, and was allotted the task of digging the trench. It took two days, and then we rested from our labours and awaited the full moon. The emptying always took place at night, so it was advantageous to have the light of the moon, and it also essential to have a favourable wind to blow the aromas of the nocturnal activities away from the farmhouse.

I was not allowed to help Gerald with the emptying, and I watched his shadowy figure from the kitchen window, laboriously ladling and scooping, his face swathed in a large red kerchief as protection against the pungent assault on his sense of smell. Eventually The Hole was empty and the pit full. The surface gently heaved as the odious mass settled; the sludge gently bubbled and a grey scum formed on the surface, obnoxious gasses fouled the sweet country air until now tainted only by cow muck. Gerald came back to the house, washed and put a clean shirt. The others were asleep and he stole into the larder for a late-night snack.

The following night, just before supper, the family was in the kitchen, playing an innocuous card game of newmarket. Gerald muttered, "Poor old Pongo, I've forgotten to feed him." Pongo was a large buck rabbit, Gerald's pride and joy, the envy of the neighbours who marvelled at its antics when they brought their does for mating. Brian assumed his determined look, the jaw clenched, the muscles bulging Gregory Peck style, and he left his chair, put on his coat and went outside. I watched him from the window, and as he walked down the yard. Later, I thought that Bacchus must have laughed as he clouded the moon for a minute. Gerald walked unseeing into his filled hole, to sink slowly beneath the surface, to disappear like our wellingtons sucked off in the cow yard after particularly heavy rain. As the moon cleared, I looked closer and saw the soil on the pit erupting, and a slimy figure dragged itself from the pit and started to crawl towards the house. "Mum! Dad! Gerald's in the pit." I screamed. Cyril was helpless with mirth, even Martin smiled.

Dad rushed outside, the rest of us crowded to the window. Dad kept well clear of Gerald, and shouted, "Go to the pump, don't take that stink near the house." Gerald changed course, and Dad rushed ahead to fill buckets from the pump in the yard. Gerald reached the yard and was immediately engulfed as Dad dowsed him with water. He helped Gerald out of his clothes, and Mum ran to the yard with a towel and clean clothes.

Gerald, now dried and covered, but still shivering came back into the house. Mum sat him in Dad's chair near the fire. His clothes were left in a heap in the yard.

We waited until Gerald warmed up and stopped shaking. Mum said he was trembling from shock, but Gerald said it was because he was hungry. Pongo went hungry that night, but we were never hungry for long; Mum took a pride in seeing us well fed. We sat down to supper of thick slices of bread and home-made butter, wedges of cheddar, pickled onions and a mug of milky cocoa. Gerald's half-closed eyes and chomping jaws confirmed that even that obnoxious ordeal could not subdue his gastronomic urges.

POTATO HARVEST

We grew only main crop potatoes on the farm; new potatoes for the kitchen were grown in the vegetable garden. Not much equipment was required for planting potatoes, all that was needed was the normal cultivation of the soil, horses and carts, and chitting trays, and casual labour to supplement the regular work force. Harvesting still needed horses and carts and casual labour, and the only machine was the potato spinner. Now, of course, all the work is done by machinery, and the potatoes go straight from the field to a factory for processing; with consequent denigration of country skills and life.

Potato chitting trays were about eighteen inches wide by three feet long and three inches deep, and made of wood. The sides were two inch by half-inch slats nailed one-and-a-half-inch square corner posts four inches long, and more slats, separated by half inch gaps, nailed to the underside of the sides. The posts projected below and above the slats so that the trays could be stacked on top of each other and allow fingers to be inserted under the trays for handling. Seed potatoes were delivered to the farm in sacks, and then laid in the trays in the barn and left to grow chits; the first growth of a stem and a cluster of roots. The potatoes would start growing immediately when they were planted, so the growing season was shorter, and also there was less chance of the seed rotting if the soil became waterlogged from heavy rain.

The ridging plough was similar to a normal plough except that the share had a double blade. It didn't just turn the soil over into the last furrow, it turned the soil both ways to form an inverted V-channel, and the soil was piled up on each side of the furrow. The next furrow did the same, but the furrows were spaced so that the piled earth made a continuous ridge, and the completed field was covered with V-shaped ridges and furrows. The skill was in judging the width to make sure that the slopes of the trenches and ridges were continuous. The spacing of the furrows allowed a cart to be pulled with the wheels running in every third furrow. Later seed potatoes were planted in the furrows, and the soil turned back on itself so that the field was flat again.

The potato spinner was a flimsy looking machine for digging potatoes out of the ground. It had an iron spine with brackets to support a single small front wheel, and a crossbar to take the chains

from a horse; the crossbar turned to steer the contraption. The other end of the spine supported two much larger spoked wheels with spuds on the rims to grip the soil. The wheels were bolted to the axle which had a bevelled gear wheel in the middle; that drove another gear wheel on a shaft that extended to the rear and operated a complex system of two concentric iron spoked wheels with connecting links and six sets of double prongs; that was the spinning part A heavy iron strip was fixed to the casing and extended below the level of the spinners and was then bent at right angles to form a flat sharp blade that was pulled through the soil in front of the spinners and below the toots of the potatoes; that loosened the soil for the spinners. When the machine was pulled forward, the machine made quite a racket as the various bits came alive. As the spinners clattered round, the prongs retained an upright position and were forced into and across the soil to dig out the potatoes; hence the name 'Potato spinner.' The spinners revolved quickly and the potatoes were thrown against a vertical sheet of heavy sacking. The potatoes and soil fell to the ground in a two-foot wide strip and the pickers could easily pick up the potatoes without darting over a wide area. The gears and shaft were enclosed in an iron casing that was pivoted to the spine and extended forward to take a large lever that lowered and raised the spinner. The driver sat on an iron seat above the back wheels. All he had to do was to position the machine in the furrows, drive the horse, and raise and lower the spinners at the end and beginning of each row. The machine dug only one row of potatoes. The seat was iron with slots and was quite comfortable but cold, so the driver usually padded it with a folded sack. The same type of seat was used on most horse drawn implements and also on the later tractors.

The picked potatoes were stored in clamps, normally on the side of the field adjoining the road. During the autumn, the clamps were opened and the potatoes sorted in a riddle. The riddle was a circular sieve about two feet in diameter with a wooden rim and iron mesh; the size of the mesh determined the size of selected potatoes. The riddle was supported on an iron rod with two prongs at the bottom to stabilize it upright in the soil, the top of the rod had two three rods welded at right angle to the rod with a ring welded to the ends of the rods; the riddle was rested on the ring and shaken about to filter out the soil and small potatoes. Rotten and misshapen potatoes were picked out and thrown on a heap. The selected potatoes were put into bags and sold to a potato merchant. The small potatoes were fed to the pigs.

***

I am now twelve, and use the school bus to go to the grammar school in town. It's the last three weeks of the long summer holiday, and I have plenty of time to help on the farm. Dad has run out of cigarettes and sends me to the pub for a packet of Red Tenners. I have to go to the back door; children are not allowed in a pub. I run there and back in ten minutes. Dad is sitting on the milk stand by the main road, waiting for his friend Alex. I sit with him and swing my legs. He says, "Tomorrow we set the potatoes. You can lead Violet with the cart. Watch what you are doing on the main road. It's market day and there will be the bus and a few cars."

About six weeks ago, I had watched while the seed potatoes were unloaded from the merchants Ford lorry into the barn. Later I helped Martin and Cyril to take them from the sacks and lay them in chitting trays. They stacked the trays on top of each other in rows about five feet high. They were too heavy for me to lift. After a few weeks, the potatoes had grown green shoots and they are now ready for setting. Everybody said that they had chitted; chits are shoots, so why couldn't they say shot? They had to be planted before the chits grew too long to avoid them being broken off while carting them to the field and planting. I stop myself from daydreaming about cowboys and their six-shooters and ask Dad, "Why do you have to buy seed potatoes? Why can't you save some from last year and set them?"

Dad shakes his head. "We have to be careful about the blight, it rots potatoes. If we did get blight it would be passed on to the crop and would be useless for seed. We get seed potatoes from places that do not have blight, and Scotland is one of those places." He becomes serious. "There was a lot of blight in Ireland and many crops were ruined. Many people starved and the country had political unrest." I didn't know what political problems were; perhaps they should have got their seed potatoes from Scotland.

Dad tells me, "King Edwards are so named because they have red skins." I can't see what that had to do with Scotland. He continues, "Arran Pilots come from a Scottish island and have white skins."

I say, "I can't see why they were named after a pilot, potatoes can't fly a Spitfire."

Dad laughs. "You have a sharp mind. You have to be careful, one of these days you will cut yourself." That doesn't make much sense to me. I watch the smoke from Dad's fag curl up over his nose. He never takes it from his mouth and puffs it like other men; he just lets it smoulder between his lips. His nose and teeth are yellow. I don't want yellow teeth, so I will not smoke when I am grown up. My brothers get dead elder twigs they pick a straight bit about four inches long. The bark is firm, but the inside pith has shrunk, so there is a gap between the bark and pith. They light one end and suck hard and get the smoke in their mouths. I don't know why they do that. I tried it and it just burnt my tongue.

"Dad! Why do you chit them in the barn? All other seeds go straight into the ground."

"It's warmer in the barn than in the soil, so they think that it is spring and start to grow. They use their own moisture to feed the chits. When they are set, they quickly take root and it takes less time for them to mature."

I ask, "Why does Mr Wright chit them in his new glass house? He has a big barn."

Mr Wright is really Alex. It would be very rude of me to use his Christian name. Dad shrugs, "He's always been ahead of himself. He bought that fancy Oliver tractor with only one wheel at the front." He went quiet for a minute, "Mind you, I must admit that it's good for working in furrows, so he probably knows what he is doing. He told me that he bought the green house to make money. It's much warmer than the barn; in frosty weather he has a paraffin heater. The potatoes chit sooner. When it's clear of potatoes, he can grow tomatoes and cucumbers and sell them at the market. He said that will pay for the paraffin and still make a profit. Good luck to him, I say."

Mr Wright is John's dad. When I went to see if John could come out to play, we were more interested in watching his dad build the glasshouse than playing. He took several weeks. He built a low brick wall, and then put up a wooden frame the same as bars in a sash window, but bigger. He then put in long sheets of glass that overlapped on the short edges. Then it had to be painted white, but I think that red would be better. Mr Wright is very clever. He filled in his earth closet, and put in a new lavatory that is cleaned with water, just the same as those at school. I grin at Dad. "When I grow up I can help you to build a glass house."

Dad laughs. "We'll have to wait a couple of years for that. Here comes Alex. Off you go and help your mother."

Highside field will be growing potatoes this year. Yesterday Cyril finished ridging it, and now we have to scatter guano, and I have to lead Violet. Cyril has already harnessed Violet and hitched her to the cart. I take it to the barn, and Cyril takes off the tailboard, and helps Martin to load the cart with sacks of guano. I lead Violet out on to the main road and about quarter of a mile to Highside. Dad said that I have to be careful, so I must not start daydreaming. I meet Tim leading Captain back to the farmyard. He has already delivered his load. Jack points to the rows; "Go along that one and keep a steady speed." I lead Violet, and Fred and Jack pull off the sacks and put them at 15 feet apart on every third furrow.

When the cart is empty, I go back to the farmyard and meet Tim coming out leading Captain with a full load. We stop carting at dinnertime, and in the afternoon Fred and Jack spread the guano. They fill buckets with guano from the sacks and hold it under the left arm and then scoop out the guano with the right hand. As the left leg moves forward the right arm swings forward and the hand opens to scatter the granules along the furrow. They would not let me try, they said that the guano would make my hands sore, and be very painful if some got in my eye. The next day we all do the same and finish the field. Fred and Jack are very graceful as they scatter the guano. I would like to be graceful. I have read about, and seen pictures of ballet dancers in the encyclopedias. I saw a drawing in the Picture Post of a man scattering seeds from a basket. It was by a Frenchman, Vincent someone or other. I thought that the drawing was crude. I showed it to Gerald, and said that I could do it better. He clipped me round the ear. "Don't be so bigheaded. It's the Impressionist style and meant to express movement." I look again and remember Old Sam saying that hoeing was like ballet dancing, and I can understand the drawing. Perhaps I will be graceful enough to be a dancer when I grow up.

I am leading Violet again today. Cyril hitches her to the farm lorry, and I take it to the barn. Martin and Cyril take the trays from the barn and stack them six high on the lorry. It is easier to handle trays on the lower and bigger bottom; the wheels are the same distance apart as the cart, so they can run in the furrows. I lead Violet to the Highside, and Fred tells me which furrow to go down. I have to stop when he shouts 'Whoa'. Violet would stop anyway. That gives Fred and Jack time to unload the trays and place them on the ridges at about three-yard intervals. When the lorry is empty I have to turn the lorry round. Tim is leading Captain again, and when we pass each other we throw small clods at each other just for something to do.

Everybody helps with the potato setting and later harvesting them. The workers' wives and older children join in. That is not enough and Dad allows Didicoys to keep their caravans and horses near the spinney in one corner of the field. They are friendly, but we are not allowed to mix with them. Trusted POWs are allowed to work on the farms. Most are delivered by army lorry in the morning and picked up at night. The really trusted ones can live on the farm. Mr Wright had two POWs, a German Fritz and an Italian Fury. They are very friendly, and sometimes we children sit on the grass verge by the road and talk with them. We are shy, and they do most of the talking about their own countries. Fury speaks good English, but Fritz can't say much, but seems to understand us. Fritz says that he misses his family and can't wait to go home. Fury wants to stay in England after the war, he said that his family had been bombed and he has nothing to go home for. He says his town of Naples is very smelly and our hamlet is nice and clean with no bad people. He tries to teach us Italian but we just giggle and can only manage 'bonazera.' He sings a lot; I just have to listen to the beautiful sound, even though I can't understand the words. He says they are arias. Fritz and Fury live in a chicken shed; without the chickens.

They invited my brothers and me for tea. Mum said that we could go, but not stay too long. We drank the tea, and we ate the biscuits, but didn't fancy the boiled strips of pastry. There was not much furniture, only two chairs, so we sat on an old carpet. There was a paraffin cooker and a cupboard for bits and pieces, and two kitbags and a couple of old leather suitcases. Two iron beds were on one wall. One was neatly made, but the other had the blankets and sheets folded and stacked at the head. Fury said that he was in the army and had to fold his bedclothes every day. Fritz was in the navy and they made their beds properly.

The potato setters work in pairs and two setters share a tray. They semi-crouch as they pull the trays along the top of the ridges and place the seed potatoes in the furrows at nine-inch intervals. Fred and Jack knew far apart the trays must be so that as one tray is empty another is with the grasp of the setters. Before they start on the next full tray they stand to stretch their backs, and put the empty tray on the next row of unplanted furrows. It's hard work setting potatoes and one woman pulls a face. "It doesn't get easier as you get older." When the setters complete one length of the field, they move over to the next set of rows. When the setters have completed three lengths Cyril guides the ridge plough to split the ridge and turn the earth back into the furrows and cover up the potatoes, so the field is level again. It is a continuous process of planting and ploughing the ridges back into the furrows to cover the potatoes, and at the end of the day all you can see is the flat field where the potatoes have been set, and the remaining ridges waiting their turn.

It is several weeks since we planted the potatoes and the field is a mass of green tops. I talk to Martin after tea and he is a bit grumpy. "I wish that I had gone to grammar school. I sometimes think that it's not fair. You sit in a nice warm classroom all day, while I slave away. As well as being cowman, I have to help on the farm." I must have looked a bit sad as he says, "I didn't really mean that. I wasn't cut out to be a scholar."

I say, "Never mind! Sometimes it's very hard, especially when we have algebra and physics." I add, "Anyway you have piano lessons. I am not allowed to learn the piano because it would interfere with my homework."

He smiles. "Don't worry, next time I practice I will teach you the scales."

I turn to Cyril. "What have you been up to today?"

He replies, "Scuffling the potatoes. When I've finished in about two days, I will have to use the ridger to earth them up."

"Why?" I ask.

Cyril looks down his nose. Because."

I reply, "That's not an answer."

Cyril grins. "Silly questions ask for silly answers." He adds, "If you really must know, the scuffler breaks up and loosens the soil between the rows of potatoes and makes it easier for the ridger." It is time to listen to ITMA so we stop talking.

I am walking with Dad to the pub; he likes a half-pint of beer now and again. He says that he will buy me a Mars bar for helping Mum. The grocery shop is over a mile down the road, and the landlord of the hamlet pub keeps some sweets to sell to local children. I ask Dad, "Why do you have to use a scuffler and earth up the potatoes?"

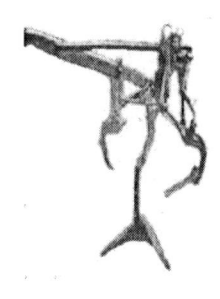

He says, "Questions, questions, questions. You will have so many answers in your brain that one day it will burst." I hold back the tears. He laughs. "Don't worry, that can never happen. I was only joking." He adds, "Anyway, the scuffler gets rid of weeds and loosens the soil between the rows, so it's easier to use the ridger to make new furrows between the rows and pile it over the plants. We have to wait until the plants are a foot high so that the green tops poke above the new ridges. The plants will keep growing but the roots and potatoes will be covered by a good layer of soil to keep out the sunlight. If they were exposed the potatoes will turn green, and not even the pigs will eat them." Dad buys me the Mars bar. I cut off thin slices with my knife and eat half on the way home. It's quite a treat so I will save the rest for tomorrow.

It is getting dark earlier as the summer ends. We have finished tea. Dad sits with one leg hanging over the arm of his chair. I don't know why he does that, I tried it and it was uncomfortable. He glances at Mum. "The potato tops have died, so I dug up a couple of roots, and they are ready for picking, so tomorrow we make a start." He smiles at me. "You are getting to know Violet quite well, so go to the stable early, and then take her to the barn and get a load of baskets and take them to Highside." Cyril had fed and watered the horses. He nods at me. "I'll hitch Violet to the cart, and while you're collecting the baskets, I will take Tinker and the spinner and get started. I have to spin out a few rows before the pickers get there."

Tim is already on the headland with Captain. He climbs in my cart, and I lead Violet down the headland next to where Cyril has spun out the potatoes. Tim throws the baskets in a line on the potatoes. He goes back to Captain and he leads him while I empty his load of baskets. There are enough to reach to the end of the rows. We both go back to the headland and wait for the pickers. He stares sat me for a minute. "How do you like grammar school?"

I shrug. "I don't like the bus ride, it stops at the market place, and we have to walk half a mile to the school. It's not fair. The girls get off at the gate to the High school, and the bus stops to pick them after school."

He nods. "Yes, but what is the school like?"

I reply, "I'm not too happy. There are hundreds of pupils and the masters wear black gowns and funny square hats and are very strict. The lessons are different and not easy to understand, and we have to do homework every night." I add, "I think that you are much better off staying at the village school; it's friendly and you will leave at fourteen. I have to stay until I'm sixteen."

Tim laughs. "I heard that you have gym and that you have to have a shower after. I wouldn't like to get undressed in front of other people."

I grimace. "Well! I don't like it either, we have to stand together in a sort of corridor, and the teacher turns on a tap and water sprays over us. It's not too bad at first, the water is warm, but the teacher turns it to cold for a couple of minutes and that is terrible."

Tim shakes his head. "A Saturday night bath is enough for me. I'm glad I didn't get the scholarship. If you go to grammar school you have to work in an office when you grow up, I wouldn't like that. I like to help Dad on the land."

While we are talking, Martin has cut some willow wands from the spinney, and pushed them in the headland about one chain apart. They marked the retches; the length of row that each picker worked on. I say, "The pickers have arrived we had better get ready for them." I am watching the pickers. Their arms move like lightening as they snatch the potatoes with both hands and drop them in a basket. As they clear a space they snatch the basket forward with one hand while the other keeps picking. When they fill the basket, they straighten their backs and reach for an empty basket. They keep doing all that until they reach the end of their retch. They walk back to the beginning of their retch. On the way, they pick up the full baskets and place them in a straight line on the side away from the spinner. The young children try to help fill the baskets, but the grown-ups tell them to get out of the way and play somewhere else. When it rains, mud cakes on the bottom of the baskets, making them very heavy and the work is hard. Before they started picking the next retch, the workers clean the caked mud from their boots, so they do not slide around.

The pickers have completed one retch and moved over to the next strip of potatoes thrown out by the spinner. Eddy and I ride in the cart and take Violet to the end of the row of full baskets. I stay in the cart and sit on the front of the side panel, and Eddy gets ready to throw the full basket into the cart. He holds an iron stay on the back of the cart and looks up at me. "You will have to do this sometime so pay attention to how I use the stay as a grip and swing of the cart to help me throw the basket. They have made a good job of spaced the baskets, so I should get one basket every other step. Let's get started."

I click for Violet to go forward. Eddy makes it look easy. He grabs the handle of the first basket, swings it up, lets go, and it flies to me upside down, and his arm goes back to catch the next basket. I grab it with both hands and swing my body so that as the potatoes spill out they go all over the cart and not just round my feet. I have to keep lifting my legs to stop them being buried. We stop when the cart is full. Eddy says, "It may look easy to you, but if the baskets are not spaced to match my step I lose the rhythm, and just use brute force to throw them. That's gut-wrenching work." He grins. "It's worse in wet weather, the mud on the baskets makes them twice as heavy."

I lead the full cart to the headland near the road. Harry is waiting for me. Harry has a smallholding of six acres just down the road. Harry and his wife are always busy looking after their chickens and growing salads and vegetables to sell at the market in town. They also sell the cockerels and eggs. Harry sometimes works for Dad during harvest time. Dad said that there is not much profit in market gardening and Harry needs the money. Harry says, "Good morning young man. Take her over there." He points towards the gate, and I take Violet there. Harry says, "Hold her while I tip up the cart." He pulls a lever over the back of the shafts and pushes the front of the cart. It tips backwards and spills the potatoes out off the back. He uses a beet fork to throw any loose potatoes into the centre of the heap and says, "Now off you go and get clear before Tim comes."

I meet Tim on my way back to the pickers. I line up Violet and keep a steady pace whilst Martin throws in another load. When I get back to Harry, the heap has grown, and when Harry tips my load and uses his fork a few minutes, the heap becomes a big ridge the same shape that a ridger makes. Harry looks at the heap. "It's taking shape now." As he works to pile up the potatoes into a ridge he explains, "You know, this is really a clamp, but our name for it is a grave." He laughs. "It's got nothing to do with a grave digger, so don't call me a sexton." He is making a tidy job of the grave, it is higher than me, and about six feet wide and Harry fiddles with the potatoes until the sloping sides are very even and smooth.

I play a game of tobogganing down a mountain. We don't even have big hills, let alone mountains around our farm. I sit on the potatoes while the cart is tipped, and slide down the moving potatoes to the grave. I always manage to end the slide in a standing position. This time, as the potatoes move under me I slide too fast and am buried under the pile. It is very heavy and black, and before I can scream Harry's worried face is looking at me. He has scrabbled at the potatoes and luckily found my face first. I am on my back with arms and legs outstretched. He asks, "Where are your arms?"

I can only move my eyes, and just say, "There."

He scrabbles away until he uncovers my shoulders and arms, and then pulls me out of the grave. Harry says angrily, "Don't ever do that again. You are lucky to be alive." I was frightened in the grave, but I forgot that when I was out and safe. I didn't know why Harry was so angry, it was only a game. He says more softly, "You could have died, and then what would your mum and dad think of me?" I laugh, I never think of myself dying.

"Well! Thank you for pulling me out. I won't do it again."

As I led Violet back to Eddy, Harry called, "You certainly won't, not when I am here."

While I am at the grave, Tim sits in his cart with Captain pulling, and catches baskets while Eddy throws them. We pass each other going to and fro, so Eddy has a little rest between loading the carts. As Tim and I go back and forth to the grave it steadily grows and by dinnertime is about fifteen yards long. Dad normally does his office work, but this morning he harnessed Tinker to the lorry and carted a load of straw from the yard and scattered it each side of the grave. He then pitch-forked a six-inch layer on the potatoes and weighted it down with a few spadefuls of earth to stop the wind blowing it away.

It is my turn to catch baskets. Suddenly there is a loud neighing and the noise of distant thunder. I like that description; I read it in a book. We all look to see Captain galloping from the grave towards us. He swerves and bumps across the furrows until he is stopped by the headland and ditch. Cyril runs to him. He holds his bridle and pats his neck. He must have spoken quietly in his ear, because Captain stops shaking. We don't see Tim until he walks up behind us. He is very pale. "I was riding on the back of the cart. Captain neighed and reared up in the shafts, tipping me out of the back. Then be bolted and galloped away."

Fred's wife looks him over. "You don't seem to be hurt, but it must have frightened you. You will feel better after I give you a mug of my cold tea."

Martin jokes, "It's lucky that you fell on your head otherwise you could have broken a leg." We have all heard that joke many times, but still laugh. Martin says, "He was probably bitten by a horsefly. Perhaps a wasp got in his ear; whatever it was frightened him enough to make him panic and bolt."

When all the potatoes are picked, we have to get rid of the dried tops. Dad likes to do that, and I help him. We take a horse rake to Highside, Violet pulls it because she is used to me. Dad makes a start and rakes the tops into rows while I wait on the headland. He stops after a couple of rows. "Now you can take over while I burn this lot. By the way since you are so clever with that brain of yours, you can use the proper name, haulm; not tops." He takes out another cigarette and lights it from the last fag end. He takes out his box of Swan Vesta matches and sets fire to the haulm; it is dry and burns easily. There is a lot of smoke, but he still keeps the fag in his mouth. It is easy work. When the rake is full, I pull a long lever, and the rake lifts up and leaves a roll of haulm on the ground. I then let down the lever and rake again until it is full. I do as Dad told me at breakfast, and raise the lever where I did at the last row, so that there is a line of rolled haulm across the field. We work until dinnertime. It takes longer to burn than rake, and there are several rows waiting. Dad calls to me, "That's enough for now. Let's get back for dinner." I finish the row, and lift the lever up and drive Violet to Dad. He unhitches Violet. "You can do some more tomorrow, so the rake can stay here. Bring her back to the yard, we will need her this afternoon." I take Violet to the stable; Cyril has left some hay and a bucket of water. I hold the bucket while she drinks, and then tie her to the manger and go in for dinner of boiled beef mince and vegetables.

After dinner Dad hitches Violet to the lorry and we go back to Highside. Violet walks along the rolls of haulm and Dad pitchforks them to me on the lorry and I make a rough stack of them. We take the load to the grave and unload it at the side of the grave. We go back and dump the next load on the other side of the grave. By teatime the haulm stretches the full length of the grave. Dad smiles at me. "You did well. I'll make a farmer of you yet. Tomorrow you can finish the raking while I carry on burning. Old Sam is coming tomorrow so you can help him."

"Help him to do what?" I ask.

Dad frowns. "You know that Mum doesn't like you to say 'What'. Old Sam will tell you tomorrow."

Old Sam takes a puff on his clay pipe and has a faraway look. I wonder what he is thinking about, but don't join him in daydreaming. There is work to do. I start to pitchfork the haulm onto the grave. Old Sam says, "Not like that boy. Just watch me." He gently shakes the bundles of haulm into long strands and lays them in horizontal layers on the straw. It takes me some time to get the hang of it, but I manage to keep up and we gradually built up a six-inch layer. Old Sam explains, "This is to insulate against the frost."

That is a new word for me. I learn a lot of new words from reading the encyclopedias. "Does that mean protect?" I ask.

Old Sam nods. "Yes, insulation keeps cold out and heat in. This layer supplements the straw, but will not keep out the rain. Later someone will have to put on a layer of earth, rain cannot penetrate that." He laughs. "Not me, I'm a bit too old for hard graft." I enjoy talking to Old Sam, he uses a lot of unusual words and I learn a lot from him. The work is not hard and has quick results. While we work Old Sam talks. He tells me how to be a good citizen when 'I grow to manhood' as he put it. That's not really learning things so I don't pay too much attention, but no doubt he is right. We stop for our packed dinner. Old Sam munches slowly, has a couple of swigs of cold tea and then has a snooze. My arms do ache a bit, so I am pleased to have a rest.

I must have nodded off. I am startled awake by a kick on the sole of my boot and Old Sam shouting, "Wake up! We are not here to sleep. The others will finish picking the Ten-acre tomorrow; and we have to finish by then so that they can do the earthing up."

I am a bit ashamed, and grin as I scramble up. "Sorry. You were asleep and I just dropped off."

Old Sam snorts. "Nonsense! I don't need to sleep during the day." It would be rude to argue with him so I keep quiet and carry on laying the haulm. We almost finish in time except for a few yards.

Over breakfast of thick porridge and cold fat bacon and pickles, Dad says, "Old Sam is not feeling too good today. He said that you made a good job of things yesterday, so you can go and finish it yourself." I feel pleased that Dad trusts me. I won't let him down.

Fred and Jack are working on one side of the grave. They are digging a trench about two feet deep and three feet wide alongside the grave, and throwing the soil on the haulm to make a six-inch layer. It is heavy work, but they dig steadily and only stop every fifteen minutes for a breather. When we stop for midmorning bread and cheese, they do not say much. I ask Eddy, "Why do you need a trench?"

He looks down his nose. "Don't ask silly questions, the earth has got to come from somewhere, and it would be stupid to get it yards from the grave." I blush, and he adds more kindly, "The trench drains away any rainwater as it runs down the sides of the grave. Without the trench, the bottom of the grave would get soaked and the potatoes would rot." When they started work again, I went home. I had finished laying the haulm, and still feel embarrassed over my stupid question and want to be by myself.

It's late autumn and my half term holiday. The teachers didn't give any homework, so I am free of school for a few days. I help Mum in the house, and do a bit of gardening and fretwork, but I have plenty of time to go to Highside and watch them make a start on the riddling. By the time that I get here, they have already spaded the soil off the end of the grave and put it back in the trench. Somebody has raked off the haulm and straw, and put it in a pile out of the way of the workers. They had put two sets of riddles near the end of the grave, and had started work. Eddy uses a potato fork to half fill the riddles. Jack works on one and Fred on the other. They push the riddles backward and forward to move the potatoes around on the mesh. The small potatoes and any loose earth fall through and then the riddlers lift the riddle off the stand, half turn and throw the potatoes into a sack behind them, and then put the riddle back of the stand to be filled again. The sack is hooked to the top of the weighing machine so that the top is open. When the machine tips the two fifty-six-pound weights, Martin eases the sack off the hooks and drags and stands it upright a couple of paces behind the weighing machine. Jack's wife sews the tops of the sack together with a six-inch needle and binder twine. She pulls the last couple of inches at the outer edges into bunches and ties them at the bottom. They look like donkey's ears, and form handles for men to grip when they lift the full sacks.

Jack tells a Max Miller joke. It was something about either meeting a lovely girl walking on a footpath and asking whether he should push past her or walk in a gutter, and Max Miller said that he fell in the gutter. I don't understand it. They all laugh so I joined in. I don't want them to think that I am stupid. I like listening to ITMA on the radio; they have good jokes. Fred says, "It's a good job that these were picked in the dry. I hate it when you have to rub off the dry mud; it's hard on the hands."

Next day I have to go on my bike to the village to change the accumulator for the radio. On the way back, I stop at the grave to say 'Hello'. An icy cold wind is blowing from Siberia; the men had hung a tarpaulin on some poles as a wind break. The riddlers have put old socks over their wrists and hands to keep out the cold; wool gloves would soon be full of holes; the socks last longer because as they wore down they were pulled down a bit more from the wrist. Some potatoes have rotted, they have to be picked off the riddle by hand; the stink is overpowering.

When Eddy has to take more than two steps to scoop potatoes from the grave to the riddles, more earth and straw is removed and the riddles and the weighing machine moved nearer the grave. Martin moves a sack about every five minutes, so he has time to take off the soil. The rows of sacks grow by the same distance. At the end of the day, some straw is put back over the exposed potatoes and covered with a tarpaulin. The rows of sacks are loaded onto the lorry. Eddy and Jack grasp an ear at the top of the sack, and pull it onto a stick held in their other hands, it is easy work to lift the sack by the stick and ears onto the bed of the lorry, Fred drags and swings the sacks to the front and arranges them in rows until the lorry is full, it is then taken to the farm yard and the potatoes unloaded into the barn. I watch Fred. He grasps a sack by one ear in each hand. He steps forward and lifts both sacks and swings them in front of him. He does that three times, and the sacks finish up at the front of the lorry. Fred grins. "What are you gaping at?"

I say, "Those sacks weigh eight stones each, how on earth can you swing them around so easily?"

He says, "Never fight the weight, always use it to help you. When I swing the sack, it becomes lighter. I couldn't lift a sack by one ear, but the swing makes it easy." He laughs. "I can even do it with a sack in each hand, don't ask me how, I just do it." I am amazed. Perhaps when I am older I will understand it when I have lessons in physics.

As soon as the riddling stops Martin has to go to his cows. It is my job to bring them back from the pasture and drive them to the cowshed. Martin and Dad and me do the milking, while Cyril attends to his horses. Later the undersized potatoes are shovelled into a cart and taken to the yard. They will be boiled and mashed and fed to the pigs. During the slump, all decent potatoes had to be sold, and the family ate potatoes selected from the heap intended for pig food. There is more money for food now, so we keep a few sacks of good potatoes back when the potato merchant comes for the crop. It takes several days to finish off the grave. All signs of the grave have gone. The straw and haulm have been burnt, all the earth put back in the trenches and levelled and all the tools taken back to the yard. After Cyril ploughs where the grave had been, Highside is just another field.

We are all still sitting round the table after tea. I say, "I've been thinking about what to do when I leave school."

Mum nods. "It's sensible to think ahead, but I don't think that you should make up your mind just yet. Anyway, you always wanted to be a teacher."

"Well," I reply, "I've changed my mind. I want to be a ballet dancer."

Everyone is very quiet for a minute, and then they all burst out laughing. Dad becomes serious. "No son of mine is going to prance around on a stage wearing his Long John underpants in front of everybody."

Mum sniffs, "I should think not. Even though you got the scholarship, it still costs a lot to keep you at school. Sometimes we have to go without things to pay for you. We are not going to spend our hard-earned money to give you a chance in life, and then to have you waste it on being a ballet dancer." Mum looked at Dad and he nodded. She looked back at me and said sternly, "You will be a teacher, and that is that."

I am shocked, but I will have to do as I am told. I have learned not to cry in front of other people, but I cry inside. Later, when I am in my bed, I know that something will get in my eyes and the tears will flow.

WHEAT HARVEST

Wheat can be sown in either the autumn or the spring. Autumn wheat, colloquially winter wheat, starts to grow and is strong enough to withstand frost, so it has an early start and ripens earlier than spring-sown wheat. The implements used in wheat production are the drill and binder; plus the normal hoes, pitch-fork, and horse and carts. The drill is used to sow small seeds such as wheat, oats, barley and peas, but is not suitable for larger seeds such as broad beans. The drill is an eighteen-inch square by ten feet long wooden box with a lid on the top, and mounted length-wise on an iron axle with wheels half the size of a cart. It is pulled by one horse; the shafts are fixed to a beam under the timber box. That beam also supports pairs of flexible funnels that poke up into the rear of the box. The funnels are made up of a series of tapered tubes loosely tied together by small chains, so they are flexible. The lowest tube is made of cast iron and goes from round to oval, the front is sharpened so that it can drag through the soil and form a shallow furrow, and the back is cut away so that seeds can be seen dropping into the furrow. The iron bottom tubes are bolted to another beam that can be raised and lowered by a large iron lever; that regulates the depth of the drills and raises the lowest tube clear of the ground when the drill is being towed on the road. The spacing of the tubes is fixed at the top, but is adjustable on the bottom beam to allow different spacing of the furrows to suit the crop being sown. The box is divided length-wise into two compartments, the front is twice the width of the rear and is filled with seed wheat. The seed trickles through holes in the bottom of the timber divider, into the rear compartment. Along the bottom is an iron shaft geared to a main wheel. Pairs of small iron rimless wheels with the ends of the spokes formed into a spoon are fixed at about twelve-inch centres along the shaft. When the drill is pulled forward, the shaft revolves and the spoons scoop up seeds and as the wheel turns the spoons upside down they discharge the seeds into the tops of the funnels. The seeds then fall down through the flexible pipes into the furrows. The driver sits on the seat to guide the horse, and another man walks behind the drill to check that the seeds are distributed evenly in the furrows from all the tubes. He

adjusts the depth as necessary with the large lever. Sacks of wheat are ranged along the headlands, and the drill is refilled after each length of the field. After drilling the field is harrowed to fill in the furrows and rolled to firm the soil. The binder is a very complex piece of machinery, and I will leave it for Cyril to explain to Simon how it works.

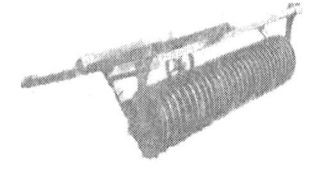

Barley, oats, and wheat were harvested by the same method. Peas however were drilled in the normal way, and when the pods were fully formed and the stalks began to dry, the stalks were cut with a grass cutter. The haulm was then forked into windrows, so called because the wind blew through the rows and dried the crop. The rows had to be forked over a couple of times, and when fully dry were carted to the stackyard and threshed. The dry haulm was stacked and later fed to the cows.

Barley, oats, wheat, and peas were all drilled by the same method. Peas however, were not harvested with a binder. When the pods were full and the stalks had stated to dry, the stalks were cut with a grass cutter; that was just the cutter part of a binder. It sliced through the stems at ground level, and until they started to dry, there was no sign that they had been cut. The haulm was then forked into windrows, so called because the wind could blow through the rows and dry the crop. The rows had to be forked over a couple of times, and when the crop was fully dry it was carted to the yard for stacking and later threshing. The haulm was stacked and later fed to the cows.

***

I have seen pictures in the encyclopedias of men in foreign countries sowing seeds by throwing them from baskets held at their waist. Farmers probably did that many years ago here, but now we use a drill pulled by a horse. I am too young to help with the drilling; I can only watch when I come back from school. Cyril drives the horse and Dad follows the drill. He said once that following the drill is one of the most responsible jobs on the farm. If the seeds do not come out of all the tubes evenly, the field would have empty lines and the crop would be less. If any of the tubes get clogged and no seeds come out, he has to shout to Cyril to stop the horse while he frees the blockage. He also refills the box at the end of each row. He said that is not really hard work following the drill, but looking down all the time makes his neck and shoulders ache, and his legs get a bit tired from walking all day.

Dad sits in his Windsor armchair; he had turned it from the kitchen table towards the heat from the range. Mum had moved her chair to the other side of the range. We boys sit at the table enjoying a supper of bread and cheese and hot cocoa. It is late summer and is still daylight at eight in the evening. Dad turns and says, "I looked at the wheat today, it will be ready for cutting in a couple of days." He looks at Cyril. "Grease the binder tomorrow, and make sure that everything works. We don't want any hold-ups once we start."

I am interested in machinery. It's easy to see how the drill works, but a binder is much more complicated.

After I have taken the cows to Green Lane and before school I go to watch Cyril. He is busy greasing the cutters; they are the same as a grass cutter, but a bit longer. He grins. "Keep well clear of these, they could cut your boots off." He laughs. "Your feet would still be inside them."

I remember that last year a girl walked in front of a grass cutter and lost her feet. I frown. "I don't think that is funny. That girl didn't laugh, she just cried. How would you like it if you couldn't run and walk, and you couldn't go to the dance on Saturday?"

Cyril puts his hand on my shoulder. "Listen Simon, you must learn not to be so serious about things. Life would be miserable if we never laughed."

I look at the ground. "Well! I still don't think that it's funny to lose your feet." He takes his hand from my shoulder, and leaves a greasy mark. "Now look what you've done. Mum will be cross with me."

Cyril smiles, "Come on! Cheer up! Why did you come here?"

I can't be cross for long. "Well! I wanted to know how this thing works."

He grins again. "In that case, since you ask me so nicely, I will tell you." Cyril points to one of the large iron wheel with a ribbed rim. "That's the driving wheel. Those ribs across the rim stop it skidding over the ground. You see that the axle is cranked down to the same level as the small wheel on the other end. Everything is driven from that big wheel.

"You see the chains that connect to the end of the cutter bar, that's got a cam that pushes the blades back and forth. This lever lifts the blades; it also opens the gears on the driving wheel, so that it turns free, so nothing works when the binder is towed on the road. That small wheel on the front keeps the binder level." The most noticeable thing is a steel and wood vane. It reminds me of the big paddle on the back of Mississippi river boats that I have seen in an encyclopedia but I think that this vane is smaller and much lighter. Cyril points to the hooks on the front. "Two horses are hitched to there, and when they pull the binder and the gears are closed, the cutters move back and forth and slice the corn, the vane makes sure that the straws all fall the same way onto the canvas." He points to the canvas belt five feet wide with wooden slats fixed to the top, held on two cylinders behind the cutters. "That takes the straw to that buncher, it gathers the straw into sheaves, and ties them with twine, and then tosses them on to the ground beside the binder." The cutters and the vane and the canvas are plain to see, but the buncher is very complicated with iron curved arms that move up and down and backward to gather the straw, and then more, smaller arms thread the twine round the middle of the sheaf, pull it tight and tie a knot. I respect the man who thought of that. He must be very clever.

I look at Cyril. "Phoo! That's marvelous."

Cyril nods. "You can see that the seat is high. I can keep an eye on everything from up there. Sometimes the twine snaps and I have to stop and re-thread it, but otherwise there is not much to go wrong providing that everything is greased and adjusted properly. I have to make sure that the cutters are the right height and that the canvas doesn't slip, and the vane is doing its job. Anyway, now that I have given you a lesson, you can it all working tomorrow. I'll still be at it when you came home from school."

Next day I have a look and it's all working as Cyril said. It makes a very loud clattering noise, and stirs up dust. Quite a few rabbits bolt away to the hedges and one or two partridge skim the tops of the uncut wheat. Martin once told me that it's difficult to get a good aim at them with a twelve-bore shotgun; if you are lucky they make a tasty dinner, but you need one for each person.

After tea Dad says, "As soon as you finish the milking in the morning, go to the Garden Ground, and do the stooking." The Garden Ground in fact was a twelve-acre field, with three acres of orchard in one corner. I don't know why it was called the Garden Ground. The only flowers were dandelions in the orchard and dog roses in the boundary hedge. Other fields are known either by the acreage, or from the name of a nearby road or drain, and even by the name of the previous owner.

It is next morning. Martin, Fred and Eddy and me look at the rows of sheaves. Martin says, "No use in looking, we have to get on with it." He looks at me.

"Fred and Eddy can work together, and you can help me."

Martin and I work on two adjoining rows of sheaves, and Fred and Eddy work on the next two. We each a pick sheaf up by the binder twine, one in each hand and carry to the middle of the space between the rows. We then lean the sheaves together with the ears at the top, to form a ridge tent shape about ten sheaves long; the air can blow though the tent and allow the straws and ears to finish drying. The sheaves are heavy for me and I can only carry one, so we fall behind Eddy and Fred.

Martin laughs. "You're doing a good job. Let the others go ahead. Remember the fable about the hare and the tortoise."

I puff. "Well! I'll just do the best that I can. Anyway, when I grow up I will be much quicker than them."

We work for a couple of hours, and then stop for a morning lunch of bread and jam and cold tea from a lemonade bottle. The bottles have a glass stopper with a red rubber-sealing ring and wire connections that can be eased down to press the seal against the bottle rim. They are ideal for water and other cold drinks. Fred and Eddy walk back to eat with us. Fred looks at the blue sky. "We are lucky with the weather. Let's hope it lasts over the harvest."

Eddy nods. "Yes! It rained last year, but we had to press on regardless. The wet sheaves played havoc with my arms."

Martin empties his mouth. "It was a bad year for thistles too." Some thistles survive the weeding, and are cut with the straw and bound in the sheaves. It is generally too hot to wear a jacket and stookers work in shirtsleeves. The sharp barbs of the thistles scratch the arms, and make the work very painful. Especially if the sheaves are still wet from a shower, the wet stalks and sharp thistles chafe the arms until they are red raw.

Eddy lights a fag. "You young'uns always grumble." He looks grim. "I agree it was a bad year, the wheat sprouted in the stooks, and half the crop was ruined." We fall silent as we remember the shortage of money and treats last year. I had heard Mum and Dad talking about the 'Slump' and looking very worried.

Martin laughs. "Well! This year is fine, let's get the crop in early." We start working again. I am refreshed by the rest and lunch, and work a little faster. Martin warns, "Slow down. You have to last the rest of the day. It's no use going at it like a bull at a gate. Any way, we don't want to catch up with the binder."

Cyril handles the binder. He cut quite a lot yesterday so can keep well ahead of us. It is sitting down job, so he doesn't need to rest, although he allows the horses to have a breather at the end of each row. He has a silver pocket watch. We know it is midday because he stops the horses and shouts, "Time for dinner." My stomach already knows. Fred and Eddy sit on a couple of sheaves and tuck into their dinner; using clasp knives to cut chunks of cheese and bread from newspaper wrapping and using the blade to pop the chunks into their mouths. Cyril unhitches the horses, and fills a bucket from the ditch and gives them some water and also some hay that he brought from the yard. The field is only ten minutes' walk from the farm, so Cyril follows Martin and me home for dinner.

Mum has cooked beef stew with dumplings and piles of mashed potatoes and steamed cabbage, followed by gooseberry tart and custard, and tea. My legs and arms ache. I am grateful for the sit down, but the others do not seem tired, and concentrate on eating. Talking is not encouraged whilst eating. After dinner, Dad looks at us. "I had to do some paper work this morning and this afternoon I have to see the bank manager. I'll work with you tomorrow."

Mum forces a smile. "Don't worry, dear, I'm sure the bank will extend your overdraft until after the harvest."

Dad looks at Mum. "What would I do without you? I give the men more wages than you get for running the home. I hope to God that the weather lasts and we get a good harvest so that we can clear the bank and get some savings together."

We brothers work for next to nothing, but Martin and Cyril have their own two-acre plots to grow vegetables to sell. We grow our own vegetables on our small plots behind the house. I have made a cold frame out of some bricks and a pane of glass. I grow mustard and cress in there. Dad really likes them in a brown bread sandwich for tea. Mum says that we need to save every penny that we can. I go with her to the town sometimes on a Saturday afternoon. It's a bit boring when she meets friends and they chat, I sometimes think that it is the real reason why they go to town. When we go in the shops I am embarrassed when she bargains; the price is marked on the shelf. Mum smiles at the man in the clothes shop; he is a second cousin, Tom, and they have a chat about the hard times. "There are not many customers; there is not much money around now-a-days."

Mum nods. "Yes, we have to pull our horns in and only buy essentials." She picks up a shirt for Dad. "This is nice, but fifteen shillings is a bit expensive." She narrowed her eyes and glanced at Tom. "Would you take fourteen?"

Tom blinked. "Come on, you know how things are. We have to cut our profit margins to the bone to survive, and now you want me to take a loss."

Mum persevered. "Well, fourteen shillings in the till is better than fifteen on the shelf."

Tom swallowed, "I can knock four pence off but no more."

Mum smiled. "Make it six and I'll have it."

Tom shrugged. "Very well, but no credit."

Mum put the shirt back, "I will talk to Dad. If he thinks that we can afford it I will bring the money next week." It's the same in all the other shops we go in,

Mum tries to get a few pence off everything she buys, and mostly she succeeds. My cheeks burn. I don't want other people to think that we are poor, and I am pleased when we finish shopping and meet Dad outside the corn exchange and drive home. Mum has bought a Mickey Mouse comic, and I am looking forward to reading it, but I really prefer the Hotspur and Champion.

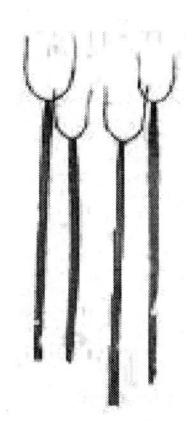

Pitchforks got their name from pitching sheaves of corn. They have two iron tapered tines, around one quarter inch diameter and about nine inches long slightly curved along the length and bent in towards an iron tapered sleeve that fits over an ash shaft about one and a quarter inches in diameter and some six feet long. Harry once challenged me to hold a pitchfork at the end at arm's length and lift it with a half-pound weight on the tines. I couldn't move it, not even an inch. Harry tried, and he couldn't move it either. He grinned. "Nobody can, not even Mr Atlas." That was my first practical introduction into the laws of moments learned later in physics lessons.

The stooks are dry and ready for carting to the stackyard. We use the carts but raves have been put on the back and front panels. They are similar to small gates with iron hooks on the end of the post that slot into rings on the cart. They make the cart longer so that more sheaves can be stacked on. I lead Violet along the rows of stooks. Jack pitchforks the sheaves onto the cart and Fred catches them in his hands and stacks them on the cart until the load is about ten feet high. Fred stays on the load and I take the full load to the stackyard. Jack loads Tim's cart. As I come back from the stackyard, I pass Tim on the way there, so the stackers are not kept waiting long for a load.

A cockney relative of a neighbour came to visit the family. He wanted to help with the harvest and was allotted the job of loader. He packed the sheaves too loosely, and when the lorry was on the way to the stackyard the load slipped and the helpful visitor fell to the ground and broke his neck. The neighbours were rather subdued for a few days, but the harvest had to be completed and the family put off the mourning until after the harvest. We were always careful when standing on straw after that.

I am leading Violet along the stooks. Jack is pitching and a rabbit runs out of the stook. Jack is startled and steps back and slips. His fork goes into his knee and he falls down. He shouts, "Get it out. Get it out."

Fred slides down the load and pulls out the fork, and pulls Jack to his feet. There is not much blood but his knee swells up like a balloon. Fred frowns. "You had better get home and lie down."

Jack moans, "I can't bloody well do that. I can't walk." I am shocked to hear him swear.

Fred says, "I will give you a hand to sit on the shaft of the cart, and when Simon gets to the stack I can unload and then Simon can take you home on the cart."

While Fred is unloading, I go to the house and tell Mum what has happened. She wipes her hands on her apron. "Well! I had better take a look at him." She goes to the door.

Dad says angrily, "What a stupid thing to do."

Mum turns back and says, "Calm down. Accidents happen."

Dad replies, "That's all very well, but now we will be shorthanded. I will have to ask Harry if he can help out."

Mum was a nurse in the First World War; she keeps her uniform in a big chest on the landing. Mum looks at me, "Come on!" and we walk quickly to the stack yard. Jack is waiting on the shaft.

I lead Violet and Mum walks alongside Jack. She knocks on the door of his cottage. Jack mumbles, "She's gone to the village."

Mum opens the door; doors are never locked in our hamlet. She glances at me, "Give me a hand to get Jack inside." We lay him on the chesterfield. Mum smiles at Jack. "I'll have to cut off that trouser leg so that I can see what the damage is." She speaks briskly. "Simon, find me a pair of scissors whilst I put the kettle on. By the time that I had found the scissors, Mum and Jack are sipping cups of tea. Mum laughs. "He needs this." She laughs again, "So do I. Simon, the kettle is still warm, find a bowl and half fill it with warm water while I cut off this leg." She grins at Jack. "Your trouser leg, not yours." Jack manages a feeble grin; the tea must have made him feel better.

Mum washes Jack's knee and says, "It's not too bad, the hole is clean, but there is a lot of fluid. I found this TCP whilst I was making the tea. I will drop some in the hole just in case you got an infection, and then put on a tea-cloth soaked in vinegar. You will have to keep your feet up for a couple of days while the fluid disappears, and then you should be ready for work."

Jack looks very serious. "Missus, I don't know how to thank you."

Mum nods. "You don't have to. It's all in the day's work. Simon, you get back to work and I will make another cup of tea."

It is tea time and we are eating boiled eggs with toast fingers, and some of Mum's marmalade sponge. Jack's wife knocks on the kitchen door. She would never knock on the front door; only important people do that. Mum opens the door, and Jack's wife shouts angrily, "What were you doing alone in my house with my husband?"

Mum looks back at Dad. He joins Mum at the door, "Come on, Ruby, there's no need for all that. She was only trying to help. Simon was there. Anyway, Jack was in no state to interfere with my wife."

Ruby tosses her head. "My Jack would never touch another woman."

Dad says quickly, "My wife would never touch another man. You know that she was a nurse. That's all she was doing, nursing, so what is all this fuss about?" He adds quietly, "You should be thanking her, not slandering her."

Ruby starts to cry. "You're right. I am very upset and angry with Jack. We can't afford to lose his wages." She looks at mum, "I'm sorry. Thank you for your help."

Dad says, "He will be back at work in a couple of days. Harry will help out." He smiles. "Don't worry, you won't lose any wages."

Ruby smiles through her tears. "Thank you." She manages a grin. "I can sew the leg back on the trousers, so I don't need to buy a new pair."

Mum's face softens. "I understand how you feel. It's best if we all forgot that you came here this evening." Ruby nodded and went back to her cottage.

When you build a stack the first thing is to decide where to put it in the yard, and then mark a rectangle with sticks, about ten yards by six for a medium size farm and much larger for a big farm. I am too small to help with the stacking; I just lead Violet from the field to the yard and stop the cart alongside the stack. I have time to watch the stackers while Fred unloads. He uses his pitchfork to throw the sheaves near the middle of the stack. The filler man pitchforks the sheaves to the stacker. He lays two rows of sheaves, with the ears pointing in, round the edges of the stack He lays the inner one first, so that the outer one overlaps it and slopes to the outside; that stops the rain from getting into the sides of the stack. The stacker makes sure that the sides of the stack are even and slope slightly outwards, to help stop the rain getting in. The binder, a man not the machine, follows and lays two more rows inside the two outer rows. He is called the binder because he presses the sheaves on the stackers and binds them tightly together. The stacker and binder do not use pitchforks, just their hands. The filler man lays sheaves over the rest of the stack, not neatly like the stacker and binder, the stacker is in charge, and often urges the filler to keep the middle full, which is how he got his name. While I am waiting and watching, I sometimes get bored and read a book; Coral Island takes me to another world. When the cart is empty, I take it back to the field. I pass Tim with a full load on the way to the yard. If the field is a long way from the yard, a third cart is used to make sure that the men on the stack are not held up.

Fred has an easy time throwing the sheaves down from the cart to the stack, but as the stack grows he has to throw them up. When the stack is too high for Jack, another man has to stand on the edge of the stack and take the sheaves from Jack's fork and toss them to the filler. As the stack grows around the man he is left standing in a hole in the side of the stack. At first, he can just swing the sheaves sideways, but later he has to lift the sheaves higher until he throws them above his head. Then it is very hard work. The shaft of the fork bends under the strain. The hole is a known as the steerhole because the man has to steer the sheaves to the filler. During unloading no one can stop. They all have to keep up with each other and develop a knack and rhythm to keep everyone busy. They can all have a short rest between cartloads.

We were all busy during harvest time, and there was no one to spare for the steerhole; so Dad did that. Mum worries about Dad working too hard. Mum told us that when we were sitting round the fire telling stories one winter's night that Dad had rheumatic fever when he was a child, and it left him with a weak heart. The doctor caught him cranking the car, and gave him a good telling off. He sometimes falls down and the doctor makes him stay in bed for a few days. He gets bored just lying in bed, so I give him one of my jigsaw puzzles, and we do it together.

Once I saw Mum looking at us, she had a very strange look, something between crying and smiling. Perhaps I will know what that look means when I grow up. When he works in the steerhole, she tells him off, but he just shrugs and says, "I can do it for a couple of days, then the field will be cleared. Anyway, hard work never killed anyone. I'm not going to let a dickey heart run my life."

Mum says, "Well! You should get someone else to do it. You could lead the horse if you want to help."

Dad grins. "Why on earth should I do that when I have a strong young lad to do it for me." He looks at me and I smile back, but I am still worried. It is very hard work in the steerhole, and he sweats a lot. I don't want him to have a heart attack and fall of the stack, he might break his neck like that neighbour's uncle.

John, our neighbour Alex' son, is in disgrace, and we cannot play for a week. He has been very naughty. He went smoking elder pith behind the straw stack. He was very careless and threw down a match without blowing out the flame. It set fire to the straw and it quickly blazed up before he noticed. John could not put it out and ran screaming to his dad. He could only watch as the stack burned; it took a long time and we all went to watch and feel sorry for John and his dad, the wheat was ruined, and the much-needed profit gone up in smoke. John sobbed and tears ran down his dad's cheeks; he said that the smoke got in his eyes, men don't cry. A few days later we were talking in front of the kitchen range. My dad says that he had been talking to John's dad, and he told him that he didn't give John a good hiding with his strap. He said that John knew that he had done wrong, and that he could never forget the hardship that he caused to the family. He said that would be the punishment that would stay with him for the rest of his life. Mum nodded. "He is a very understanding and wise man." That night I cried for John, and his family.

THRESHING

By the late autumn the crops had been harvested and work started on muck spreading and preparing the land for the next crops. Other work included maintenance of buildings and implements, making and repairing chitting trays, mending sacks, ditching and hedging. The normal work of feeding animals, milking, and bottling milk had to be done regardless of the weather. On the domestic side, there was plenty of activity making jam, bottling fruit, preserving eggs and pickling onions. Late autumn brought the eager anticipation of cheques from the potato and corn merchants; then the financial situation became less tight. The bank overdraft could be cleared and money set aside for seeds for next year. Not much money was left, enough to purchase essentials but very little for luxury items.

The most important autumn event was extracting corn from the straw; we knew it as threshing. The first step was to book the threshing tackle, and then buy special coal for the steam engine. The coal was delivered in large lumps that had to be broken down with a club hammer. It was not suitable for domestic use; it was slow burning and smoky; however, we did mix any left over from the threshing with domestic coal and logs for the fires. On the appointed day, the threshing tackle would drive into the yard. It was an impressive sight, the steam engine resplendent in black gloss paint with green and red embellishments and polished brass fittings. It consisted of a large horizontal cylindrical boiler and firebox, and a platform behind with a seat for the operator, and open fronted box for the storage of coal. The steam produced powered two large cylinders and pistons with operating valves on each side of and lower than the boiler. The pistons drove a horizontal crankshaft, athwart and below the driver's seat, which had a gear box to drive the large and heavy iron rear wheels, and a separate gear to drive a heavy vertical flat-rimmed iron flywheel on the left side in front of the operator. Smaller wheels at the front were turned by a system of chains attached to the front axle and treaded round a horizontal wheel under the chassis that was turned through shafts and gear wheels to a much smaller iron wheel with a handle for the driver.

The drum was the main component; it was a very large timber box on wheels with several pulleys and belts and levers on the sides. The main driving pulley was near the front of the right side and was connected to the flywheel of the engine by a stout canvas belt. Straw from the stack was fed on to a wide canvas belt on top of the drum, similar to that on the binder, and was distributed to a series of large moving boxes that pulverised the straw and separated the grains of corn; they were taken by a series of channels to the front of the drum to a container with two outlets with steel flaps that allowed the grain to fall into sacks hooked to the drum. Blowers inside the drum blew the ears and dust out of a hole in the side of the drum, and the straw was pushed from the rear of the drum on to the elevator, known locally as a jackstraw.

The elevator was a combatively simple machine consisting of a long chassis with four wheels. A long adjustable ramp was mounted on pivots at one end. At each side of the ramp, a series of small wheels supported and guided two loops of chain; they had timber cross members with steel prongs pointing up. The chains were moved by sprockets on an axle driven by belt from the rear side of the drum. Straw from the drum fell on the prongs and was conveyed to the top of the ramp and then fell to the ground below. Men then arranged the straw to form a stack. The angle of the ramp was adjustable to suit the height of the stack as it grew.

It was all rather cumbersome and everything seemed to be in slow motion. It took some time, and considerable skill, for the operator to either tow or push the drum next to the stack, with the elevator just behind, and the engine facing the front of the drum. Lining up the engine flywheel and main driving pulley on the drum, and getting the correct tension on the driving belt was highly skillful, considering the primitive steering and poor maneuverability of the engine.

***

Harvesting is over, and it is now Harvest Festival Sunday. The ladies and girls have decorated the church with sheaves of corn and stalks of wheat twisted into many shapes. The crosses and wreaths don't look too difficult, but the animals and birds are very complicated. I don't know where they learned to do that. I have read something about folklore; perhaps that is where they learned it. Anyway, they are very interesting shapes. Apples and plums and pears and other fruits are all over the place, with a few swedes and mangolds and sugar beet and garden vegetables. There are bunches of flowers tied to the columns and pulpit and lectern and altar rails, and there are several flowers and leaves arranged in bowls and vases; the best one gets a prize. All the boys in the hamlet, including my brothers and I, are in the church choir, but only two girls, perhaps they are too shy. We enjoy Harvest Festival hymns; they are happy. Funeral hymns are very gloomy, we always have to sing 'Abide with Me', that makes us sad. Anyway, funerals are sad.

Everyone is relieved that 'All is Safely Gathered In'. The next Saturday, the vicar arranges a garden fete. All the church decorations are piled onto stalls and sold and the money is given to the Church. The Women's Institute has a stall full of homemade jam and cakes, and there are lots of games like being blindfolded and trying to pin a tail on a drawing of a donkey; guessing how many peas in a jar, hoopla, and there is always an ankle competition for the men.

A few days after the Harvest Festival, I was with my best friend Tim. There are only eight other boys in the hamlet, and we play together. We don't mix with the girls, they like to play silly games with dolls and toy tea sets. We play cowboys and Indians; we climb trees using wagon ropes and pretend that we are climbing Mount Everest. Sometimes in the winter, we make tunnels through a straw stack; we just do that without pretending anything.

Tim and I are lying in the orchard munching apples. I was reading about coal mining in the encyclopedias last night. I finish my mouthful; Mum says it is rude to talk with food in your mouth. "Did you know that miners dig coal from deep under the ground?"

Tim snorts. "Don't be such a twerp! Of course I know that. Everybody knows that."

I say, "Well! I didn't until last night. I bet that you don't know that they have to crawl in tunnels and use a pick axe and shovel lying down to dig out the coal."

He snorts. "Yes I do. Yes I do. I also know that it is very dirty work and the dust clogs up their lungs. They have to have a bath at the pithead before they can go home."

I reply, "Yes. That's so their wives will know who they are."

Tim grins. "You must have been reading those books again. What else did you learn?"

I think a bit while I swallow another mouthful. "They have to go up and down in a lift, that's the pithead. They also bring out the coal in a lift. They build a small railway in the bigger tunnels and load the coal into small wagons to get the coal to the lift."

Tim sputters as he talks with a mouthful of juicy apple. "Farmer's sons work on the land. I suppose that miner's sons go down the mines."

I nod. "I saw a picture of boys loading the trucks, they only had short trousers on, and they were covered in black grime and sweat."

Tim sighs. "That's a terrible way to earn a living. We are lucky to live in the clean open air. I feel very sorry for them."

I sniff. "So do I, but I feel more sorry for the poor ponies. They have to pull the trucks, and have to live down the mine. They go down as soon as they are strong enough to pull the trucks, and never come up again. They never see the sun and go blind."

"If those men and boys want to have such a hard life, well that's up to them, but they shouldn't be so cruel to those poor ponies."

I agree. "Yes, but I read that they can't do anything else; mining is the only work that they know. I read something about a Mineworkers Union. It was all a bit beyond me, but I think that some people are trying to make life easier for the miner's children."

Tim and I have eaten enough apples, and haven't got room for any gooseberries even though they are nice and mellow and juicy. We think that it might be fun to pretend to be miners in a tunnel. We go to the stack yard to start a tunnel. We both claw at the straw and make a hole about eighteen inches round in the side of the stack.

There is not room for two of us to go in the hole, so Tim goes in first; he pulls out the straw and kicks it behind him, and I pull it out of the stack. After a couple of yards, he comes out sweating. "It's like a furnace in there. You have a go." I go in and claw away at the straw and stuff it behind me. Tim has to go in and out of the tunnel, and soon there is a wedge of straw behind me that shuts out the daylight and air. I cannot back out. There is no room to turn round. I am trapped. I cannot hear Tim. I gasp for air. I try to scream but no sound comes out. It is dark and dismal. I think of miners trapped underground and start to sob, but I cannot breathe. I am sure that the straw will fall and squash me. I am afraid. The dark gets darker. My head is spinning. Everything stops there is nothing but blackness.

The sun dazzles me. I am lying on my back beside the stack. Martin is bending over me shouting, "Simon. Wake up. Simon. Wake up."

I move my head and see Tim kneeling down crying. "Please God, don't let him die." I hear Martin.

"Your prayer is answered; his eyes are open."

He looks at me with the same misty eyes that Mum sometimes has. "Are you all right now?"

I nod and manage to sit up. "What happened?"

Tim wipes his eyes, "You were stuck in the tunnel. I couldn't pull you out. I ran for help and saw Martin coming into the yard and we ran here."

Martin continues, "I couldn't make much of Tim, he was crying so much. He pointed to the tunnel, so I assumed that you were in there. The hole was too small for me, so I had to make it bigger and I went in until I could feel your boot, and then I pulled you out." He goes misty eyed again. "I thought that you were dead."

***

After tea Mum looks at Dad and nods. He has his stern look. "After what happened this afternoon, there will be no more tunnelling in my stacks." He glared. "Is that clear?" I nod. He continued, "You have given us all a terrible fright. We could have lost you. Think yourself very lucky that Martin was on hand to help." He looked at Martin and back at me. "Martin saved your life. Mother and I will never forget that." He looked around the table. "None of you should forget that. Let it be a lesson to you in helping each other." He pauses. "I will speak to Tim's father."

He looks at me. "I think that your experience of dying is punishment enough. I will ask Tim's father not to give him a good hiding. According to Martin, he helped to save your life, and was very upset. You are lucky to have such a good friend."

Mum adds, "Of course I agree with everything that Father has said. We will now consider the matter closed. Simon, you can clear way the table, and Cyril and Martin can wash up." She smiles. "Then we can all have a nice game of newmarket."

"Simon! Run to the road and let me know when you can see the threshing tackle coming," Dad orders as he looks down the yard. He calls to Fred and Eddy, "Best to get those sleepers out of the way." He mutters to Martin, "The tackle is very expensive and I don't want any time wasted clearing a way for it."

I see a black shape, puffing black smoke and steam, coming down the road, and rush back to Dad. "It's coming. It's coming." Dad walks with me back to the road and we wait for the tackle. I am fascinated by machinery, and I get this once a year thrill from this seemingly living monster. Our gate is set back from the road so the driver can turn into the drive, but it does churn up the grass verge. We follow it into the yard, and the driver spends a lot of time setting up his machinery. The driver is also the owner of the threshing tackle.

I sit with him, looking at it, while we have our mid-morning lunch. He is very thickset and stocky, and looks as strong as his engine. I say quickly, "Sir, it's beautiful."

He laughs. "I'm not your school teacher. You can call me Geoff. It should be a beauty, I spend enough time cleaning and polishing it."

I grin. "I have to polish Mum's brasses. You must take a long time to polish all those brass bits."

Geoff laughs again. "It's a labour of love."

I think that I know what he means; I get the same feeling when I clean the chrome on my bicycle. We munch in silence and then I say, "I looked up traction engine in the encyclopedia. The cut-away drawings showed how the steam drives the pistons and connections to the back wheels, but I couldn't find out what the big flywheel does."

Geoff grins at the other men. "My! My! We have a bright one here." He looks at me and this time he doesn't laugh. "The flywheel keeps the momentum going in between piston strokes. Without it the engine would stop and if the valves were in the closed position, the boiler would blow up." I must remember to look up momentum in the dictionary. He continues, "You can watch me tomorrow when I start it up."

It's still half term holiday, so I can help with the threshing. I get my chores over early so that I can meet Geoff. He is early too. He has to get the tackle working in time for when the others start work. He climbs the ladder to his seat and I follow. He says, "Stand over there and don't get in the way. You can just watch and if you don't understand, then I will tell you what I am doing."

He opens the furnace door and pokes around with his rake. "I just damp down the fire when I finish work, so there is still a bit of pressure in the boiler." He shovels in some coal. "I leave the door open to get the draught to the fire; it will soon liven up and make some steam. I have to keep an eye on this gauge to make sure it never reaches the red line." He grins. "You can make yourself useful while we wait. I am a bit low on coal, so you can take the barrow and bring me some from the heap." I do as I am told. I am pleased that Eddy has already broken up the coal; otherwise the lumps would be too heavy for me to handle. By the time I get back the gauge is showing a working pressure of steam. Geoff says, "The valves are closed so I have to start the engine to relieve the pressure, I could let off some steam, but that is a waste of good energy. I only have to give the flywheel a push to open the valves, and as soon as the steam goes into the cylinders the engine starts." He nods to the yard. "Just in time, here they come to start work." He adds, "You will notice that the wheels are not turning. This lever opens the sliding dogs on the axle to engage and disengage the drive. All that the engine has to do now is to keep the flywheel turning. You can see that the belt is a bit slack. It's absorbed the dew and will soon tighten up as it gets warm. It looks as though everyone is ready to start, so off you go and get on with your job."

I smile and say, "Thank you very much. I would like to own this when I grow up, but I really want to be a teacher."

Eddy and Fred are on the stack, Eddy picks up a sheaf on his fork and pitches it to Fred, and he passes it to Martin who is standing on the drum. Martin cuts the binder string and spreads the straw on to the canvas belt; that takes the straw to the crushers that smash the grains from the ears. I climb the stack ladder and can see the belt and the crushers, they are timber boxes that move up and down and through a small arc, they seem to eat the straw and it disappears inside the drum. Spreading the straw on the belt is dangerous work. Dad once told us about a man who slipped onto the belt and his legs were taken into the crushers. The crushers jammed and the driving belt outside the drum slipped on its wheels. The engine was stopped, and workers managed to pull the man off the belt. He was rushed to hospital and the doctors had to cut off one leg, but managed to save the other. That is why I am not allowed to go on the drum.

The grains come out of two chutes at the end of the drum facing the engine. The main driving belt from the engine is to one side and is quite high, but it pays to keep out of its way; it could really damage anyone standing near it if it came off the wheels. Cyril looks after the grains. He hangs sacks under the chutes and controls the flaps so that they can be closed when the sacks are full. By filling alternate sacks, he has a steady supply of full sacks. When a sack is full Cyril lowers the hooks and pulls the sack onto a sack trolley to a weighing machine.

Fred's wife either adds or takes out grain, to make sure that the sacks weigh eighteen stone; she then uses a big needle and binder string to sew up the mouth of the sack. While she is doing that Cyril hangs an empty sack on the hooks, and then takes the sewn-up sack on the trolley and lines it upright on a tarpaulin spread on the ground. At the end of the day the rows of sacks are covered with another tarpaulin until a grain dealer's lorry comes to take them away. The sacks are very heavy and not easy to move. Cyril is very strong which is why he has that job. The threshed straw is pushed out of the back of the drum onto the jackstraw; that drops it on the ground. Harry helps with the threshing. He and Dad gather the straw as it drops from the elevator and make it into a stack. Geoff tends to his engine and looks around to make sure that all the belts are tight and that everything is working properly. He also raises the jackstraw as the stack gets higher.

My family and Geoff go the house, and Fred and his wife and Eddy go to their cottages for midday dinner. After we have had our fill of Mum's cooking, Dad says, "If I get a good price for the wheat, I might invest in a jackstraw. I could use the Lister donkey engine to power it. It would make stacking a lot easier, do away with the steerhole, and save some wages."

Mum said, "That would be a very good investment. It is a worry to see you sweating in the steerhole. You know that the doctor told you not to do it."

Geoff looked at Dad. I thought that he seemed a bit sly. He said, "If you are serious I might think about selling mine. It is past its best, but would certainly last you several years. New jackstraws are expensive. Mine has given good service and more than earned its keep, so I wouldn't ask too much for it."

Mum smiled. "We might be interested, but we have to wait for the wheat cheque before we can make up our mind."

Geoff smiled. "Take your time." He got up from the table. "I will just go and stoke up the fire." He winked at Dad. "I mustn't waste your money by keeping the men waiting while it builds up pressure."

Dad smiled. "I am not worried about the boiler, but I am worried about the weather. The moon had a haze last night. I hope that the rain holds off until we finish threshing."

Geoff grinned at Mum. "Thanks, Missus, for the dinner. It was almost as good as my wife's cooking." He looked at Dad. "Don't worry, if it rains I can give a discount for not working."

Mum flushed at Geoff's compliment. "That's what I like to hear. A discount is always welcome."

My job must be the dirtiest in the world. I have to rake away the husks and ears of the wheat as they are blown out of the side of the drum, so that they do not clog up the opening. It is known as the muck hole. There is a fog of grey dust and husks. I have to wrap a wet handkerchief over my mouth and nose, otherwise I would choke. I have to wash the grime from the handkerchief in the cow trough every fifteen minutes. Mum says that she has to wash my clothes twice to get them clean, and when I wash for tea, the water is filthy. I don't really think that it is the dirtiest Iob in the world; I have seen a photograph of those poor miners coming out of the cage at the pit head, and they are all black from coal dust. After tea, I tell Mum that. She nods. "It's as well for you to realize that you have a better life than many people. It's not only the miners, but also the factory workers who have a hard life. At least you have plenty of food and fresh air. She went quiet and then said softly, "Don't forget our brave boys fighting the war. I worry about Gerald."

I don't know what to say. I just say, "Never mind, Mum."

Greta is like a chimney sweepers brush, black bristly hair and body as thin as a stick. She has a crooked smile with black teeth but merry eyes. She is married to Fred; they have one daughter but I don't know her very well; we didn't mix with girls. I talk to Old Sam about Greta. "I don't like her because she has black teeth, and a harsh voice, and she says, 'I aren't' instead of 'I'm not.'"

Old Sam says, "Don't judge people so harshly. Never consider them ignorant if you think that you know more than they do. Greta is an avid reader of the classics; she has probably forgotten more that you will ever learn. You spend a lot of time reading, so perhaps if you bother to talk to her and be pleasant, you will find a friend." He winks, "Here's another thing. There is always someone who can use fine words and phrases to prove that you are wrong, even though you know that you are right." He smiles. "That raises the eternal problem that has no answer. What is absolute right and what is absolute wrong, and indeed, what is the truth?" He pauses. "Remember my words. Later as you gain knowledge, you may understand their profundity."

I am lost in respect for him and can only stare and nod.

One Sunday we have only bread and jam for tea. Dad says that this is the first time that we will leave the table hungry. He and Mum talk about the benefits of living on a farm now that everything is rationed. Mum sighs. "How can I feed a hungry family with only four ounces of butter, cheese, lard and sugar a week for each one of us?"

Dad nods. "We are very lucky to live on a farm. At least we have plenty of eggs, and milk, and chickens, and vegetables from the garden and swedes from the fields."

When we kill a pig, we have to forego our bacon and meat ration for a few months, but we still shoot rabbits and pheasants and have plenty of salt pork and ham. Dad says, "We have a life of luxury compared with the miners and factory workers. They have to survive on their rations. They work just as hard and under more dangerous and difficult conditions than farmers. They produce coal and machinery, but they cannot eat those." He looks sternly round the table. "It's no hardship to be hungry once in a while. It teaches you to be thankful for the good life that we have here." We all nod in agreement. I know that there are eggs in the chicken house and food in the pantry, but I realise that Mum has given us only bread and jam to teach us a lesson about not taking things for granted.

After evensong, I call on Old Sam. Greta is having a cup of tea with him. Greta offers me a biscuit. I tell them about leaving the table hungry. Greta nods. "That is good advice, but you must realize that there are always two sides to a coin." I look away from her black teeth, but pay attention because Old Sam likes her. She stirs her tea. "My sister works in the kitchen of that big American base in Norfolk. She says that it's criminal the way they waste food. They eat only half of their enormous platefuls of food and throw the rest in the bins. Local farmers buy it to feed their pigs." She says angrily, "My sister says that they are not allowed to salvage any of the food to take home to supplement their rations. Those G.I.s don't have rations they have too much of everything; sweets and bananas, and American food like peanut butter."

I remember eating bananas and oranges before the war but cannot remember the taste, but sometimes Mum finds a tin of pineapple when she goes to town. That is a real treat. Dad uses his sweet coupons to buy a large bar of Cadbury hazel nut milk chocolate every Saturday, and after Sunday dinner, we each have two squares. We use coupons to buy a milky way and some aniseed balls in the village shop, but they don't last long. Old Sam looks up. "Yes, it's a scandal to waste good food. Not only that, the G.I.s entice our girls with nylon stockings and sweets. The girls are entranced by their accent; it probably reminds them of American film stars. Several are tempted to marry G.I.s but I've heard that they are very disillusioned when they see where the man comes from. Those brown stone apartment blocks are not at all what they expected. Some men are quite unscrupulous in telling the girls about their fine house and life style; they are just figments of their imagination to persuade the girl to marry. Of course, once they are over there, there is no easy way to come back."

Greta nods. "Thank goodness I am too old for that sort of thing. I am more than happy with my husband thank you very much."

Old Sam laughs, "Those Yanks are overpaid, over sexed and over here."

I am sorry that they don't like Americans. I would like to go there to see the cowboys and also the Red Indians.

THE DANCE

During the Second World War there was a shortage of temporary workers in England; all able-bodied men and women were enlisted, either in the armed forces or in factories, or mines, except for those already in reserved occupations such as agriculture and mining. Many civilians, either too young, or too old, or unfit for conscription, came from the East End of London to spend working holidays in the Fens to help with the harvest of fruit and other crops. They were accommodated in 'Holiday Camps'; fields full of rows of army tents, with temporary cooking and sanitary amenities. They were probably the precursors of holiday camps such as Butlins. The camp nearest to our hamlet was three miles away. The campers worked hard all week and relaxed on Saturday nights at a dance they organised the local village hall. The local youth had an open invitation, and mixed their shy country ways with streetwise cockneys. It was a comfortable intermixing of the two cultures. Alcohol was not allowed in the hall, and those worse the wear from a visit to the pub were denied access. There was neither friction nor any trouble between the two groups.

I was fifteen, Cyril was coming up to seventeen and Martin was nineteen. I was still a school, but worked on the farm during the school holidays. Cyril and Martin were exempt from military service, but Gerald was called up into the army. Martin had a motor bike and sought his entertainment at the Town Hall dances.

Cyril and I really looked forward to the Saturday night hop. We would have our weekly bath in a galvanized tub filled with hot water from the coal-fired copper; put on our carefully creased flannel trousers and tweed hacking jackets with open necked shirts, and leather brogues highly burnished with Cherry Blossom polish. Normally we would wear a suit and tie to go to a social function, but the cockneys were very casual in their dress and we met them half way. Many local lads wore a suit, so Cyril and I felt very daring to go wearing sports jacket and flannels and open neck shirt neatly folded over the collar of the jacket without a tie. We did not wear our peaked caps; lashings of Brylcreem kept our hair neatly parted and in place despite the worse efforts of the wind cutting across the Fens as we rode our bicycles to the camp. We folded our jackets across the handlebars so that we would not be too sweaty when we arrived.

When the harvest moon rode high we could see for miles across the countryside, and sped with the wind in our back to the hall, but on pitch-dark nights our battery lamps cast a small pool of light six feet in front of the bike and we crawled along. On arrival at the hall, we added our bikes to those ranged at the side of the hall, confident that they would not be stolen. Country people took a pride in being honest; the only thieves were poachers who trapped rabbits, hares and game birds; that was not looked on as criminal thieving, just a sensible way to control pests and provide cheap food. We put on our jackets and paid our entrance of one shilling in the entrance lobby and went through the double doors to the hall to be met by the un-amplified sound of the band. We found a seat on the benches that lined both sides of the hall, lads on the left and girls on the right. We sat during a couple of dances, eyeing the girls. Some we knew from previous dances; some were new arrivals. We could catch only a glimpse of them through the swirling couples dancing clockwise round the floor. Expert dancers normally used the centre floor to display their talents. They obviously had taken lessons; we had neither the time nor money to indulge in such luxury, and learned the various dance steps from the Sunday papers. A famous ballroom dancer, Victor Sylvester, wrote instructions accompanied by diagrams of footprints to show positions for the feet with movements indicated by arrows for forward, backward, sideways and arcing curves in all directions. They were very simple lessons but an excellent introduction to the basic steps for the waltz, foxtrot, quickstep, and more advanced techniques for the samba, rumba and tango. The tango was the ultimate achievement; only a few experts took the floor for that dance whilst the rest watched with a mixture of admiration and envy.

There was a short interval between each dance, during which time dancers looking for a change of partner went back to the benches, and those wishing to hang on to their partner, stayed on the dance floor, chatting quietly whilst waiting for the next dance to start. Normally the experts were first on the floor when the music started. It took great courage for a simple farm boy to get up, walk across an almost empty floor to the other side of the hall under the full gaze of everyone, and then very politely ask a girl, "May I have this dance?" Should the girl refuse, the boy hurriedly asked the next girl in line; regardless of appearance; anything rather than face the humiliation of returning to the left of the hall after being rejected. It was not acceptable behaviour for a girl to ask a boy to dance. When a boy walked across the hall the girls' eyes followed hoping that he would walk in their direction. Some girls were never invited to dance; they were known as wallflowers; however, it was quite in order for those girls to dance with each other. In those far off days, before the baleful influence the mass media and sensational reporting, we were blissfully unaware of homosexuality; girls dancing together did not engender thoughts of lesbianism, but for some reason or other, young men never danced as a couple. Half-way through the evening the band had a break.

There wasn't much to do except chat, but sometimes one of the cockneys would be urged by friends to stand on the small stage and sing; one man had a pure tenor voice and his rendition of 'The Donkey Serenade' always received applause. Most dancing involved no close contact, but the last waltz was something special. The prime object of the evening, for the boy, was to have the last dance with the girl that he particularly fancied as a prelude to further activity after the dance. The lights would be turned low; the plaintive moan of the saxophone; the soft scraping of wire fanned sticks across the kettle drum and cymbals; an almost inaudible main drum marking beat, and the heart beat thrum of the double bass, encouraged the dance to become a slow shuffle of short steps and close body contact. The feel of brassiere-protected breasts on the boy's chest and his probing thigh on the girl's crotch in the slow turns, caused the half-embarrassed pulling away as the music and contact roused primal feelings and rampant manhood.

At midnight, we all stood to attention for the National Anthem, and then most dancers passed a few pleasantries on the floor before dispersing to the cloakrooms and disappearing into the night. Those who had made trysts during the last waltz met outside the hall and retired to the shelter of tree and hedge bordered fields near the hall. There was a strict unwritten code of behaviour. Pursed lip kissing on the mouth and cheeks, low talking, normally standing leaning against a tree, perhaps a gentle squeezing of a brassiere. On the third tryst with the same girl, a probing hand might be permissible, but little could be discovered through the layers of skirt, suspender girdle and thick knickers. The girl was mostly passive, but 'No' really meant 'No'. Rape was very rare, and unheard of among youngsters. After the inept fumbling and a walk back to the holiday camp entrance hand in hand and a promise to meet the next Saturday, and then the cycle ride home.

In my innocence, I enjoyed my first real contact with the opposite sex, and became very friendly with Gill, a dark-haired girl of seventeen. She wore make-up and her hair was permed; even though she was rather chunky I thought that she was very sophisticated. As the summer holiday progressed we danced more often; all week I looked forward to the last waltz and subsequent petting. She was keen to learn about country affairs and I was interested in the world of the town. We talked more than we petted; I loved her friendship more than her body, and thought that was a sure sign that we really were in love. I made plans for the future; when I was old enough to drive a motorcycle, I would get one with a sidecar with a cover to shelter her from the wind and rain. I wanted to take proper dancing lessons so that we could be first on the floor. She giggled when I told her my plans and said that I was very sweet.

After the harvest, Gill went back to London. Our last waltz and our last tryst prompted declarations of love and the promise to be pen friends. We exchanged letters every week. They were passionate declarations of love and contained phrases that we were too shy to say to each other. My love blossomed; I wrote comparing it with the roses round the porch of the church. She wrote that she loved the yellow roses blooming in a park near her home, and how she played games with her friends round the trees when she was young. Her last letter was very brief. She wrote that her fiancé had seen our letters and forbidden her to write to me again. The letter coincided with the first hard frost. The roses on the porch withered and died. It took some time to realize that she had been playing with me. A long time later, I acquired my own toy; a gleaming motorcycle; without a sidecar.

GERALD'S STORY

I am the oldest of three brothers and a sister. As was the custom in the old days, I helped to raise the family. Farmer's wives had many arduous duties and needed any help that was available; I was available. Not that it did me any harm; in fact, it probably made me aware of the necessary sense of responsibility. Simon has recounted work and life on the farm, I will not elaborate on his narrations. Naturally I had to participate in helping with farm work as well as raising the children, but I still found time to read a lot. I was what was known as a bright child, and easily absorbed what I read. The headmaster of the local primary school made me one of his favourites and gave me extra lessons; consequently, I passed the scholarship with flying colours and went to the grammar school in town. I was soon nicknamed Brains; that was later changed to Bronx, probably we had been reading about prohibition and the Bronx area in New York. I must say that I preferred Bronx rather than Brains. I had homework in the evenings, but still helped out by making sure that my siblings washed behind their ears before bedtime, and reading them a bedtime story.

Mum had put Lilly, my sister to bed, so I read a bedtime story to my three brothers. They all slept in the same bed, so I made myself comfortable by stretching out beside them and reading them Coral Island, and sometimes Aesop's Fables. I could only do farm work during the day during school holidays and weekends, but had to feed the chickens and pigs before catching the school bus to town. My sister is twelve years younger than me, and six years younger than my youngest brother, Simon, so we were not really involved in her upbringing. That was because she was a girl, and also because Mum and Dad wanted a girl, and made her their favourite. We didn't mind, at our age we didn't know much about girls, and they were not interested in our games; they preferred dolls and toy tea sets. When we were a bit older, I did teach her to ride the pony, and that is when we really began to get to know each other, and we have been good friends ever since.

During the winter nights after supper we would often sit in the kitchen in the warmth from the range, and listen to Mum and Dad telling stories; they were told and retold many times, but we still enjoyed them. One story was about a neighbour, we nicknamed him Yaddy. Dad said that one night, Yaddy's hair slipped down to his chin, and that was why he is bald as a coot and has full set of bushy bristly red whiskers. Yaddy lived in the large house opposite ours, next to the church yard; in fact, the side of his house was built on the boundary, so it couldn't have been any closer. He was very old and inactive but his body seemed firm and strong. He was unusual to be a retired farmer, most farmers died in harness. His only relative was a spinster sister; she was pert and spry as a sparrow, and always dressed in Victorian clothes. She was Yaddy's surrogate wife and looked after him in his old age, even though she was only one year younger.

Yaddy spent most of the day watching the world go past his dining room window; not that there was much to see apart from the small birds twittering in the front garden and the chattering crows in the rookery in the ancient elms in front of the vicarage next door to us. Only about six motor vehicles passed in a day; most of the traffic was farm workers plodding to and from the fields with their horses, and children scurrying to school and back. I thought that he must be lonely and used to wave to him, but he never responded. He just sat there, looking at nothing; perhaps his mind was busy.

Sunday was a day of rest and dinners were eaten in the dining room instead of the kitchen. There were several rituals involved including an elaborate carving of the joint and the family on their best behaviour. One ritual was for Dad to glance across the road at Yaddy's shiny pate and smile as he said, "When he pops off, it will be a simple funeral. All they have to do is tip him out of the bedroom window, straight into the grave below." We children didn't think that was funny, but sniggered dutifully. Mum just ignored the remark. Dad would follow it with, "When he does go, I will buy the farm and we can live in his house." I remember that I didn't relish the prospect of living next to the graveyard. I had been reading about vampires and ghosts and didn't want to be a victim.

The day before one bonfire night one of my younger friends went round the hamlet collecting a penny for the Guy. He knocked on the back door of Yaddy's house, and the sister invited him into the kitchen. Yaddy sat at the table. He glowered at my friend. "I don't like children." He pointed to a large cupboard in the chimney recess. "How would you like me to lock you in there?" Yaddy started to rise and the sister giggled. My friend shook with fear and bolted through the still open door.

When he arrived home in a state of panting frenzy, his mother scolded him for making a mess in his trousers. He never told his parents, just his friends. After that, the children kept clear of Yaddy's house, except for rolling a very large snowball into his gateway every winter, and scrumping his apples and gooseberries. His orchard was at the back of his house, and we made an adventure of crossing the adjoining fields for the raid. We were playing at storming a German machine gun post, and always won and ran off with the spoils of war.

Bert did casual work for the local farmers; he helped during threshing on our farm. He was small and sturdy, with ruddy face and a mop of unruly blonde hair that he attempted to keep in place with lashings of Brylcreem. Most locals had brown air; there was only one blonde girl in our hamlet, she was the envy of other girls, which is probably why she was so aloof. Bert was a natural comedian, and entertained us during breaks from work. His facial contortions and expressions, and body movements were funnier than his stories; some had a cruel streak. One day he stood up and posed in front of us, his captive audience, and winked. "My woman is not too healthy, she can't work for long, so I have to earn most of the money. When work is scarce and money short," he paused, rolled his eyes, cocked up his head, slowly raised and lowered his hand palm down to waist level and delivered the punch line, "I put her in the Grubber." He repeated his gesture and made a loud 'Ooooh.' That humour would elude the present generation, but we had a good chuckle.

Thinking of the Grubber reminds me of the weak-porridge like soup served at the workhouse; the inmates had to force themselves to drink it, so perhaps the term 'Grueling Time' came from that. The workhouse was a charity that provided accommodation including a small hospital for the poor; several were built in both the countryside and in the towns. People only went there as a last resort; they swallowed their pride with the food, hence the term Grubber. The inmates had to work for their keep. There were workshops for a variety of trades, the laundry, cleaning and the important vegetable garden to supply fruit and vegetables to the kitchen. Some workhouses in the country had a working farm to supplement their income. Quite a few tramps came, they were known as Roosters.

When they came past our house, some would knock on the back door and ask for water. Mum always gave them a cup of tea and a sandwich. Dad said that many were Great War veterans; their experiences in the trenches of Flanders' fields so upset them and destroyed their faith they that could not settle and had to constantly be on the move. Dad said that they were casualties of war, and we should be grateful for their efforts in securing victory. They were not beggars, most were able bodied; they had to be to tramp the endless road in their search for what lay beyond the horizon. If additional labour was needed on the farm, the tramp could sleep in the barn and have free food and a little money for his efforts. If no labour was needed, Dad would find a job just to give them a helping hand. When the wanderlust became irresistible they continued their endless search.

Tramps used the workhouse as a staging post in their travels. They could take a bath, have their clothes laundered and perhaps replaced, sleep in a dormitory bed, and be fed. When they entered the portals, the tramps were searched; any valuables were confiscated. The equivalent value of the cost of accommodation was deducted and the remainder handed back to the tramp. Tramps put signals to warn other tramps that they were nearing the workhouse. They could then secrete their valuables somewhere, such as in a hollow tree trunk, and have little of value in their pockets when searched. They would of course retrieve their possessions after leaving the workhouse. The tramps were not great talkers, so I didn't find out much about their past and why they were tramps, but I did hear a story several times of evil men who watched out for tramps on the road near workhouse, saw where they hid their bits and pieces, and then later stole them. I thought that was a terrible thing to do to war veterans, some of them might have been heroes.

Another of Bert's stories involved sharing a bed with a man who tried to 'brown him'. I didn't understand the joke, and when he explained it to me I was disgusted. He said that he also didn't have any time for that sort of thing and the people who did it. In fact, homosexual behaviour was illegal then, but I have heard that it was a covert practice in some public schools; I had not seen any evidence anywhere, and certainly not in the grammar school, although later in the army there were several hints and rumours. The BBC was very prim and correct and never mentioned it, and the papers were very discrete in their reporting of cases. Quite unlike the scandal-mongering sensationalist reporting in the media of today. Now no-one, neither the living nor the dead, not even royalty, is immune from the snide intrusion into private lives and the consequent shredding of character in the media My sister had a good education, and our chats over tea invariably end with a mutual regret over the denigration of all the standards that we still hold dear. She bemoans the current debt-burdened running of both the country and family finances, and says that that is the road to ruin; I tend to agree with her. We only half joke when we agree that workers in Victorian times were factory fodder; in the wars they were cannon fodder, and now they are financiers fodder.

Grandfather on my mother's side died when I was very young and I have no memory of him. Dad told me that he was not tall, but well-proportioned with the usual crop of whiskers, with a steely and determined look but also a kindly glint in his eyes, and the mien and manners of a typical Victorian gentleman. He was descended from the French aristocracy, one of the few families who managed to escape Madame Guillotine. They anglicized their name and adopted English habits, but could not shake off a slightly superior air, which was an advantage as class distinction was acceptable in English as well as French society. Everyone knew their place, but it was praiseworthy for a man to work hard and claw his way up in life to achieve the same financial status as the upper class, but there was always a slight barrier of snobbery. I remember the remnant of that attitude. My brother Cyril was having secret trysts with a village girl of poor status. He brought her to the house. I cannot forget the look of scorn and superiority on my mother's face as she exclaimed, "How dare you bring that girl to my house?" I felt so sorry for the girl. I liked her; I could not believe that my loving mother could behave in such a cruel way.

Grandfather married an English lady and made a valiant attempt to perpetuate the family tree by siring fifteen children, but as was the norm in those days many died either at or soon after birth. Seven lived, of course my mother was one. She was the eldest and was kept at home to help raise the rest of the children. Uncle James was next. In due course, he tired of living on the family fortune, and embarked on a business career selling seeds to farmers. His first office was a small brick and slate building in our hamlet. The business thrived and he built a fine retail shop for farm and garden seeds with a suite of offices behind, at the end of the market place in the town. He also built a monumental warehouse on the outskirts of the town. He married into a well-to-do family, which probably helped to finance his buildings. His wife was an only child; her parents had passed on and she lived alone in their large house in the snobby part of town. Uncle moved in with her when they married. He tried to emulate his father with no success, and they remained childless. He wanted an heir to his fortune, and since I was the oldest of his nephews, he chose me as his successor. I was quite bright at school and had set my heart on being an English teacher and perhaps a writer, but Mum and Dad were very firm about my future, and in those days we respected and obeyed our parents. When I had finished school, I worked on the farm for a year. Uncle said that I needed more experience of farming so that I could talk to farmers on equal terms and so be more successful at selling them seeds. I joined Uncle's business and started at the bottom and worked my way up to be Uncle's partner and eventual owner of the business. Uncle James had some French and Victorian traits of snobbery, but he was always very kind and helpful in guiding me through the intricacies of general business practices, particularly related to seeds.

Mum had a spinster friend; she ran a lodging house in town. She was too refined to accept lodgers; only paying guests were allowed access to her rooms. Perhaps she had reason to be proud; the house was a rather grand Georgian town house fronting the market place. She took in only respectable people; four teachers from the grammar school and the district nurse. Mum told me that I was going into 'digs' but didn't elucidate so I just accepted her description of a lodging house. I was very shy when I moved into the house but the other guests gave me a warm welcome even though I was much younger. The teachers remembered me, one was my English teacher and she wanted to know why I was not studying to be a teacher. When I told her, she was sympathetic. "Well! Perhaps it's for the best. You can always take up writing as a hobby; who knows where that will lead you when you are older?" Each guest had a private bed-sitting room and shared the dining room and lounge. A pair of teachers often exchanged meaningful glances, and always sat together at the dining table. They were models of propriety, but in the witching hours a creaking floorboard on the landing signalled that they were enjoying nocturnal canoodlings. Later they married and shared a room so that we could all sleep undisturbed.

Miss Hampton, the district nurse, had the nickname 'Dicky Nurse' so given because her duties included making periodic tours of schools to inspect pupil's scalps for nits, fleas and ringworm. If she was aware of the nickname she showed no annoyance; she was always calm and placid and had a gentle smile that sat comfortably on her matronly figure. She managed to squeeze herself into a small Austin Seven to do her rounds. Any person sitting beside her had to be as thin as a beanpole. I always addressed her as Miss Hampton, and she became a good friend. I was happy to talk to her and often took her advice, but I firmly rejected her attempts to mother me. I already had a mother and couldn't cope with another. She gave me a nickname; 'Squid'. Thank goodness no one else knew it.

Miss Hampton loved flowers. She maintained that it was a crime to cut flowers in their prime for display because they faded so quickly. She had a small garden of pot plants on the flat roof over the stairwell at the back of the house. She climbed out of her bedroom window, inched along a narrow ledge and stepped over the parapet to the flat roof. That was no mean feat for a woman of her girth, particularly as there was a three-story drop to the paving below. She asked me to visit her garden, but even though I could shin up a high stack ladder I couldn't face that sheer drop. She diverted a gutter on the main roof, to spill into a galvanized tank to collect rainwater to satisfy her precious geraniums and pansies.

My room was at the front of the top floor. It was small with linoleum on the floor, and furnished with a bed and wardrobe, a small chest of drawers with a swivel mirror on top, and a small table and dining chair. The latter was useful as I was taking a bookkeeping correspondence course, paid for by my uncle. The room overlooked the market; I developed a bad habit at gazing at bustle below instead of working on my course. In March a traveling fair, known as The Mart, set up stalls and rides on the market square, and all normal activities were suspended for a week. It was interesting to watch the coming and going. People enjoying hoopla, coconut shies, shooting galleries, roll the penny and other stalls. The Noah's ark, the whips, and dodgems catered for older customs. Children enjoyed the merry-go-round, and penny on the mat; a tower with an internal spiral staircase and an external spiral ramp. A penny was enough to take a mat, climb the stairs get a view of the town from the top of the tower, and then slide on the mat down the ramp to crash land on a pile of mats on the pavement. The painted wooden horses on the carrousel gave children a gentle rocking ride; the parents waited and they and their children waved to each other as they passed in a never-ending circle of ups and downs. The swing boats were popular with all ages. Some bold young men had to be checked when they tried to swing the boat upside down. There were no health and safety rules then, but the only serious accident that I can remember was when a slightly tipsy man walked under a swing boat, and was scalped. There was a flood of blood, but he still staggered around. His friends bundled him into the sidecar of their Norton motorbike combination and they roared off to hospital. Layer he was known as 'The Hairless Wonder' because the doctors couldn't understand why he was not killed.

There was only a general rumble from the machines and murmuring from the crowds, but some squeals penetrated my room. The worst noise was the music from the Noah's ark. A record of a Jamaican female singer bawling, "Me 'usband lies dead in de market, stone cold dead in de market, I killed no-body but me 'usband." It was a new style of music quite different from the soothing tones of crooners such as Bing Crosby. The din echoed round the square from midday to ten at night, and penetrated the church, offices, shops and house. The local traders gladly tolerated the noise, after all the fair brought in customers from the country. I didn't get back from work until six in the evening. The noise was quite faint in the dining room at the rear of the house. When the table had cleared after dinner, I studied my course there until nine, when I normally went to bed, but sleep was impossible until the Mart closed for the night. A couple of times I skipped my studies and met my friends. We stroll around looking at the stalls and ogling the girls, before going to the pub at the end of the square for half a pint of bitter. We never had more than two; it was unacceptable behaviour to get drunk.

The Mart was eagerly anticipated by young and old, they enjoyed a break in their routine, but the main purpose of the Mart was as an unofficial labour exchange for farm workers. There was labour exchange in the town, but it was difficult for farm workers to go there during normal working hours. Farm workers wishing to find work on a different farm wore a feather in their cap when they went to the Mart. Farmers seeking new workers would approach them and negotiate terms. A handshake was all that was needed to seal the arrangement. Most farms had tied cottages for workers, so a worker changing jobs had to move his family to the new farm. The new farmer would send a horse and lorry to move the family and possessions of his new worker to his new home. Most exchanging of workers was above board, but the few workers who had not told their farmer that they wanted to move, had to take care to avoid their present employer, otherwise he might be angry at being deceived and send the worker and his family packing. That was a serious matter; there were none of the myriad of rules and regulations to protect workers in those days.

Farmers and wholesale buyers conducted their business in the corn exchange; uncle also went to chat with his customers. Farmers came to the cattle market on Saturday and the general market on Wednesday, so it was convenient to meet in the corn exchange on those days. The corn exchange was a two-story building with a large room, lavatories and cloakrooms, and small café on the ground floor, and offices on the first floor. The front was rather ostentatious with stone walls and roman style columns flanking a large door. When not required as a corn exchange, the ground floor was rented out for various functions such as exhibitions, antique fairs and trade fairs. Saturday nights were reserved for the local dance. Young people from the town and villages came to listen and dance to a local amateur octet with saxophones, double bass, drums, cornet and piano. Glen Miller numbers were firm favourites, with old-fashioned Valletta, Gay Gordons and waltzes, followed by the new craze of jitterbug and jive. The wailing moan of the saxophones gave a romantic feel to the last waltz.

Long working hours, studying my bookkeeping and reading library books left little time for socializing. We had Sunday off, and I went home for the day. On Saturday night, I gave myself a treat with my weekly bath, and dressed in my best to go the dance at the corn exchange. I had a lively time and had about six regular partners. If the film looked promising I went to the pictures on Thursday night, I took a dance partner a couple of times, but really had no time to develop a liaison. A weekly hot bath was the norm in those days. When I worked in the warehouse I would lose a lot of sweat. I wondered why a teacher guest became very aloof and changed her place at the dining table. My landlady tactfully advised me to have a stand-up-strip-down wash in the bathroom, paying particular attention to my armpits, before coming in for dinner. I followed her advice and the teacher resumed our friendly talks.

I soon picked up the rudiments of the seed business. Uncle James would arrange for a farmer to grow a set acreage of grain under a contract. Uncle would provide the specially selected and prepared seed, and the farmer would drill it, weed it and tend the crop. When the crop reached the stage of forming ears, uncle would send men to take out any impure plants. This was known as roguing. The farmer would then harvest the crop, and deliver the sacks of grain to the warehouse.

After a short time in the office when Uncle instructed me on the business, I went to work in the warehouse. That involved much heaving and lugging of sacks weighing up to eighteen stone. I had done that on the farm, that and other hard work with a good stoking of wholesome food made me strong, and I could cope with the warehouse, but there were times when I wearily trudged the mile from the warehouse back to my digs.

The warehouse had ground, first and second floors each about nine feet high, connected by sturdy flights of stairs. The building was solid brick walls with a slate roof, set back from the road to form a forecourt. There were not many windows and there two large double doors. The main feature on the front was a steel gantry projecting from the top floor with an arrangement of hand-operated pulleys and chains and a large steel hook. The farmer would drive his lorry of sacks under the gantry, the hook would be lowered and slid under a doubled loop of wagon rope to form a cradle for the sack; it was then hoisted to the top floor, and pulled on the gantry into the building and taken on a sack trolley to a storage bay. The hook would swing in the wind when lowered. I hadn't been warned and received a heavy thud on my shoulder that knocked me down. Luckily, I was only bruised; if my head had been in the way it would have cracked open like an eggshell. The foreman grinned. "You've learned your lesson. I bet it won't happen again."

The seed grown under contract was in fact the seed for next year's crop, and had to be treated, we knew it as dressed. A sack was trolleyed from storage, and the grains carefully spilled at a controlled rate into a timber hopper in the floor; at the bottom of the hopper, a timber chute directed the grains into the top of a blower on the floor below. The blower was a miniature threshing drum with a fan driven man-powered handle; all the seeds in the drum were agitated and the fan blew all husks and other debris not removed by the threshing drum on the farm. The perhaps wrongly named tares were blown into lightweight chaff sacks and later burned in the area behind the building.

The clean seed then spilled into another hopper and another chute to a dresser on the ground floor. The dresser was similar to a large butter churner; a timber barrel fixed to steel pivots and trestles, and turned end over end by means of a cranked handle. The barrel was turned upright and the removable top opened to received grains from the chute until it was half full, a quantity of WBM powder was added and the top closed. The barrel was revolved until the grains were coated with powder, and then the barrel was inverted to spill the treated grain into sacks supported and held open on a steel frame. They were then taken to the treated grain storage areas on all the floors by trolley, to await delivery to farmers just before winter and spring sowings.

The whole process had to be carefully controlled to ensure an even flow of grains; sliding wooden flaps at the bottom of the hoppers were used to cut of the supply particularly when the dresser was refilled. The main control was by the men who spilled the sacks into the top hopper. The whole process generated a lot of dust that penetrated clothing; dust that came from the opened dresser was particularly bad; the WMB made the eyes smart and dried the throat. Apart from the occasional cough we did not think too much about the consequences. The WMB was an insecticide to kill the bugs that burrowed into the roots of grain crops and killed the plants. Perhaps it had very dangerous long-term effects on workers, but since I was only in the warehouse full time for one year I think that any effects would have been felt now that I am old. I don't know how it affected the other workers, and I doubt that they would have associated any effects with the dust.

The hard graft was manhandling sacks up and down the stairs between floors. There was a sack lifter on each floor near the stairs. A trolley man would bring a sack, ease it onto the lifter and crank it up to suit the waist- height of the man picked to do the carrying. He would press his back against the sack, crook his arms over his shoulders, grab the top of the sack and ease it forward to rest down his back. He would then walk crabwise up or down the stairs. No mean feat with an eighteen-stone burden, even though it was distributed down the back. I watched a man do it while the foreman instructed me. "This can be very dangerous. Pay careful attention; I'm not going to tell you again. You will never get up and down stairs in the normal way with that weight. You will either rupture yourself or fall over. Watch how Joe goes up sideways, and how he balances himself. He faces the wall so if he overbalances forward he can support himself on his elbows and get his balance back. If he overbalances backward the weight of the sack will take him though the handrail and probably land on top of him on the floor below. If you feel yourself going backward, let go of the sack. It will probably crash through the handrail, but with luck you will end up sitting on the stairs." The foreman frowned, "Better to have a broken handrail than a funeral." He grinned. "Especially if it's the gaffer's nephew."

He carried on with the lesson; "Look at Joe now. Watch how he rocks. When he sways to the right he puts most of his weight on his right leg, he can then lift his left foot to the next tread. As he sways to the left he moves his weight to his left leg, at the same time straightening it and moving his right foot just in front of his left, so he has gone up a step." He laughed. "Don't look so puzzled. You will soon get the knack. It's stupid to fight the dead weight of the sack, use it to help you. After you have done it a few times it will become second nature. Anyway, I will keep an eye on you."

Later I spent a few days sitting with casual women workers sorting bean and pea seeds. The crops had been through the threshing machine on the farms, and needed only a short time in the blower to remove debris. The seeds were taken to a sorting area and spread on a large table. The women sat down each side and picked out all the bad, damaged and misshapen seeds; they were dropped into baskets between the women and later disposed of. It was a boring occupation; the women relieved the tedium by gossiping, sometimes singing and telling jokes. They were nice to me, but didn't spare my blushes when they made lewd jokes about me. I mentioned it to the foreman; he just laughed and told me that it would develop my sense of humour. After getting my eye in on the sorting table and becoming proficient, the next job was to take the baskets of rejected seeds to the back yard and burn them on an incinerator.

The seed grains were delivered to farms in two Ford lorries. I had to go in one and help to unload the sacks into the farmer's barn. That made a nice break from the confines of the warehouse; I enjoyed being driven through the countryside. Another time when we could get out of the warehouse was to go roguing; we went to the farm contracted to grow seed grain and inspected the crop and took out all impure strains, known as rogues.

Mum's younger brother Nelson went to public school. He probably tried to live up to his famous namesake and became rather pompous and primped up with self-importance. From my readings that was probably due to an inferiority complex. After school, he spent some time doing nothing and so did not have a reserve occupation at the outbreak of war. He was called up into the army. He made good progress and became a captain in the Indian Army. Despite his prowess at sport, his overbearing posturing made him unpopular with his fellow officers, and he was posted to a remote part as district supervisor. The nearest Englishman was miles away. He soon adapted to the loneliness and accumulated several servants to fulfill his every whim. When he was demobbed he found it hard to drop his lordly ways. He came to stay on the farm for a few days and Martin told me that Nelson asked him to empty his chamber pot. Martin blurted out, "I'm not your servant," and later received a good telling off from Mum for being cheeky. Nelson was at a loose end, so Uncle James took him into the seed business. He was too overbearing to deal with the farmers so helped out in the office, but his work mostly entailed delegating to the clerk and typist. Nelson was quite good at shooting and golf, and was more popular with the more aristocratic land owners; Uncle gave him plenty of time off to play with them because it brought in large orders, and it also got him out of our hair and we could do our jobs free from his burdensome interference. He was not well liked. Uncle James thought that it would be a good idea to take him down a peg or two, and sent him to rogue a field of wheat. I went to tell him how to do it. He was not pleased to take advice from a nephew, but soon understood what was required.

The wheat was almost fully grown, and the work involved stooping down at the end of a row of wheat, looking at the tops and remembering the plants that were taller than the rest. They were tares, and had to be removed. It was not difficult to walk straddling the row and pulling out the tares, and tucking them into a bag slung over one shoulder. It was not so pleasant when it was raining, then we had to wear waterproof trousers otherwise the wet stalks brushing against the crutch would quickly make it unbearably sore. On this occasion, it was pouring with rain, but the work had to be done. My constant reading made it necessary for me to wear spectacles. I couldn't see properly though the streaming lens, and had no spare hand to wipe them. Nelson forged ahead. He stopped and looked back. "Just buck your ideas up and get on with it. My God, if you were as idle as that in my empire, I would have you flogged. I knew that my future was safe with Uncle James. I just ignored Nelson's ravings and pressed on at my own rate. An hour later he said, "I have had enough, this is servant's work." He went to the van and sat drinking something probably stronger than tea out of his thermos flask. I was the victor on that day. I was proud of knocking him off his high horse, but I kept it to myself.

Thinking of Nelson reminds me of one of Bert's stories. An Indian Army officer named Caruthers was posted to the back of beyond. A messenger went to collect dispatches, and when he returned, the C.O. asked about the welfare of Caruthers. The messenger replied, "He felt a bit lonely, so he is now living with a gorilla."

The C.O. raised an eyebrow – aptly expressed by Bert – and asked, "Male or female?"

The messenger looked surprised. "Female of course."

Bert did his characteristic downward sweep of the hand and an 'Oooooh', paused for the punchline, "There is nothing queer about Caruthers."

Uncle James came to see me in the warehouse. I met him on the forecourt. We exchanged pleasantries as uncle and nephew; we talked about the digs, and my weekly visits home. Uncle looked at the front door. "Once inside it's a business matter. I have to treat you as am employee in front of the others and show no favouritism, you understand?" I nodded agreement.

Inside, uncle went on a short tour of inspection with the foreman, and then called me into the small office. There was only a desk and chair and filing cabinet, so I had to stand. Uncle looked up from the desk. "Well, Gerald. The foreman tells me that you are not afraid of hard graft and that you get on well the other men and also are not shy when dealing with the women. That will stand you in good stead when you deal with customers."

I shuffled my feet in embarrassment and wondered if he was going to increase my wages. He went on, "I am moving you to the main office next week. I hope that you have been diligent in your bookkeeping course. You will be able to put your learning to good use. The clerk will instruct you in working with the accounts, receipts, invoices, and other paperwork. I don't expect you to learn shorthand and typing, unless of course you want to, but you will help the typist with the filing system. It's not too difficult, and if you pay attention and don't rush things, you should not make any mistakes. You will also help out in the shop. By the end of a year, I expect you to have a sound understanding of our office and shop procedures, and we can then talk about training you to work with the farmers."

I nodded. "I will do my best, Uncle, I don't mind the hard work, but I don't want to do it all my life, I want to use my mind as well as my muscles."

Uncle laughed, "I will make sure that you do, especially later, you will have to very sharp witted to strike a deal with my farmer customers." He became serious. "Back to work now, and tell the foreman I want to see him."

***

The next year seemed to fly by. I remembered Great Uncle Joseph advising me, "Get an office job, then you will only wear out the seat of your trousers, not your body." I now know what he meant. I was no longer physically tired after work, but often my head was in a spin, and when closed my eyes to sleep, I could see rows of words and columns of figure floating around inside my head. The office was only a few minutes' walk from my digs, and I spent a lot of time on a chair so I didn't get much exercise. The large meals served in the digs we more than sufficient for my needs and I began to put on the pounds. I continued to go home on Sundays. Mum often frowned and told me to either eat less or get more exercise. The cycle ride home got some air in my lungs, but as my weight increased I began to worry about being made fun of. I went to the local baths and had a grueling hour's swim twice a week, and also joined a tennis club and sweated a few pounds off. I eventually managed to persuade my landlady to give me smaller helpings and I lost my sagging belly.

Mr Williams, the clerk, was short and thin, always immaculate in dark grey pinstripe suit, glossy black shoes, starched white shirt and grammar school old-boy tie. He had a fine thatch of brown hair, but a very high forehead gave the impression of a receding hairline, although he did have a slight widow's peak. At first, I was fascinated by his habit of creasing his brows. I counted ten furrows. I later learned to ignore his wrinkled brow, but was always amused by his look of surprise when he lifted his eyebrows, he did that as a prelude to all his actions; he was in a more or less constant state of surprise. He never raised his voice, was always courteous to customers and staff, and despite his brow raising habit, he was my idea of a gentleman. He was very patient with me and taught me everything that he knew about the office side of the business. Perhaps he found his perfect behaviour in the office a strain, and I was very shocked to hear rumours that he was in the habit of beating his wife, however I couldn't help but wonder whether or not he raised his eyebrows either before, or during, or after the beating. I never knew his Christian name; he was always referred to as Mr Williams.

I enjoyed my spell of work in the shop. We sold mainly vegetable and flower seeds and a few potted houseplants. I learned a lot about flowers and vegetables from trade literature that came to the office, and from library books; I had time for a quick visit there during my lunch break. Many customers sought my advice before buying seeds, and quite a few out-of-town customers just came in to say hello when they came to the Saturday market. During slack periods, I had to weigh out two ounces of seeds on a balance, and put them into small printed packets with the business details and photo of the seeds on front and cultivation instructions on the back. Once I put the wrong seeds in the wrong packet. A few weeks later the customer came in and joked, "The beetroot went well with the colour of my marigolds, but I was really expecting pansies." Uncle was very annoyed when he heard, but since the customer had joked he let me off with a stern warning to pay attention. The packets of seeds were stored in pigeonholes on the wall behind the counter, but I had a bit of fun in arranging eye-catching displays in the shop window.

Rosemary, the typist, was middle aged, rather dumpy and dowdy. Each morning she would take dictation from Uncle and Mr Williams. I was amazed to see her fingers fly over the keys of the office Underwood typewriter; she seemed never to make a mistake. When she had finished typing for the day, she would put a carbon copy of the letters into a large leather-bound book with flimsy pages, she would insert a damp cloth between each letter and its page. She closed the book and placed it on the bed of an iron press and turned a wheel to compress the book. After half an hour she released the book, took out the carbon copies and cloths, and by a strange process that I never understood, a perfect copy of the letter was printed on the page. Every letter sent from the office was recorded in date order in the book. There were several identical books going back to the time when grandfather started the business. He maintained that the books were admissible evidence in a court of law. The business never had to go to court, but the ritual was continued every day. Carbon copies of letters were put in their respective brown envelope files with invoices and receipts and other papers for normal everyday use.

The following spring, Uncle summoned me to his office; it had a large desk and chair, a filing cabinet, a safe, a small table and three dining chairs. Uncle nodded to the chairs, he stayed behind his desk. "Sit down. It's time for another talk." I felt more comfortable looking at him at the same eye level. Uncle smiled. "Well, young man, Mr Williams has given you a good report, and tells me that you are ready to move on."

I grinned and nodded. "I now know all about the warehouse and the office. I suppose that the next step is being a salesman. I am looking forward to getting back to the land."

Uncle frowned. "Don't be so cocky. You can never know everything, there is always something new to learn, particularly new methods of agriculture. You know the effects of the insecticide WMB from the warehouse. I have been reading about weed poison and a new insecticide DDT, will soon be available to spray on growing crops. I have mixed feelings; they may make a lot of farm workers redundant. One by-product of DDT is Derris Dust, intended for use as an insecticide for vegetables and flowers; I will order some for the shop; once the word spreads, it should sell well." He paused. "Back to the matter in hand. Yes, I have decided that you are ready to visit farmers. You have probably heard that Thomas is ready to retire, he has served the business well as a salesman for thirty years, and the business will look after him. I'm about throw you in at the deep end, it's up to you to keep your head above water and do a good job. You will start by going with Thomas for the two weeks until he retires. Keep alert and watch his every move and listen to how he talks to the farmers. Being a salesman is not easy; you have to know how to treat people. When you visit farmers with Thomas, speak only when you are spoken to, just be polite and don't say much, let Thomas do the selling. He will also teach you to drive the combination; later you will have to take a driving test. When Thomas leaves, you will be on your own. You will make a start in your own village.

"You know the farmers, so should have no problem talking to them. They are already customers and know what seeds they want to buy, so you will not have to use any hard selling. Later when you have got the hang of it you will spread your wings and go to all farmers in our area, both to present customers and to the others; your job then will be to persuade them to change their seed merchant and use us instead."

Uncle gave me a piercing look. "Well, do you think you are up to the job?"

I looked Uncle in the eye. "I will do my best not to let you down."

He nodded. "I am sure that you will. Let's hope that your best is good enough. The salesman is a very important man, if he doesn't buy and sell there would be no business." Uncle dropped his stern look. "Don't let that responsibility lay heavy on your shoulders. I know that you won't let me and the family down."

I picked up several tips from Thomas and liked the work. He taught me to handle the motorcycle and sidecar, and I had my share of fun roaring along the almost deserted county roads on the 500 c.c. BSA outfit. I passed the driving test. I was very pleased with myself when I tore of the red L-plates after the test. I had enjoyed talking to the customers in the shop, and I enjoyed talking to the farmers. I heeded my uncle's advice about not talking too much: they took advantage of ability to be a good listener and unburdened their problems. I was too inexperienced to give advice, but often just the talking helped them to sort the problem out. Consequently, many were on very friendly terms with me, and that made my work much easier, and the orders flowed in, particularly from the new customers that I found. Uncle was pleased with my progress. "Well done, my boy. Keep up the good work." In fact, he gave me a five shilling a week increase in wages.

At first, I was just selling seeds, and passing the orders back to Mr Williams in the office to arrange delivery from the warehouse. Later Uncle entrusted me to arrange for farmers to grow grain for seed on their farms, but I was not allowed to sign contracts. The farmer had to visit the office and Uncle handled that business. I also inspected crops grown under contract, and advised the warehouse foreman when they were ready for roguing. The main selling seasons were from January to March for spring-sown grain, and June to October for winter-sown crops. The later including strawberry picking time, and farmers would often give me a couple of punnets. I passed them on to my landlady and we all scrunched fresh strawberries and cream for desert at dinner. Strange how the other paying guests became friendlier as the strawberry season approached. During the periods between selling seasons I helped out in the office, shop and warehouse.

I had to visit all types of farms, from smallholdings to large estate farms; I never received a cool reception. Farms did not have many visitors and it was a pleasure for the occupants to talk to a relative outsider. When I was selling near my village I always called to see my family. As I drove into the farmyard, I would herald my arrival by opening the clutch and throttle, the crackling exhaust warned of my coming. I always timed it for midday. I was always welcomed at the kitchen table to share the meal and exchange family news.

One day when I was scouting an unfamiliar area, I noticed a sign Grove Farm. I left the main road and had to fight and coax the combination to negotiate the muddy track. At the end were a small cottage and a barn. As I spluttered to a halt the door opened and I had the shock of my life to see the most beautiful girl in our village; at least to my mind she was the most beautiful, and the sight of her long dark hair and sultry looks of a gypsy confirmed my opinion. She left some time back to look after a relative in another village. "Daphne! What a surprise," I exclaimed. "I've often wondered what became of you."

Daphne smiled coquettishly. "Gerald! I remember you. You've grown up. What brings you here?"

I said, "It's been a long time. You have changed too. I am the salesman for the seed merchant in town. I'm looking for new customers and I saw your sign on the road."

She nodded. "I know the firm; we deal with one in the next town. Since you are here, come in and I will put the kettle on."

She invited me into her kitchen, large by town house standards, but comfortable by farmhouse standards. As she busied herself she told me, "I married about a year ago. Timothy's father set us up in this place." She glanced at the table. "Please sit down." I sat at the table and watched her make the tea. I thought that I was silly not to have designs on her when we were younger, but we both had other things on our minds then. She continued, "This land is difficult to work, so we are thinking of laying it down to pasture and starting a dairy farm, with a few pigs and chickens." She giggled. "The Grange is a bit grand, but we have big ideas for this place."

She poured the tea into thick china cups and put a couple of ginger biscuits on the saucers. "It's nice to see you. We don't get many visitors here; the tradesmen and postman won't come down the lane, and I get a bit lonely." She arched her lovely eyebrows and cocked her head. "Next time you are in the area, call in for a chat."

I choked on the biscuit at such a blatant invitation. She laughed. "My husband will be back soon; you may be able to sell him some grass seed."

As though on cue a man came through the door. Daphne said briskly, "Just in time for a cuppa. This is Gerald, we went to school together. Timothy put out his hand. I stood up and returned his iron grip. We both said, 'How do you do', and mutually relaxed our grip.

"I have heard of you. You are making quite a name for yourself. Apparently, you are good at selling." He grinned. "You will not have much luck here I'm afraid. We are still struggling to make a go of things."

I took a liking to Timothy and the feeling seemed mutual, and I regretted my lewd thoughts about his wife. We had a chat about this and that and I got up to leave. "Thanks for the tea. I noticed that your land is heavy; I have a contact in the lime spreading business if you are interested. It makes the soil more pliable."

He nodded. "Thanks, but not just yet." He smiled at Daphne. "We have a few plans, when we have decided what to do we will get in touch."

Daphne came with me to the motorbike, "Don't forget. When you are in these parts, call in for a cup of tea." Her look suggested something more interesting than ginger biscuits to go with the tea. I breathed a big sigh of relief when I reached the road.

Colonel Harper's estate was quite a contrast to Timothy and Daphne's cottage. Large wrought iron gates opened to a broad gravel drive, lined with Lombardy Poplars, leading to a large Georgian manor house. I kept the engine revs down as a sign of respect. As a tradesman, I had to go round to the back entrance. A servant escorted me to the colonel's library, knocked gently once on the door, and opened it for me. The first time I was overawed by the grandeur of the house and furniture and by the colonel's appearance. He was large with a ruddy face, blue eyes that seemed to pierce right into your brain, and short white hair. He dressed in tweeds and brown brogue shoes white shirt with a thin blue stripe, a detachable starched winged collar and regimental tie. A monocle would probably an affectation on other people, but on the colonel it seemed absolutely proper.

He quickly put me at my ease; he got up from his desk, pulled a cord hanging from the ceiling, and sat on an easy at near a low coffee table, "Come in, sit down, lad. I know your uncle well. He has told me about you, I hope that you make a fine future in the family business." A single knock heralded a maid. She waited by the door. The colonel said briskly, "Doris, we will be two for tea today." He turned to me. "I was expecting you, so I have written out my order for you."

By the time that I had stammered my thanks, the maid came in with a silver tray and laid the table with thin bone china crockery, silver teaspoons and cake knives, the meal consisted of cucumber sandwiches and seed cake. Doris served the tea and cut the cake and quietly left the room. On subsequent visits the ritual was always the same. The colonel was a bachelor. His only close relative was a nephew; he was following the family tradition of having a spell in the army. The colonel liked to regale me with tales of his army career. He had told me how he wanted to learn about the army from the bottom up, and had enlisted as a private instead of going to Sandhurst Military Academy straight from university. He was very proud of his rise through the ranks to receive the King's commission in an infantry regiment. When the colonel served in the Boer War, he was regimental sergeant major. On one visit, he told me an episode.

The colonel swallowed his sandwich. "In those days, army discipline was harsh." He looked into the distance. "I could have men flogged, but never resorted to that cruelty. I was expected to maintain discipline in the regiment. Normally my orders were obeyed to the letter, and only minor offences such as being untidy and having dirty kit warranted a punishment, usually a couple of days' jankers, degrading work around the barracks, and extra guard duty. The adjutant agreed with my methods, and supported me by issuing a standing order that the men must shit, shine and shave before breakfast." He paused and laughed. "I heard that I was known as the 'Three S's'.

"We had a small skirmish when out on patrol. As I was dealing with one Zulu, another slashed my forehead with his assegai." He pointed to long scar, like an extra wrinkle on his forehead, and continued, "I reacted by opening his guts with my bayonet." The colonel paused for a nibble of cake and a sip of tea, "I was brought up to kill cleanly and not cause suffering. When I have shoots on the estate, I always ask my guests to shoot to kill. We shoot for food, not for pleasure, but we do enjoy the social side and camaraderie of a shoot." He gave me one of his piercing looks. "I couldn't see the poor bugger suffer, he was screaming in agony, so I finished him off by sticking my bayonet into his gullet."

The colonel nibbled his cake. "Yes, it was hard in those days. Now-a-days young people have it all too easy. It all started with those flappers flaunting themselves on the dance floor to that noise, I can't say it is music, imported from America." He lifted his head and sniffed loudly. "No dignity don't you know." I could only nod in agreement; I respected the colonel and understood his old-fashioned ideas, and enjoyed his tales. He had many acres of arable land and pasture, and I always left with a substantial order.

Many years have passed since those early days learning the seed business. I had an enforced break of four years when I was called up into the army. During that time, I was posted to the other side of the county. There I met a local girl, married her and eventually we raised a family. Of course, that is another story. I rejoined the seed business after the war and soon picked up the ropes. Nelson had kept his interest in the army and was a major in the Territorial Army. He was called up at the outbreak of war. His regiment was sent to Singapore, and he finished his life under appalling conditions on the death railway in Thailand.

Uncle James was pleased with my abilities and made me a director. He retired and fulfilled his wish to keep the business in the family by making me managing director. I made a few changes. I installed electric hoists and trolleys in the warehouse, and removed the hard graft. The BSA. was on its last spokes, and I replaced it with a new Jowett van. When he died, Uncle James bequeathed the business to me. During the war, there were many personal tragedies; I was grieved to hear that Colonel Harper had been killed by a stray bomb jettisoned by a German plane on the run from Spitfires. I respected him and admired him and we became very friendly, but I was still very surprised to learn that he had left me his manor house. I was able to live and raise my family in a style befitting a prosperous seed merchant. I did not feel guilty over his nephew. He inherited the estate; he already had a large mansion as part of the settlement when he married. He was not interested in the estate and employed a manager who lived in a nice house.

I can look back over an eventful and successful life. My daughter had a good and successful marriage to a barrister; my two sons joined the business and I trained them to take over. I will stop working soon and let them take over the business to allow me a contented retirement with my beautiful house and lovely and loving wife.

LILLY

Mum wanted me to be baptised as Victoria because the Old Queen was so dignified and respectable. Dad preferred the name Violet, but Mum insisted that no daughter of hers was going to be named after a carthorse, even though it was Dad's favourite. Mum was a bit like Queen Victoria – very determined – and Dad gave in as usual. He suggested Lily because it had a nice sound and would be a suitable name for a pretty girl. Mum agreed, but insisted that it should be spelt Lilly, and not the common form Lily. Anyway! That's how I got my name. I've heard the story many times during family reminiscing round the kitchen table. I am happy to tell you my name, but wild horses would not force me to tell you my age. A lady never discloses her age, and I am a lady even though my hands show my hard life as a farmer's daughter and wife. Mum often says – boasts – that she had four sons in six years, and then had to wait six years for me. Dad always adds that I was worth waiting for. I was the family pet during my early childhood, but the age gap meant that I had to wait a few years before I got to know my brothers. In those far off days, boys were boys and girls were girls and they didn't mix. In fact, intimate, and indeed, general knowledge of the opposite sex was not discovered until after marriage, and even then, the two sexes – there were only two in those days – was of a passing nature; men did men's things, and women did women's things. Quite different from today; when blatant sex is constantly featured in advertisements, and through the media of television and newspapers and journals.

My oldest brother, Gerald, is twelve years older than me. He left home to work in the seed business at sixteen, was called up in the army at eighteen. There was a large farm near the barracks. The farmer's daughter was the dream girl of all the soldiers. Gerald wooed and wed her and was the envy of all his fellow soldiers. After he was demobbed, he went back to the seed business. He inherited a house near the town and proved his manhood by siring five children. During my early childhood, I didn't see much of him, but I remember him calling to see us when he was visiting farmers in our area. He would arrive at midday in time for dinner, shovel in the food and be off on his business again within the hour. Of course, now we are more sophisticated; we have lunch at midday and dinner at six-thirty in the evening.

My second brother is Martin. He is ten years older than me. He was exempt from military service, and has spent all his life farming. He worked hard and was careful with money, but he indulged his whim to cut a dash; he bought good quality clothes and worked his way up from second hand motorbikes to a smart green MG two-seater sports car. He was indeed a handsome lad, and caught the eye of a farmer's daughter from another village. After the obligatory courtship, they married. Dad had recently bought a large field with a substantial house on the frontage. He let Martin have it rent-free; of course, Martin continued to work on the farm and his wife helped out during the harvest.

My next brother is Cyril, and he is eight years older than me. He was the horseman until a new Fordson Standard tractor made horses almost redundant; they were eventually sent to the knacker's yard. The milk round and cows had been sold, and Martin was granted his wish to be the tractor driver. With only two cows to provide milk for the family and only one horse for odd jobs, the only work left for Cyril was labouring on the farm. He wanted a better life and left home. He had saved his money. He bought a Bedford lorry and became a gangmaster. His business thrived, and eventually he sold it and started a haulage business. He married a town girl and bought a house far from the farm.

The next brother, Simon, always either had his nose in a book or fiddled around in his shed with a fretsaw machine. He is six years older than me. That's no barrier between adults but a big gulf between a young girl and teenager. Simon studied hard, went to college and became an engineer. He did spend a year on the farm between grammar school and college, but decided that labouring on a farm was not his ambition.

My first memory of getting familiar with farm animals is around the age of ten. Cyril would take me on the cross bar of his bicycle to bring the cows back from the pasture to the milking shed. We walked back and he put me on a cow's back. He wheeled his cycle with one hand and held me with the other so that I would not slide off. I loved the rhythm of the cow walking, quite different from the cross bar. Feeling the cow moving probable probably led to my joy later when riding my pony.

Farmer's children were unpaid workers; now it would be considered slave labour with many dangers. Exploitation was not recognised and the work was considered as an apprenticeship to learn all aspects of farming, so that children would carry on the tradition.

When I was ten I joined the others in picking potatoes and riding in the cart, taking a turn to catch full baskets and spilling them into the cart. After I acquired the knack it was easy, though hard on the hands. That started my history of rough hands and broken nails. I enjoyed the sway of the cart and felt superior as I looked down on the other pickers, but I did pity them as they stood to stretch their aching backs.

The age gap between my brothers and myself; the fact that I had few playmates, not mixing with boys and only two girls around my age in the hamlet, all contributed to my rather lonely childhood. I went to the village school until I was ten, and then I was sent to a private boarding school for girls in order to make me a better catch by having a good education. Several pupils were farmer's daughters so I made many friends and was no longer lonely. On leaving school, I went back home and Mum completed my education as a potential farmer's wife by teaching me the harsh routines on housework and cooking. Mum was a hard taskmaster, but I am grateful now for her help, and can turn my hand to everything that is required from a dutiful wife. Mum was often ill, so I then had complete charge of the household. It was hard work even with only three in the house and the use of electrical appliances. I still don't know how Mum coped after I was born, with five men and a baby with neither electricity nor tap water.

After my brothers left home and were busy raising their own brood, there was only Mum and Dad and myself in the house. I was still lonely, even though I was Dad's pet. He said that he wanted me to be a good farmer's wife. He took me around the farm, explaining the whys and wherefores of farming, and on Saturdays he took me to the cattle market in town and taught me how to discern required features of cattle. Once at the auction, he even let me bid for one; it became my favourite. I named it Gus. We bought only steer calves for rearing as beef beasts. I was very upset when it was time for Gus to go to the cattle market. I knew he would go to the slaughterhouse and his carcass bought by a butcher. I couldn't eat beef for a few weeks after that. The cattle market was also a meeting place for farmers to gossip; Dad introduced me to them, particularly to those who had strong sons. After the market Dad always took me to a fish and chip shop for lunch.

After I left school, electricity was brought to the hamlet. Our house now had electric lights and a few 15-amp sockets. There were not many appliances then and we had only an electric iron, radio, and vacuum cleaner. Dad and a couple of farm workers built an extension on the back of the house, with timber walls and a slate roof, containing a bathroom, scullery and verandah. Mains water was connected to a tap by the gate to the main road; we had to carry it in buckets to the house. Dad and his helpers laid a lead pipe from the tap near the gate and connected it to new taps in the washhouse, scullery and bathroom.

I was kept very busy helping Mum with the general housework such as cleaning, washing and ironing clothes, scrubbing the front door step every Saturday, and other chores. When we worked together, Mum liked to talk a lot, mostly reminiscing about the past. "In the days before electricity we used a stiff hand-brush and dustpan to sweep the carpets, crawling on hands and knees. It's not very common now, but every year we would do the spring-cleaning, one room at a time. Dad and a worker would move the furniture and roll up the carpet; they would take it outside and drape it over the clothes line and give it a good thrash with bamboo carpet beater to get rid of the dust." She smiled. "I used to threaten to thrash your brothers with the beater when they misbehaved. Of course, I never hit them; the threat was enough to bring them into line." She looked into the distance.

"I would get the chimney sweep in then to clear out the chimneys. He was very careful to drape an old sheet over the fireplace to contain the soot, but after he had gone there was a fine dust everywhere. Everything had to be wiped with a damp cloth, and I washed the paintwork and windows. The men would then relay the carpet and move the furniture back. Every five years or so, I papered the walls, and touched up the paintwork. It was hard work but very satisfying to live in a nice clean house." Mum shrugged. "Wives don't spring clean anymore; these electrical cleaners have made them lazy."

I retorted, "Well! Just because you were a slave to the house doesn't mean that I have to be. There are plenty of other things to do that are far more interesting than housework. I am pleased to have time for myself, to do the things that I like, rather than working all the time."

Mum sighed. "Yes, I suppose that you are right. My generation finds it difficult to adapt to new ideas, things change so quickly now, but I must admit that life is easier now than in the old days." She gave me a meaningful look. "Of course, life was simple then, now there are so many temptations for curious young people."

I remember the sheer drudgery of Monday washday. I had watched Mum do the laundry, but now she gave me a lesson. I had already filled the copper from a hose on the tap, and lit the fire and the water was almost boiling. Mum said, "Next time use the water from the pump, tap water is very hard and water from the cistern is soft and makes better suds. That's why I told you to always use pump water to wash your hair, tap water makes hair brittle." Mum frowned whilst giving me instructions. I threw in a couple of handfuls of carbolic soap flakes and a handful of soda crystals, and stirred up the suds, and then put the sheets and pillows and white clothes in the hot water and let them boil for half an hour. I had to use a length of old hoe shaft to lift the whites from the copper to the machine. I then had to half fill the washing machine from the copper, and close the lid, it had a handle on top of a rod going through a swivel joint to an aluminium slotted paddle inside the machine. When I stirred the handle, the paddle went to and fro and around to agitate the clothes. When I had got the hang of agitating the lever she said, "Keep that up for ten minutes while I go a make myself a cup of tea." When she came back she nodded approvingly. "That should do. Now give them a rinse and put then through the mangle." She added, "Use soft water." I dutifully filled a bucket from the pump and lifted the clothes from the hot water into the bucket and rinsed the clothes. It took several buckets and rinses before Mum was satisfied.

Mum nodded. "I've already filled the old tin bath behind the mangle with pump water and put in a couple of cubes of blue whitener. Don't use any more, the whites will turn out blue and it will take two washes to make them white again. Now just turn the handle slowly whilst I feed in these clothes." The rollers squeezed out the water, and they dropped into the blue whitener water. "Leave them there to soak, we will mangle them again after we have washed the smalls." We went through the same process with the smalls - socks and underwear, and then did the coloured clothes. Of course, we did not put all those in the blue whitener, but just rinsed them in pump water and mangled them once straight into the wicker clothes basket. Mum said, "Now give me a hand to carry it to the line. I don't want to strain my back again." I thought, 'Me too! If you do that I shall have to cope with all the housework for a few days.' We lugged the basket to the path beside the vegetable garden and hung the clothes on a long line fixed to the top of two old railway sleepers

231

planted in the ground. The posts had to be strong to resist the blustery winds that swept across the Fens. The line needed two wooden props to raise the clothes above the ground. The long line was full and straining under the load. I remember that it once snapped and the clothes fell onto the mud. I wept quietly as I washed the whole lot again.

When the clothes were dry, we ironed them all including socks and then put them on the clothes-horse in front of the dining room fire to air. Simon told me that when he was small he liked to sit on the hearth between the fire and the clothes-horse; he said it was his safe place. When the washing was finished I had to swill out the washhouse floor with the water from the copper. I had to lug buckets of water from the pump in the washhouse to swill the concrete paved back yard and path to the outside earth closet; I used the long handled heavy bristle brush that was normally used to swill out the cowshed, including the dung channels. When I said to Mum that it was very hard work, she replied, "Hard work! You don't know the meaning of hard work. It's not that many years ago that I had to do it all by hand. At first, I had to use a wash board, and then the dolly and tub to clean clothes. Now you have a machine; no doubt they will soon have an electric machine that does everything apart from ironing." How right she was.

In cold weather, the clothes froze as I hung them on the line. The carbolic soap and soda and the frost made my hands very chapped and red and sore. Mum caught me crying. "What's the matter?"

I held up my hands. "They are so ugly. I wish that I had a lady's hands, nice and soft and white."

Mother snorted. "You should be proud of your hands, not ashamed. They prove that you are not afraid of hard work. When you dance with those farmer boys, they know that you will make a good wife. They may fancy those office girls with their fine clothes and soft hands, but they know that they would be useless on a farm."

I nodded. "You may be right, Mum. I am never a wallflower; the boys say that they like to dance with me and during the evening quite a few ask me for the last waltz."

Mum smiled. "Well! You are a very attractive girl, especially since you took my advice about make-up. Remember a little goes a long way, too much plastered on makes you look cheap and vulgar. A natural look is far more appealing to man looking for a decent wife. I don't want a son-in-law who wants a tart for a wife."

I looked at the floor. "Mum! I need some more advice. During most of the dances I don't get too close to the boys, but during the last waltz, when the lights are low, they hold me very close. We can't dance properly them, just shuffle around. They press their legs between my thighs, especially during the turns, and I feel something pressing against my stomach. Perhaps it's just a box of matches in their trouser pocket, but it makes me feel uncomfortable." I looked at Mum. "Do you think that I should push them away?"

Mum giggled. "It's just nature taking its course. You've seen the bull get aroused when it services a cow. Well! Men are the same." She frowned. "I know that you young people like a goodnight kiss after the dance, it was always so. If the boy gets too aroused just push him gently away and tell him that that sort of thing must wait until you are married." Mum grinned. "You can let him fondle your breasts if you like, but nothing more, and don't let yourself get too excited." She frowned. "We don't want any shotgun weddings in our family."

Thank goodness my brothers had left home, so there were only two beds to make every morning. The bedclothes were pulled down over the brass foot rail, and the pillows placed on a chair. The feather mattress lay there in crumpled lumps. A vigorous shaking and plumping soon restored it to pristine condition. I spread the sheets and three blankets and tucked them in round the bottom and sides, and folded the top six inches of the sheet neatly over the blanket. I spread the counterpane and then the eiderdown, plumped up the feather pillows and laid them above the top sheet. Each head needed two pillows. The bed looked very inviting; I understood why Mum took such a pride in her housework, I wasn't exactly proud but I did feel satisfied with a job well done. Feather mattresses are now considered unhygienic; perhaps they were but there was nothing as cosy as lying on a plump feather bed and wriggling to make a hollow, the mattress pressed around the body and the blankets and eiderdown kept the heat it. It was a luxury of warmth, comfort and safety, almost like being back in the womb. The three blankets were needed in the winter;

as the weather warmed, the blankets were removed as required, and only a sheet and eiderdown were needed in the summer.

Of course, in those days we didn't have central heating; an open fire in the rooms and hot water bottles were the only source of heat. The fireplaces in the dining room and lounge were modern grates with glazed tile surrounds; they needed only a wipe with a damp cloth to make them gleam. One of my many duties was to lay paper and sticks and coal in the grates ready for lighting, and to fill the coal and log scuttles. The bedrooms had a small ornate cast iron fireplace. Mum said that she didn't like the dust soiling her beds, so they were only lit when someone was ill in bed. I still had to black-lead them once a month and lay crumpled red tissue paper on the grate. We had stone hot water jars to warm the bed, old vinegar jars were ideal; warming pans were seldom used, only to hang on the wall as decoration. The copper pan had to be polished with Brasso, along with the brass candlesticks, ornaments, door knobs, crumb tray and brush, lounge coal scuttle and furniture handles; the silver cutlery was only used for special occasions and did not need polishing every week.

Every month I cleaned the windows with water and vinegar and polished them with crumpled newspaper. I had to stand on a stool to reach the ground floor windows, but the outside of the first-floor bedroom windows was not so easy. I had to raise the lower sash and sit on the window sill with my legs inside the room. I puller the outer top sash down to my knees so that I could clean the top of the lower sash and then pushed up the outer sash and pulled down the inner so that I could clean the bottom. It was then simple to clean the outer sash, but I always finished the job with wet pinafore and skirt. It was rather dangerous; I could have fallen backwards and smashed my head on the ground below. I could have used a ladder to clean the upper windows, but I didn't want anyone to look up my skirts and see my bloomers, especially on a windy day.

I enjoyed going into the chicken run to collect the eggs. The chickens amused me with their clucking and scratching the earth, and I liked the warmth of feeling under their bodies while they sat on their boxes. I tried to guess how many each hen had laid; and it made me smile when I was proved right. The rats were a problem. I was afraid of them when I was young but when I got older I learned that they would not attack unless provoked; I could tolerate them and even found their twitching noses and scurrying amusing. They ate the corn and drank the chicken's water, but never touched the hens; perhaps they had received a good pecking. I suspected that they stole eggs but they were too stealthy to be caught in the act. Dad used to set traps; he used a wire cage, he said that gin traps were too cruel, the rats could suffer all night, but they had no pain in a wire trap. He killed the rats humanely by sinking the trap in the water trough. Eventually he gave up saying that he was making no impression on the numbers, they were breeding faster than rabbits, and that is saying something!

We kept a few cocks to service the hens. They were very vain and strutted around jerking their heads and flapping their wings, and then suddenly pouncing on any hen that came within jumping range. By the time that the hens had stopped laying eggs they were too old and tough for eating, even if boiled; we just buried the bodies when they died. Year old cocks were good for roasting and we always kept a supply for dinner. We sold about half the eggs to a market stallholder in the town. We ate some and preserved the rest in a large earthenware tub. Mum and I washed the eggs and then gently layered them in the tub and then cover them with water containing Water Glass; that sealed the shells and the eggs would keep for a long time, so we always had a good supply of eggs for the table even when the hens were off lay and broody. If a hen went broody it was allowed to keep its eggs and sit on them until they hatched. That mainly sustained the chicken population. After I left school, I persuaded Dad to invest in a small hatchery. That was just a box with two deep drawers and glass sides with a paraffin heater in the bottom and a flue on top. The eggs were kept at the body temperature of a hen by checking with a thermometer and adjusting the wick as required. The eggs had to be turned every day and after three weeks the chicks pecked their escape from the shell. They soon dried off and started cheeping. I made sure that they had a good supply of finely ground wheat and topped up the water trough; when I did that, I loved the feeling as their soft yellow fluff snuggled against my work-worn hands. Some of the chicks were packed into cardboard boxes with holes for ventilation, and sent to the market to be sold as day-old chicks. After a few days those remaining were moved to a brooder; a wire cage on a table with a paraffin heater placed in the middle. The chicks huddled round the heater; they probably thought that it was a hen. As they lost their fluff and grew feathers, they became livelier and soon became more interested in the water trough and tray of bran. They progressed to eating whole grains of wheat at about six weeks old. We kept enough to maintain the flock, and sent the rest to market.

Dad gave me some bantam chickens; a cockerel and four hens. I liked to watch them scurry in the dust, their colours looked lovely in the sunlight. I cosseted them and they thrived and began to lay eggs. The eggs were stolen by the rats, so no chicks were hatched. The rats liked the eggs and took a fancy to bantam meat. The bantams were no match for the rats and soon there was nothing left but small scatterings of bloodied feathers.

Dad sold the milk round after the war, but kept a couple of cows for domestic use. He taught me how to milk, and we each milked a cow every morning and evening. I chattered to him but he didn't say much, probably because of the cigarette that drooped from his lips; his hands were fully occupied so he could not take it out to talk. The cows gave more than enough milk for drinking and making cream, most of which was made into butter; the rest was fed to the pigs.

The morning milking would yield enough for twenty-four hours' domestic use. The evening milking was poured into a large shallow earthenware bowl, covered with muslin on a flat wire frame and left overnight. By next afternoon all the cream had risen to the surface and was scooped off into a half-gallon bottle with a wide mouth and a screw top fitted with wooden paddles inside the jar and a handle on top. It took half an hour of vigorous churning so that the paddles agitated the cream into solid butter and liquid buttermilk. The butter was scooped out onto a marble slab and made into blocks with wooden pats about eight inches long and three inches wide and quarter of an inch thick with a handle at one end. One side of the pat was flat and the other grooved, so that a grooved pattern was left on the sides of the slab of butter, the top was smooth and a deep groove was made along the top with the side of the pat. Some people added salt before patting, but we preferred our butter natural. The buttermilk and skimmed milk was fed to the pigs. If there was only a small amount of cream we put it in a kilner jar and shook it to form butter, but that was very hard on the arms. Some milk was kept until it went sour and started to solidify. It was then put in a muslin bag and hung outside until all the liquid drained off, the result was cream cheese, and it needed a generous sprinkling of salt to give it a taste. The butter was stored on a marble shelf in the pantry. Most food was stored there. Flour was bought in half-hundredweight sacks and stored in a wooden bin; I had to pick out the mouse droppings before we could use the flour, it was the same with the sugar bin. The rows of jam and bottled fruit were safe in their jars, but nowhere else was safe from those hungry mice.

In addition to the other animals we had a couple of sows; they were taken to a neighbour's boar for servicing, and we sold the subsequent litter at the cattle market. Every year we would select the best from a litter and stuff it with plenty of food. When it was big and plump the butcher from the village would come and slaughter it. He came in his van, loaded with the tools of his trade. Dad helped them to take the pig from its sty and string it up by the back legs from a tree at the side of the farmyard. The butcher took a large tub from his van, put it under the pig's head, and slit its throat. Blood spurted and the butcher directed it into the tub until the pig stopped wriggling and jerking. I was not allowed to see the slaughter and had to stay in the house, but I could still hear the piercing squeals; it seemed to take ages to die. Mum didn't want the blood, and Dad helped the butcher to load the tub into his van. Mum and I then went to the yard to help. Our job was to take boiling water from the copper to the pig. The butcher used it to scrub the carcass and a metal scraper to remove the hair and bristles. The butcher put another tub under the pig, told us to stand clear and cut the belly open. Blood and guts spilled into the tub. The butcher groped in the mess and the carcass, cut out the heart, liver and kidneys and the layer of fat over the stomach known as pig's fry, and put them into a washing-up bowl held by Mum; I took that to the kitchen. By the time that I returned, the butcher had removed the lungs and put them and the large intestine in the van. Mum didn't want those either, she later said that the butcher used them to make tripe and black puddings, and she didn't want her family eating that dirty stuff, so we never ate what other people referred to as delicacies.

The butcher then cleaned the inside of the pig with hot water, and Dad helped him to put the carcass on a trestle table that was unloaded from his capacious van. The butcher got busy with his knives and choppers and quickly and expertly cut the pig into joints. Mum and I used milking pails to cart the meat to the kitchen; we were careful to close the window and door to keep out the cat and dog. The butcher cleaned his tools and hands in the still warm water, and loaded his paraphernalia into his van. As he turned to drive away he laughed and said, "The only things that we can't eat are the pig's squeak and the curl in its tail." He may have talked to Mum and Dad while I was busy, but they were the only words that I heard him say. He was a very quiet and busy man.

After the butcher had gone work started in earnest. There was a frenzy of making pork sausages, haslet, pork cheese, and rendering down fat into lard. Some joints and pork chops were put in the larder and the rest, including hams, hocks, sides of bacon, were taken to the dairy and laid in a large lead-lined tray. They were given a thorough rubbing with salt. We had to turn and rub salt into the meat every morning for three weeks. The various pieces were then suspended from stout hooks in the edges of the kitchen ceiling. They matured there until needed to make a meal. Most joints were soaked in fresh water overnight to leach out the salt. The pigs were usually very fat, and there were several joints of pure fat. They were soaked overnight and then boiled. The fat was then eaten either cold with bubble and squeak or fried with tomatoes and eggs. It must have been very high in bad cholesterol, but we were blissfully unaware of that danger in those days.

The hanging bits of meat were part of the kitchen scene and we never thought about them until one was needed for a meal. One ham was hung over my kitchen chair. Once at teatime, when I was very young, I had to rush to the hole. During my few minutes' absence, the hook came out of the ceiling and the ham fell on my chair shattering it into splinters. Had I been sitting there I would have been killed; so undignified to be slain by a ham. The family, including me, was in a state of shock. Dad pulled the table out of the way and Mum cleaned up the mess. Cyril's laugh was a little too shrill; he joked, "Well! At least the ham isn't damaged." We all laughed, more in relief than fun. That night their laughs were more genuine as they made up an epitaph: -

A ham above where Lilly sat.

Deserted its hook like a rat.

It squashed Lilly flat.

And that was that.

***

After Gerald and Simon had left home, Martin and Cyril went out to balls and dances wearing dinner jackets. Of course, they enjoyed the dancing, but the ulterior motive was to cultivate the prospects of marriage with a healthy, strong and only daughter of a farmer with plenty of land to bequeath. I was responsible for preparing the accoutrements; I polished the black shoes, starched the white collars and cuffs and fronts of the dress shirts, and pressed the trousers to a knife-edge. I must say they were a well turned out and handsome pair. The ruse succeeded with Martin, but Cyril liked the thought of just having the last waltz and a good night kiss rather than a more permanent attachment. It was a two-way seeking; the girls vying for the last dance with the most eligible farmer's boy.

When I was about nineteen, my pleasure was to go down the back grass field, sit on a tree stump and dream of boys. The neighbour's son was strong and handsome, and I hoped to catch a glimpse of him riding his tractor in his nearby field. We saw each other at church on Sundays, but we were both too busy to socialize. Later when we joined the Young Farmer's Club in town we had a chance to talk and eventually we went together in his car. One thing led to another, he proposed and I accepted. We married and lived in a cottage on his father's farm. Unfortunately, his parents were killed when driving their car across an un-gated level crossing and the train squashed the car and them. Every cloud has a silver lining; my husband was the only child and inherited the farm, so we moved to the big house. Dad and Mum were getting on, and they let Martin take over the farm and they went to live in the town. Several other farmers did the same thing so they could enjoy each other's company.

The hard times during Great Depressions ended with the outbreak of war in 1939. After the war, rationing continued but the national economy gradually improved, and there was more money to spare for luxuries. Mum bought new carpets and clothes, Dad changed his Flying Standard for Rover Ten, and we had a comfortable standard of living without being ostentatious. Farming methods changed, the tractor replaced horses; the binder and threshing machine were made obsolete by the combine harvester; mechanical potato planters and machines for harvesting sugar beet and potatoes made seasonal labour unnecessary, but it was still needed for fruit picking. The cows and milk round had been sold off, and the farm was just arable.

When Dad sold the milk round, he used some of the money to buy an electric cooker. It took some time to learn how to use it, and Mum and I spoiled a few meals in the process, but eventually we got the hang of it and wondered how we could have lived without it. It was much cleaner and easier than the old-fashioned way. We still have the old cooking range. Mum refuses to have it removed; she says that it brings back many happy memories of cooking for the family, especially cooking the Christmas dinner. My memories are not so nice. I was still at primary school when I started to clean the range every two weeks. The fire was allowed to die down and when the ironwork was cool, I removed the ashes; cleaned out all the ducts around the oven with a very small hoe and flue brush; washed the outside and then rubbed black lead all over it with a shoe brush and polished it off. Mum wouldn't allow me to clean inside the oven; she said that it was too dangerous for me to use caustic soda. Later Mum taught me how to use the dampers to regulate the flow of hot air round the oven and to the hobs on top on the range.

Before the arrival of the electric cooker, we had a paraffin stove used mainly in the summer for cooking food, and a primus for boiling the kettle for cups of tea. The cooker had a frame of metal to support a top with three holes covered with cast iron grills. Under the grills were separate round wicks in a metal globe open at the top to let the heat out. Paraffin was stored in an inverted glass bottle with a valve to control the flow of paraffin into a tube leading to the wick containers. I don't know why it worked, but it never overflowed. A lightweight metal oven could sit over two of the grills so we could bake cakes and roast meat. It was not difficult to use; the only disadvantage was that we used tractor paraffin and when the wicks were too high the black smoke had a foul smell. When the bottle was empty we had to take it to the tractor shed for a refill, which was a nuisance in dirty weather. The cooker and primus were in the scullery, which was not too convenient; Mum said that she would not have the smelly thing in her kitchen, and anyway there was a fire risk and it was better to lose the scullery rather than the kitchen. The paraffin cooker was used only during the summer, in winter we needed the range to heat the kitchen: Mum thought that is was a criminal waste to not make use of the range for cooking when the fire was alight.

Mum said that the old cooking range distributed heat throughout the oven and maintained a constant temperature, and baked more evenly. Much more efficient than the flimsy pressed tin oven on the paraffin heater; that also gave a tang of paraffin to the food, but I couldn't taste it. I was quite proud of my cooking, especially the Sunday roast dinner. The joint was usually beef, with at least three vegetables and thick gravy. Of course, Yorkshire pudding was important. We had it with gravy as a starter, then another slab with the joint, and then finished off with a dessert of Yorkshire pudding with either homemade raspberry vinegar or golden syrup. Dad liked his Yorkshire pudding to rise up the sides of the baking tin and to be light in texture and nicely browned. He hated a flat dense slab in the bottom of the tin. The joint was large enough to give good helpings for Sunday dinner, and then cold slices on Monday; the remaining bits were added to a stew on Tuesday. The dripping was enjoyed later in the week spread on hot toast as a midmorning lunch.

***

Great Uncle Joseph lived about two miles outside the hamlet, with his wife, Jenny, in a large new house; the nearest neighbour was half a mile away. When he married Jenny, my father's aunt, they lived in a small cottage with a range of outbuildings and about thirty acres of mixed arable and pastureland. Uncle Joseph supplemented his farm income by dealing in cattle; he had a reputation as an expert at judging the value of cattle; also for driving a hard bargain, and he saved his money. They had a son and christened him Henry. We have an old sepia photo of him in the family scrapbook, aged about thirty. He cut a fine figure of a man, and looked handsomely dapper and dashing in his bowler hat, well-tailored Norfolk jacket and riding breeches with highly polished leather boots and leggings; long side boards and a walrus moustache and a silver topped cane completed the ensemble. He was a fine catch for the post-master's daughter and they became engaged to be married. His parents dug into their hoard of gold sovereigns and built a fine new house for them to live in after they were wed.

Henry was slashing and laying a hedge. He impaled his thumb on a thorn. He pulled it out and sucked the wound clean. He did not make a very good job of it; a week later he died from blood poisoning. There were no antibiotics then and not even hot bread poultices could move the poison. His parents were distraught and became withdrawn and reclusive. His fiancé never married. Great Aunt Jenny never left the farm; Joseph did the weekly shopping in the town. They had always been careful but after their great loss they became miserly; they never spent money on clothes and luxuries, and lived on the bare minimum of food.

I think that Dad took the place of Henry. Joseph would help out on Dad's farm during harvest, and Dad would use his men to farm Joseph's land. Every Sunday, Mum would cook two extra portions of dinner, and during the afternoon they took them to Joseph and Jenny.

They never ate the food then, saving it until Mum and Dad had gone. Mum used to comment, "At least they have one good solid meal a week."

Dad would nod and say, "I bet that they don't eat it all at once; it probably lasts two or three days."

One-day Joseph arrived with his horse and pig float to collect a litter of pigs from Dad; he was going to deliver them to someone he knew, he winked as he said that it's stupid to pay auctioneer's fees when you can sell privately. I was about ten at the time, and watched him back the float to the sty. I must have stood too close; he unfastened the tailboard and it fell on my shoulder and knocked me down. I cried with the pain. Joseph was upset and helped me up. "You don't seem to be hurt, just frightened. You had better run home to Mum." I couldn't run and managed to walk slowly to the farmhouse.

Mum took one look at me, "Whatever happened to you?"

I sobbed, "Mum. My shoulder hurts. Uncle Joseph dropped the back of the pig float on me and knocked me down."

Mum was very concerned. "Let me have a look." She was a nurse in the Great War. She gently felt my shoulder, "Your shoulder is going to have a bad bruise, but I think that I will take you to the doctor."

Fortunately, Dad had just arrived back from town in the car. Mum nursed me on the back seat and Dad drove slowly to the doctor in the village. The receptionist was also the dispenser. She looked at me and said to the waiting patients, "We have an emergency here, I hope that none of you will object if Lilly goes in next." They all nodded and smiled. Mum took me into the surgery. "Good morning, Doctor. It looks as though Lilly has a broken collarbone as well as getting a bad bruise. The tailboard of a pig float fell on her. Fortunately, it missed her head."

The doctor knew Mum very well and nodded to me. "Come here, young lady; let me take a look." He gave me an encouraging smile. "I'm just going to sit you on my desk; that will make it easier for me to strap you up and make you more comfortable." Mum helped him to take off my blouse and vest, and he wrapped sticky tape quite tightly round my shoulder and upper chest, and then put my arm in a sling made from a cloth triangle. I whimpered when he straightened my shoulder, and then it didn't really hurt any more, just an ache. He pinched my cheek. "Good girl. That should do the trick." He turned to Mum. "You know what to do. No exercise or sudden movements. Bring her back in a week, and I will check that it's still in position. Fortunately, it is a simple break, otherwise she would have to stay in hospital."

The doctor was a proper doctor in those days. He could do almost anything, certainly setting bones and minor surgery was well within his capabilities, and of course there were no stacks of forms to fill in and inspectors checking his every move. The doctor's treatment was quick and efficient. Many patients owed their life and sometimes a limb to him; he was the most respected person in the community; next came the vicar, then the head teacher, and then the policeman. All children were taught from an early age to be polite to those four; as a result, crime was unheard of in the village, the only misdemeanors being riding a bicycle without light or some such triviality. In such cases the policeman would give the culprit a good telling off, get an apology and the culprit would not reoffend. Doors were very rarely locked, and possessions never disappeared.

When we got home, Uncle Joseph had already left. "Just as well," said Mum, "otherwise I would have given him a piece of my mind." She was quiet for a minute and then said, "We don't want any unpleasant rows, so when I next see him, I will just tell him what happened, I know that he will be upset; he just didn't realise that Lilly had a broken bone, otherwise he would have carried her home."

Dad nodded. "Even so it's bad luck. I will have to someone else to help with the potatoes."

There were tears in his eyes when he looked at me, "Thank goodness it missed your head. What would Mum and I do without our little Lilly?" He patted my head and smiled. "It couldn't have happened at a worse time. Now I will have to get someone else to catch the potato baskets."

As Uncle Joseph became older he gradually became less active and seemed to live in his own dream world. Mum took him to the doctor, it was over forty years since Joseph and Jenny had seen a doctor. They were healthy despite their frugal life and they treated any minor ailments with 'Old Wives Tales' remedies. The doctor diagnosed senile decay, and that there was nothing that could be done apart from nursing. Aunt Jenny looked after Joseph as best she could, but she was showing symptoms of the same complaint. When he was eventually confined to his bed; Mum and Dad went every morning and evening to help her out. I went with them sometimes and the last time that I saw Uncle Joseph he didn't recognise me, even though he was bright-eyed. He was more interested in telling anyone who cared to listen about the magnificent bulls and pigs that were running round the picture rail. He seemed happy and pain-free. He escaped his mortal coil peacefully during his afternoon nap.

Aunt and Uncle never showed much emotion; if she grieved she kept it to herself. That was normal in those days, none of the overt out-crying of mass hysteria that

that is so common now. Aunt Jenny deteriorated quickly, perhaps she felt incomplete without Uncle Joseph. The doctor gave the same diagnosis and advice. Dad bought a bed and put it in our lounge, and Mum settled Aunt Jenny in her new home. She liked the bed and preferred to stay there most of the time, apart from necessary sitting on the commode. She developed gangrene on her ankle. Mum gave her aspirin for the pain; there were very few painkillers and antibiotics then. Mum had been hardened nursing soldiers during the Great War. Perhaps raising her family had softened her.

One morning after tending Aunt Jenny and cleaning the gangrene, she staggered into the kitchen and collapsed on a chair. Dad looked alarmed, "Mother! Whatever is the matter?"

Mum sobbed, "Poor little soul. She is so brave. She just whimpers when I dress that horrible wound. It must be agony for her, but she thanks me and tries to smile. It really tears at my heartstrings. I just can't do it anymore."

Dad put his arm round Mum's shoulders. "Come on, Mother. Bear up now. We must do the best we can until she is released; it can't be long now."

Mum pulled herself together and stifled the sobs. "Sorry, but it's been a bit of a strain coping with the nursing as well as the usual chores, even though Lilly is a godsend." She stood up straight with her stern look in her eye. "It won't happen again."

Dad smiled. "That's my girl."

A few days later I was sitting with Aunt Jenny; we took turns to keep an eye on her. I held her hand. She said dreamily, "Henry came to see me today. It was wonderful to see him again after all these years. He hasn't changed a bit, still the same handsome man with a nice smile." She paused and her look of bliss brought tears to my eyes. She continued, "He couldn't stay long. He promised to come back soon and take me away in his smart car." She turned to me. "I'm waiting for him now."

I didn't know what to either say or do. I just kept holding her hand. She seemed to go to sleep and started to snore. She had never done that before.

Dad came in. "I will stay with her for a while. You can bring me a nice cup of tea."

Mum was peeling vegetables in the kitchen. She seemed calm and perhaps relieved. "It won't be long now, that's the death rattle. Best to let her sleep undisturbed." By the evening the noise increased and echoed within the house, I had to go into the pasture to escape the awful sound. Mum was sitting with Aunt Jenny; at midnight, the noise stopped. I like to think that Henry kept his word, and came for his mum to drive her to a place free from pain.

Families looked after their own in those far off days. Most old people faded away in their own beds. Those without a family finished up in the Workhouse, colloquially known as The Grubber. I went with a friend to visit her old friend. She was well cared for and the nurses were very kind and attentive. It is all so different today. Everything is so institutionalised; we have lost our humanity.

***

The next Christmas day, we had the usual family gathering. We had consumed a large goose dinner and were relaxing listening to the King's speech. After he finished, I went to the lounge to tend the fire. As I entered I heard the death rattle. I froze in terror, but managed to whisper, "Aunt Jenny. Is that you? What do you want?"

A giggle drowned the rattle. Gerald's wife had come in, she laughed, "It's only baby Bess, she has the sniffles." She bent behind the chesterfield and lifted the carrycot. "I have just come to feed her." I poked the fire viciously and threw on more logs to hide my embarrassment.

Mum and Dad died several years ago. Mum had a stroke and died at once; Dad waited to see her decently buried in the afternoon. At the family gathering, he seemed distant; he did not eat the food and drank only a cup of tea. The only words that he said were, "Mother and I had a good life. I won't keep her waiting long." The next morning, he lay in bed; the blankets were warm but he lay in the chill of everlasting sleep.

My loving husband was crushed by a stallion when he was helping it to service a mare. The only way that I could cope was to make a joke of it and tell my friends that he died in harness. Of course, one can never really recover from such a personal tragedy, but life must go on. I stayed in the farmhouse, and rented out the land and buildings. I couldn't have children, so I hope that one of my nephews will carry on the tradition of family farming when I have gone. I am the youngest of my siblings; most women live longer than men and I went to all my brothers' funerals. Dying is the only certainty in this life, and I have no fear of the Grim Reaper.

I am old now, which is probably why my story has rambled along. It may be a sign of senile decay, so please make allowances for my diversions; I was quite bright at school and I seem to have lost some of my learning. I have only two friends left. We go to church for Sunday morning Service, and since my house is close to the church, they come back with me for tea and fruitcake. When one of us has a birthday during the past week, we celebrate with a couple of glasses of nice dry sherry. We talk of the good old days, of how simple life was then, and how we cannot cope, indeed have no desire to, with the intricacies of this technological age. In our young days, the modern fads such as political correctness, racial and sexual equality, excessive concern for minority groups at the expense of the normal people, and the legal intrusive interference and probing in to the life of a loyal subject of Her Majesty the Queen, did not exist. It troubled me when officials in Brussels decreed that we were to be known as citizens and not subjects. Computers and mobile phones are beyond us, and since they are a requirement for almost any transaction we have to enlist the help of younger members of the family.

We just don't understand the younger generation, and the way that they disregard all the values that guided us to live a decent and rewarding life. I suppose that has always been so, but progress was much more casual in the olden days and was more easily assimilated. My friend says that progress today is like a snowball rolling down a hill; it gets bigger and bigger and eventually destroys itself under its own weight. He says that technology will destroy the world and all this talk about nuclear war and climate change is used to distract the gullible public from the really serious issues of an excess of technology.

I have left instructions in my will that I must be allowed the dignity of dying in my own bed; not for me the vegetable state of a worn-out body trapped by the artificial extension of a life that craves for release. I have done nothing to be ashamed of in my long and fruitful life, perhaps my only regret is being barren. I have no handsome son to come for me to take me on my last ride in a fine car.

REMINISCING

As I approach my dotage, I often muse about the past; those times so long ago, yet so clearly remembered, when I was a lad. Life was mainly good with only a sprinkling of bad events. Life on the farm was not all work and uneventful routine. The complete lack of present health and safety rules and the myriad of directives from the Brussels and our own Nanny State, the use of child labour, imposed discipline and self-control, all gave a spice to life; so different from the dependency syndrome that is now so prevalent in Western countries. Some aspects of work were dangerous and life threatening, but very few people succumbed and most lived to tell the tale. In fact, vehicles are one of several essentials to modern life that wreak more havoc than old fashioned farming and child rearing. The following recollections are recorded for your diversion from the trials and tribulations of the present day, albeit either amusement, or nodding agreement, or scorn and derision.

***

We did only essential work on Sundays, such as feeding livestock and milking the cows. Sunday was a day of rest; apart from Sunday school, morning and evening services and a heavy midday meal and high tea, we enjoyed the luxury of idleness. Many adults went to sleep in the afternoon, and children played games, often board games and such like received as Christmas presents. When Gerald worked in the seed business he came home every Sunday for the day and night, cycling the six miles back to the town on Monday morning. We enjoyed being a complete family at weekends. Of course, when war broke out Gerald, not being in a reserved occupation such as farming, was called up into the army, and we saw little of him for months at a time, and so were deprived of his company on Sundays.

Before the war when I went to the grammar school in the town, I visited a very old uncle occasionally in the lunch hour. His name was Charles; he was a distant cousin of my parents, but I always knew him as Uncle Charles. Had I been caught creeping out of the school I would have had to wait outside the headmaster's study for a dose of the swish for breaking school rules, but the visit to my uncle was well worth the risk. He was a gunsmith. He lived in a terrace house with a shop in place of the front room with living accommodation behind and on the first floor. Uncle Charles had covered his back yard with a wooden building with a corrugated iron roof that he used as his workshop. As well as guns, he also sold bicycles; he was equally adept at assembling a cycle from the various parts, including the wheels, as he was at building a double-barrelled shotgun. He bought the barrels, but made all the other parts including the wooden stock. When I visited, I walked into the shop and the bell on a coiled spring over the door announced my arrival. I didn't wait for service, but walked straight through the house, smiling at old Aunt Flo rocking in her chair immersed in her own thoughts, and then I went to the kitchen and scullery into the workshop. They had an early lunch and had finished by the time of my visit. Uncle was always singing songs from the First World War, sometimes they were rather lewd; he had a cracked voice, but that was no deterrent to his fervour. I used to sit on anything that looked reasonably comfortable and marvel at his skill with a file as he formed intricate trigger parts from lumps of steel. The stocks were a work of art in seasoned walnut with brass trimmings. Each gun was the result of years of experience and genuine interest in his art, for it was truly art and not just work. Would that there were more of his ilk today; the only incentive to work is often the rewards of payday and the consequent sating of materialistic appetites. Uncle made a living and after living expenses there was little left for savings, which is why both he and his ladylike and birdlike wife ended their allotted span in the workhouse.

Uncle Charles had a 1925 Sunbeam motorbike lying derelict his workshop. I really wanted that motorbike; I could have brought it back to life. Uncle just laughed when I told him of my dream. "You're far too young to have such a powerful machine. Just wait until you have grown up a bit more." I don't know what happened to the Sunbeam when he was taken away to the workhouse, but I still regret not having the opportunity to renovate it.

Before the war, Gerald was very friendly with Uncle Charles, and visited a couple of times a week. He liked Aunt Flo, and they had tea together; the old-fashioned way. She was a bit senile, but had her lucid moments, and then she could make interesting conversation. Gerald told me that one day she had her hair plastered down with Brylcreem. She said that a friend had told her that it was good for her hair. Gerald told her that her fine white hair was beautiful, and didn't need anything; it should lie naturally, and not be plastered down in a man's style. She gave the Brylcreem to Gerald and reverted to her old style; presumably she gave it the obligatory fifty strokes of a brush every night. She was barren, so they treated Gerald more as a son than distant relative. Uncle gave Gerald a handmade bicycle; I borrowed it sometimes. It was a racing machine with drop handlebars and only one very high gear. That was very fast when riding the open Fenland roads with a tail wind, but going into a head wind was hard work; standing on the peddles and straining on the handlebars resulted in a slow crawl. It was easier to walk. A three speed Sturmey Archer hub would have made it a more practical bike.

Uncle Charles gave Gerald an old twelve-bore shotgun that he had taken in part exchange for a new model. Gerald used it on his Sunday visits, he kept it on the farm; he was not allowed to keep it in his digs. We had heard of exploding barrels killing someone somewhere up north. Gerald was apprehensive and devised a test to ensure that the gun was safe. He tied the gun to a fence rail, and then tied a string to both triggers and laid it on the ground to behind a straw stack twenty yards away. He loaded the barrels, and we four brothers retired to the safety of the straw stack. Gerald pulled the string tight and gave it a jerk. Both barrels roared in unison. We rushed to the gun; it was still in one piece, but there was a neat circular pattern of holes in the fence post. Gerald declared the gun safe. He untied it, reloaded, told us to stand clear, clasped the gun to his shoulder and squeezed one trigger. His shoulder jerked back. Gerald grinned, "It's got a kick like a mule, but if I pull it tighter into my shoulder I can control it."

I could handle an air rifle from the age of nine, and mostly shot at homemade targets, however I did go hunting sparrows. I restricted myself to bushes and did not stalk the hedgerows. A freshly shot sparrow, plucked and drawn and cooked in the middle of a baked potato and a smear of butter and salt was delicious. Martin was hunting with the air gun. He fired through a hedge at a blackbird and missed. The pellet grazed Cyril's neck; he was walking unseen on the other side of the hedge. The pellet passed only a couple of inches from his Adam's apple; a hit there would have had dire consequences. Dad was very angry, and gave us a stern lecture on the use of guns. He went through all the rules, emphasizing that we should never fire a gun unless we had a clear view of the target and making sure that no one was in the line of fire.

From the age of eleven, when one of my brothers brought back a shot rabbit, I could skin it, joint it and cook a rabbit stew with onions and swedes. Whoever shot the rabbit would gut it and leave the entrails in the field, so I didn't have that rather smelly task, but after watching my brothers do it, I am sure that I could have done the same. At that age, I had not yet mastered the art of pastry making, so could not make a rabbit pie. That was delicious, but even better cold with a dollop of homemade redcurrant jelly.

From the age of fourteen I was allowed to use Cyril's four-ten shotgun. It was lightweight and a third of the size of the twelve-bore. It had two positions when opening the breech for loading, one was normal, allowing just enough room to insert the cartridges, and the other allowed the butt to be folded against the barrels, so it could be easily hidden by slipping it down a trouser leg. Obviously that type of gun was favoured by poachers. I was careful to follow my older brothers' instructions on handling a shotgun. I always opened the breech when jumping across a ditch and climbing over a gate and never fired through a hedge, in fact I never fired the gun unless I had a clear view of the target and I could see that no-one was in the line of fire. Rabbits were easy targets and just sat waiting to be shot; hares were very timid, the closest I got to one was when it jumped out of a tree that I was passing and sped away. I was so surprised to see a hare in a tree, that by the time I had got my sights on it, it was out of range. Once I walked across a frozen snow-filled ditch, with the breech open of course. The frozen crust of snow gave way. I floundered my way out, the noise disturbed a covey of partridge a few yards along the ditch. They flew away low over the snow-covered fields. I was sorry to miss a shot at the partridges, but pleased that I had obeyed the rules. It only needed a sleeve or something to get caught on a hammer and partially pull it back, when the sleeve or whatever came free the hammer would close and fire the gun. There have been several cases of shooters climbing obstacles with a closed breech and shooting themselves, mostly in the leg, but sometimes fatally.

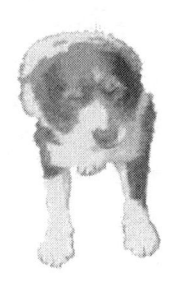

Gerald had a sheepdog named Woof. He was not allowed to keep it in his digs; anyway, it was a farm dog and wouldn't survive in the town, so Martin, Cyril and me promised to look after it on the farm. During the first week, it pined and went mad with joy on Sunday when Gerald came home. The next week it just went mad, and killed three chickens. Dad put Woof on a chain, it barked a lot for a day, and then went moody. Next Sunday, Dad told Gerald about the chicken killing. Gerald said that he was sorry. Dad said, "Being sorry isn't enough. You know that we can't allow a chicken-killing dog on the farm." He nodded to Gerald's twelve bore leaning in a corner of the kitchen. "Woof has got to go."

Gerald nodded. He left the table and collected the gun and a cartridge and went outside. I followed and walked beside him. He looked straight ahead; I had never seen him so serious. We reached Woof; it leapt up to greet Gerald. He knelt beside it and held Woof close while it licked his face. Gerald took a pace back and said, "Stand back." He pointed the muzzle at Woof's throat and squeezed the trigger. Gerald said gruffly, "Get a spade."

When I returned Gerald was cradling Woof. He took the spade, dug a hole and buried Woof while tears streamed down his face. When he had finished he looked me in the eye. "Promise not to tell anyone that I cried." We walked back to the house. I held his hand. Gerald was very subdued for the rest of the weekend, as indeed were we all. I cried myself to sleep that night.

The barn was a general storage area, and included cake for the cattle, meal for the pigs and wheat for the chickens. It was a happy hunting ground for rats. In the days before warfarin, they were uncontrollable. Traps could catch only a few; a hose pipe running from a tractor exhaust into rat holes probably killed some but the only evidence was a smell for a few days. Going into the barn at night with a paraffin lantern revealed countless pairs of tiny eyes reflecting the light. One night, I took the four-ten and a lantern, opened the barn door and had the unnerving experience of all those staring eyes. I steadied myself and let fly with both barrels. The noise was deafening inside the barn. The twinkling eyes vanished. There was neither a drop of blood nor a dead rat on the floor, just pellet holes in the boards. Those rats had a charmed life.

The war was the main topic in the newspapers and on the BBC radio news, with reports of loss of planes and life on both sides in the war. There were particularly harrowing articles and pictures of the Blitz in London and other targets of the Luftwaffe. The constant reminders of death from far away made me fear for Gerald's life; we were relatively safe in the Fens, but we did have casualties caused by jettisoned bombs and shot-down aircraft. I realised that the only certainty in this life is the inevitable journey towards the Grim Reaper.

Martin and Cyril had left school and were working on the farm. That made a worker redundant and he had to leave the tied cottage and find work on another farm. The cottage was requisitioned by the government, and evacuees moved in; just a wife and child; the husband was in the army fighting as one of General Montgomery's Desert Rats. When the Desert Rat – he never told me his name – was on leave I watched him make a model dredger from a Hobbies pattern; I had tried to do it but his model was much better. We both used hand fretsaws.

Later a family friend gave me an A1 Hobbies fretwork machine with a drill attachment, and that made the work much more accurate and easier. It had a foot treadle similar to my aunt's sewing machine. She said that she could use both hands for guiding the cloth to the needle, and it was quicker. My mum had a Singer sewing machine. She had to work it by a handle on a wheel, and had only one hand to use to guide the cloth. She said, "It was good enough for my mother, so it is good enough for me. Anyway, we can't afford a new one so this will have to do."

I made a galleon from a Hobbies pattern; it was a model of the boat on the back of a halfpenny. The grocer from the village used a horse and large covered lorry to deliver his wares to the surrounding hamlets and remote farms. Mum used to give him a cup of tea in the kitchen. I was putting the finishing touches to the galleon on the kitchen table. The grocer sipped his tea and said, "That's a very nice galley."

I thought it strange that he didn't know the difference between a galley and a galleon, grown-ups should know everything. I said loudly, "It's not a galley it's a galleon." The grocer dropped his smile and looked sad and left. Mum told me off, and said that I should never be scornful and never think that I knew better than adults. Later I made a proper model yacht from a Hobbies pattern. I sewed the sails on Mum's machine. It sailed well. I resolved that when I grew up I would take a holiday, make my own yacht, and sail round the world.

The Desert Rat was killed in the desert. He was buried out there. There was no corpse to help the wife with her mourning. She had no friends in the hamlet, she had not been there long enough to make friends, just acquaintances, it took years to get the complete trust of the locals. Mum comforted her. The vicar tolled the death bell as a token of respect for the dead soldier. I was helping to pick potatoes at the time. At eleven the lowest church bell tolled the knell of his death, one ring on a single bell for each year of his life. Everything stopped, the horses and workers just stood in silence, out of respect for the dead soldier. It seemed to go on and on, the slow ringing echoing across the fields. Twenty-seven times, once for each year of his life. When the ringing stopped we all got busy again. One woman was weeping, "My God! I hope that Trevor is all right." I think that the others must have been worried about their own relatives who were fighting abroad because they worked very quietly for a long time.

One night, a soldier home on leave was riding his motorbike home from the dance in town. He swerved to avoid a stray cow, and hit a telegraph pole. He was thrown up into the wires and was cut to pieces. The church bell tolled 19 times. It went on and on, and I thought of death, and the family grave in the churchyard. When grandfather died, they opened the vault under the marble cross in the churchyard. The side of one of the coffins had split open, and the bones inside were disturbed. It was the remains of his young daughter. The story was that she must have been buried alive. Grandfather left instructions that his wrists must be cut before burial. It seemed that he had good reason to fear being buried alive.

Before the war boys often played cowboys and Indians, and we were no exception. We had other games, such as pretending to climb mountains when we climbed trees; exploring when we trekked across the fields; pretending that our bicycles were motor bikes, and sailing a land yacht made from a fruit crate nailed to a plank with pram wheels, and a sack for a sail, the roads were usually deserted and the yacht would sail down the road faster than we could cycle. The boy on the yacht always had a thrill of a narrow escape; the only brake was both boots pressed onto the road. News of the war in the papers and illustrations in the Picture Post prompted a change from cowboys and Indians to a new war game of English and German. We no longer used the potentially lethal bows and arrows made from willow, but we retained the six-shooters improvised from a small forked branch. We became more ambitious and built a forward observation post from timbers and corrugated iron sheeting on one side of the farmyard. On the other side, we put a much larger forked branch into the ground and tied on old cycle inner tubes to make a big catapult; it was as tall as me. It would hurl half a brick over the two hundred yards to the observation post and smash with a dreadful clatter onto the iron sheeting. I wore Dad's steel helmet from the First World War but I doubt that it would have given much protection from a flying half brick. It might have saved my skull from being smashed, but the force would have snapped my neck. We had a 'war' with some neighbouring boys. We decided who should be either English or German by having a spitting contest. We brothers won and chose to be English. The Germans went to the observation post and suffered a punishing bombardment. After the noise stopped, the Germans came out looking rather dazed. They later told their dad of our adventure. He told our dad, and he immediately ordered the destruction of the observation post and consigned the catapult to the woodpile.

Many items were rationed during and after the war. Books of coupons were issued to each person, and shopkeepers cut out the appropriate number for every purchase. Shortage of clothes stimulated a cottage industry in dressmaking; silk from an unserviceable parachute was ideal for wedding gowns, and could be dyed for more normal dresses. Old knitwear was unravelled for the wool and re-knitted into new pullovers and socks; the click of needles accompanied after-work listening to the radio. Petrol for private cars was also rationed, but petrol for commercial vehicles, including farm tractors and other engines, was dyed red, and not rationed. Anyone caught with red petrol in a car was heavily fined. Food rationing during and after the war contributed to a healthy diet, with no surfeit of fat and cholesterol laden food, but of course we knew nothing of such dangers then. Most people had sufficient calories, but there were very few fat people and even less obese people to be seen. People were generally healthy, which was just as well because there was no National Health and Social Services then. Country people were dependent on the local doctor who treated most illnesses and complaints, and those needing more specialist treatment had to go to the cottage hospital in the town. There was also an isolation hospital for the rare cases of scarlet fever and other infectious diseases; they did not include flu; sweating it out in bed for a couple of days with hot water bottles, plenty of water and aspirin was an effective treatment.

In my family, if one child caught a mildly infectious disease, such as measles and chicken pox, all the children were put in the same bed, so that they were ill together. That saved Mum's nursing time. Bilious attacks, now known as food poisoning, were common. The treatment was staying in bed with the chamber pot handy for the inevitable vomiting and diarrhea, plenty of water and a light diet of soup and fish, and swigs from a medicine bottle collected from the dispenser at the doctor's surgery. We had to return empty medicine bottles; there was a shortage during the war. Once I had a poisoned finger. I developed a high fever, and Mum called the doctor. He prescribed the new M and B big yellow tablets. They made me feel really ill. The doctor said that he knew that would happen, but they killed the infection. He said that without them I would certainly have died.

Hot bread poultices were applied on boils and infected cuts; the sting of scalding was worse than the pain of the boil. Some mothers put hot water in a bottle, then quickly poured it out and pressed the open end of the bottle over the boil; as the air in the bottle cooled it created a vacuum that sucked the pus out of the boil. Mum never did that to us, she said that it was too painful. Fever and headaches were eased with a handkerchief soaked with vinegar across the forehead. Wintergreen ointment and horse oils were used for relieving aches and pains.

We brothers used to make model boats and sail them on the ponds that the cows used for drinking water when they were out on the pasture. The boats were very primitive, just a twelve-inch length of four by one, pointed at one end, and rigged with a square brown paper sail on a mast and crosstrees made from willow wands. They just drifted aimlessly, but when weighted with a dollop of wet clay on the stern, the front lifted and the boat would run before the wind. I carved a small boat about six inches long, with a proper shaped hull. I cut a slot in the bottom and hammered in a halfpenny, and put on a square-rigged sail. It would sail slightly off the wind, and I was quite pleased with myself when it sailed faster than my brother's larger boats. Those early experiences with model boats aroused my interest in real boats. Much later I sailed and raced dinghies and progressed to small cruisers that I bought as bare hulls, and fitted them out. Eventually I acquired an eight-metre catamaran, renovated it and sailed into the sunrise. I spurned the romantic dream of sailing into the sunset; that ended in darkness. I wanted a new life with many new dawns. I sailed into the light. The new life was much better than the old; no more petty and obstructive restrictions from dictatorial officials, and no more oppression from materialistic, self-serving and unscrupulous commercial and financial exploiters. Now I enjoy a haven of peace and contentment to spend the last precious years of a fulfilled life. It seems appropriate to finish this book with a little episode to commemorate the end of one of my many phases in life. Please chuckle.

THE DINGHY

Several decades have passed since those idyllic childhood days on the farm. The skies are still much the same. The space and ever-changing clouds still inspire artist and poets and lesser mortals. My place of abode has changed from the flatness and peace of the Fens to the vastness and turbulence of the sea. The threat of second childhood urged me to realize the aspiration to discover what lay beyond the ever-retreating and unapproachable horizon, before the inevitable beckoning skeletal finger of the Grim Reaper. After ten years of living with the sea, I dropped my last hook in Far Eastern waters. This little story is one of my last incidents as a lone sailor, before I embarked on yet another stage of my life.

***

The replacement dinghy lay waiting above high-water line on a beach in southern Thailand. The previous dinghy was a very stable inflatable that had served faithfully for 12 years. In common with old people it lost wind easily; it was past its prime. I pumped out all the air, folded it neatly and reverently laid it to rest at the back of the carport; the tiller, dagger board, sail, mast and boom arranged on top formed a memorial to our past adventures. The glass fibre replacement was very tender (no pun intended) and unstable compared with the inflatable, and I made a mental note to handle it with care. I dragged it to the water and rowed to my ketch-rigged catamaran anchored 300 yards off shore.

Minor maintenance of a boat can be therapeutic. Just concentrate on the job in hand and all other problems fade away. Calmness and serenity prevail. I had retreated from the troubled world to a haven of peace. I was just messing about – a common occupation with boat people – with a bowl of water and some wet and dry abrasive paper, cleaning the salt and grime from the teak taffrail and handholds on the cabin roof. My mind drifted back over the good times during my over three score years and ten sojourn on Earth. A sudden gust of wind blew the plastic bowl into the sea. The bowl cost all of ten baht, (sixty baht to the pound sterling) and was scratched and stained only a little, so had a few more years of useful life remaining. It was just drifting away, giving the paper a free trip. I sprang to the stern, and leapt into the dinghy, untied the painter and rowed to the bowl that floated serenely on a calm sea. In seamanlike fashion, I shipped the oars and let the offshore wind push the dinghy to the bowl. So far so good, but I misjudged the 'tender' trait of the dingy and I leaned out too far. The gunnel went under the water and the sea surged in. This Old Sea Dog just sat as the dinghy sank beneath me. The bowl went calmly on its way; oblivious to the embarrassment and danger it had caused by its untimely and unnatural wish to seek an adventure. The small buoyancy tank in the bow gave sufficient support to hold the dinghy vertically in the water, with about six inches showing above the surface. My habit of lashing the oars to the rowlocks proved worthwhile; they were still attached to the dinghy.

So there I was, in the sea treading water beside that foundered dinghy, 100 yards from the boat with an offshore wind, fortunately offset by an incoming tide. It all happened so smoothly, my hat and spectacles were still in place, but one shoe preferred the freedom of the sea to the odour of my foot. Nobody was around either to see my stupid mistake, or indeed to render assistance. I grasped the painter between my teeth, fortunately capped and not detachable, and swam with a back-frog stroke, towing the dinghy towards the boat; not an easy task as it was still vertical in the water. The dinghy cost 2,000 baht, second hand; my mean streak would not allow me to abandon it. It took an age to swim that 100 plus yards. I cleated the painter to the boat, and clambered aboard. It was then a simple matter to lift the dinghy by the painter vertically out of the sea, so spilling out most of the water, then refloat it and bail out the rest.

The bowl was still in sight; as was the shoe, the left one of a pair bought only a few days before for the princely sum of 70 baht. Since I still have two legs it was essential to retrieve the shoe; I didn't relish the thought of hopping everywhere in order to wear out the right one. I rowed off in the dinghy again, eased alongside the shoe, gingerly reached out and with a quick scoop it was lying in the bilge unfazed by its adventure. The bowl's joyous flight to far-flung shores was scuppered by a similar deft sweep; unfortunately losing the wet and dry paper in the centrifugal force of the graceful, yet strong movement of a left arm swing. A slow row over the now 200 yards back to the boat; there to indulge in self-congratulatory excesses and plaudits that there was life in the Old Salt yet.

Great is the fall that follows false pride. The weightless feeling on my right buttock indicated that something was missing; that familiar reassuring feeling of a plastic wallet just wasn't there. My heart plummeted with the realisation that that most treasured possession was even now floating to the destination so earnestly sought by the bowl. That miserable, scratched, and stained excuse for a bowl; that troublemaker, sitting on the worktop, dared me to vent my fury by throwing it overboard. I resisted the temptation and took more satisfaction from denying its epic voyage to an unknown shore. The wallet was out of sight. 1500 baht, credit card, OAP card and its promise of cut prices in UK all gone. Money, even more important, family honour, was at stake. No scruffy plastic bowl would get the better of a male descendant of those respectfully interred by the porch in an English country churchyard.

Head erect and straight-backed I stepped over the stern into the dinghy. A rapid calculation of wind and tide to establish distant waypoints astern and ahead, and the quest started for that Holy Grail of a wallet. I rowed 300 yards, 400 yards, and no sign. I rowed farther and farther out to sea. Suddenly there it was, just a few yards to starboard. It was still closed, floating and gently rocked by the ripples from the dinghy. A simple retrieval, and then I rowed over the now 500 yards back to the boat. A cup of tea was much needed, but the milk had curdled, so I decided to go home. I eased into the dinghy, rowed ashore, lugged it up the beach, made all secure, and loaded the oars and bits and pieces in the car. All was ready to make course for that cup of tea.

I had a quick look around before leaving. Further along the beach someone had his knickers in a twist. An Australian friend was beaching his boat to work on the hull at low tide. It was on the top of the tide, the right time to prepare for beaching when the tide ebbed. He had a line ashore and another to an anchor astern; but half a dozen Thais were trying to get a powerboat out of the water onto a trailer, and they were carelessly fouling the Aussie's lines. His was a keelboat, so he had rigged a temporary cradle to keep the boat upright at low tide. He couldn't get the boat out of the way, and he was in danger of having his lines snagged and his boat pulled off the cradle. He was single-handed and I shouted, "Can I pull anything?" The Aussie waved in greeting, and shouted, "Thanks mate, I can cope," and he shook his boathook at the Thais, who just grinned.

I waved back and walked away. I understood the love/hate relationship that sailors have with the sea. I understood the need to survive adversity, alone; to endure the vastness of all that water, the predictable and relentless rising and falling of the tides; the tides that can either help or hinder, even kill; the tides that will continue to ebb and flow into the eternity of time, long after the Human Race has self-destructed through the abuse of knowledge. All that paled into insignificance, as I walked with two shoes, and with the wet wallet dripping down my right buttock. I'd had enough of calmness and serenity for one day. The teak fittings could wait a little longer for varnishing.

ACKNOWLEDGEMENTS

Many people have contributed information for this book, either by direct advice or by personal contact in times long past. I would like to thank the latter for being part of my pleasant memories. The book is based on my recollections and experiences of farming in the 1930s, but this is a work of fiction and actual people are only used as inspiration for the characters, and the book is definitely not a true account of their lives.

My thanks to the Gressenhall Farm and Museum, Dereham, Norfolk, NR20 4DR who gave me free access, and allowed me to use photographs of their exhibits and library, for inclusion in this book.

Thanks also to an acquaintance who allowed me to use some of his extensive range of photographs concerning Norfolk history.

Invaluable help was given by a family proud to go by the name of Foster, and I thank Brian, Dick, Graham, Mary nee Brooke, Ashley and Hilary.

Finally, my heartfelt gratitude to either whoever or whatever gave me the gift of a life full of interest, activity, happiness and the pure joy of living.